Summer's Cauldron

The Young Sorcerers Guild
Book Two

G. L. Breedon

Kosmosaic Books

For more information:
www.kosmosaicbooks.com

Chapter One
Dead Forest Dance

Centuries-dead branches clicked and clattered as feet stomped and arms swung past desiccated tree trucks, frayed strips of leathered bark falling in wild, windless clouds.

"Mmm, I think it went this way," Clark said, his long, half-giant legs carrying his large form briskly through the trees.

"Where?" Ben said, struggling to catch up, his short, dwarf legs flying furiously to match Clark's pace. "I can't see anything around all these trees."

"Ahh, would you like me to pick you up?" Clark asked, looking down to Ben.

"No," Ben said, glaring up at Clark. "No, I would not like you to pick me up."

Bone-like twigs snapped and popped as feet pounded the coffin-dry forest loam, eddies of ancient lichen dust drifting upward to clog the air and lungs.

"Hermes' hemorrhoids, it smells in here," Daphne said, waving her slender hand before the scrunched up nose of her half-Indian, half-Dryad face.

"They do call it the Dead Forest, after all," Rafael said, ducking under yet another dead tree branch.

"I hope we don't have to chase that gorping thing all day," Daphne said.

"Do you really think we're going to be that lucky?" Rafael asked, a frown filling the gentle Hispanic features of his face.

Cadaverous underbrush, brown and paper-like in its mummification, crumbled and turned to ash at the slightest touch, clinging to the pant legs of those running past.

"Are you sure he's headed in the right direction?" Nina asked, her long, Iroquois-Italian face drawn tight with exhaustion. "Because

1

this doesn't look like a place where you would plant a Rune Tree and even if you did plant one, it doesn't look like a place where it would grow, because nothing grows here, not leaves, not grass, not weeds, not nothing, just dead trees and dead leaves and dead, dead, dead for miles and miles."

"Did I mention it's called the *Dead* Forest?" Rafael said.

Hooves skittered, sliding this way and that, dashing around death-grey trees and leaping over the coal-black bones of animals dead so long no semblance of their living life could be discerned.

"We have been running around this Dead Forest for nearly the whole of the day," Victoria said in a clipped British accent as she leapt over a long dead log, her centaur hooves leaving small clouds of soot-like soil trailing behind her. "Are you quite certain that animal knows what it's about? I love running as much as anyone, but I'm beginning to suspect he thinks we're playing a game of tag."

Branches parted, cracked and crumbled, chalk-like ash covering everything and everyone as a clearing came into view and all motion stopped.

"What is it?" Alex Ravenstar asked, running around his friends of the Young Sorcerers Guild to stand at the edge the parchment-brown grass. He wiped the sweat from his forehead and brushed his jet-black hair from his eyes.

"Cerberus's canker sores," Daphne panted. "We ran all this way for that?"

"Hmm, seems like it was important to him," Clark said, bending down to breathe deeply.

"Same," Ben said wheezing. "Wish I could say the same."

In the middle of the small clearing of lifeless grass stood a solitary dead tree, its leafless branches statue-still in the motionless air. At the base of the tree trunk, one leg cocked high, stood a small beagle.

"I certainly hope that's not the Rune Tree," Rafael said, brushing Dead Forest dust from his shirt.

"Are you sure it's a magical beagle, Brother?" Nina said, leaning against Alex as she gasped for air.

"It must have a magically large bladder," Victoria said with a flick of her tail. "He's been marking this forest as his territory all afternoon."

"He hasn't gotten the scent yet," Alex said as he watched the beagle finish his business and turn to cock his head at the young mages assembled at the edge of the clearing. The small dog seemed surprised to find they had followed him once again.

"You can't blame him with this stench," Rafael said. "It smells like a carcass that's been rotting in the sun for a month."

"Sun?" Ben said. "There is no sun." He stared up at the dark clouds hanging motionless above the lifeless trees like great, capsized leviathans of the sky. There was never any sun in the Dead Forest.

"Hmm, there could be a carcass nearby," Clark said.

"Yuck," Nina said. "Smells like a million carcasses."

"What's that you're standing on?" Rafael asked Nina.

"Very funny," Nina said with a grimace. She waited until Rafael looked away before checking the ground beneath her feet.

"So many trees," Daphne said, her voice tinged with sadness, "and all of them dead. Silent. I can't hear anything from them."

"Have I mentioned it's called…" Rafael began to say.

"Yes!" everyone except Alex said in unison.

"It seemed worth repeating," Rafael said, trying to hide a smile.

"Beowulf, come," Alex said to the dog, ignoring his companions. Beowulf gave a quick bark and trotted over to Alex.

"Who names a dog Beowulf, anyway?" Daphne asked.

"Our dad," Nina said. "As the official warlock tracking dog, Dad got to choose his name."

"Very Medieval of him," Victoria said, "but are you sure this dog can track anything other than a place to relieve himself?"

"I told you," Alex said, bending down to the beagle, "Beowulf can track anything you want to find. He just needs the right scent." The problem, Alex realized, was that he really had no idea what the Rune Tree might look or smell like. All he could tell from the stories the Guild had tracked down and read to each other every night in the Guild House was it was a magical tree, which somehow possessed all the possible runes of magic in its branches, bark, and leaves.

Beowulf barked and licked Alex's face.

3

"Ahh, I think he's hungry," Clark said, pulling a handful of nuts from his pants pocket and plopping them in his mouth.

"Give up," Ben said. "Maybe we should give up."

"The Rune Tree could be our one chance to make sure the Shadow Wraith can never escape its prison again," Alex said. That was why they were looking for the elusive tree — in the hopes of finding a rune they could use to permanently destroy the Shadow Wraith's grip on the world.

"Valley," Ben said, "We've been looking for it all over the valley and we haven't found anything."

"Well, we haven't tried the Crimson Forest yet," Clark said. "Or the Silent Swamp. Or the Copper Blood Mountains. Or…"

"Nope," Ben said, "but we've tried nearly every place else. Are you sure there really is a Rune Tree?"

"We've all read the stories of the Rune Tree," Victoria said. "Or what stories there are to read. And they all point to the tree being somewhere in the Rune Valley."

"Besides," Alex said, "this is the first time we've had Beowulf with us."

Beowulf turned his head toward a small copse of corpse-like trees and growled.

"What is it, boy?" Alex said, standing up to see what had spooked the dog.

Beowulf barred his teeth and growled even louder.

"Something is in the woods with us," Rafael said, squinting. "I can't quite see it, but I can smell something different."

"All I smell is death and decay," Victoria said with a dainty sniff.

"This is worse," Rafael said, his nose twitching.

"Mmm, I can smell it too," Clark said. "Smells like bad magic. Like sour milk on a moldy cake." Clark had a nose for sniffing out magic.

"Everybody get ready," Alex said as Beowulf barked again and the trees in the distance began to sway and crack, seemingly of their own accord.

"Get ready for what?" Nina asked.

"Get ready to run," Alex said.

"Always the running." Rafael sighed.

Alex could now hear whatever it was coming through the trees. It shook the ground and made the heretofore dead-still wind whip around them in small cyclones of decayed tree dust. He could smell it now, too. Like something deceased and decomposing for days in a pool of warm water. It stung his nostrils and made him gag. Then he saw it.

Rushing through the forest, dried branches sticking to it like burs on animal fur. However, it was not an animal. It was something alive that could not be alive without some manner of dark magic. Dead moss and ash-dry earth packed tight with twigs, branches, and black-brown leaves matted and twisted with fibrous bark strands. A skittering mass of rotted forest matter, half-rolling like a living tumbleweed, propelled by eight crustacean-like legs formed from broken, but bending dead branches. In the center of the mass — eight eyes of night-black granite stones circling a mouth of broken animal bones arrayed like the teeth of some nightmarish threshing-machine.

"I think running is a brilliant idea," Victoria said, slightly mesmerized by the sight of the monstrous thing hurtling through the trees toward them.

"I like running," Rafael said, turning to do just that. "I like it a lot."

"Hmm, would you like me to carry you?" Clark asked, looking down at Ben.

"Seriously?" Ben said. "You seriously have to ask?"

Clark scooped Ben up into his arms as Nina turned to Victoria and said with an almost pleading voice, "May I?"

"Certainly," Victoria said, helping Nina swing up onto to the horse half of her centaur body.

"Demeter's death wish, wait for me," Daphne said as she ran alongside Victoria, who helped the slender girl up to ride in front of Nina.

Beowulf growled once more and then dashed into the trees, dead leaves flying through the air like confetti as he rushed toward the monstrous thing bearing down on them all.

"Beowulf!" Nina cried.

"Don't worry," Alex said as he turned and began to run from the clearing with his friends, "that's one dog that can take care of himself. Remember, stay together."

"And no magic," Daphne said.

Unsurprisingly, magic did not work correctly in the Dead Forest. Rune-spells could have an unpredictable and potentially disastrous effect. It occurred to Alex that the creature crashing after them through the woods might be the result of a spell gone wrong.

Alex glanced over his shoulder to see the Dead-Tree-Monster, as he had begun to think of it, was gaining on them. He could hear the growls and barks of Beowulf, but whatever fight the dog was offering, and his father had assured him it could be considerable, it wasn't enough to slow the Dead-Tree-Monster.

Alex ran beside his friends, crashing through the forest, creating more dust and debris than ever. A cloud of Dead Forest wreckage billowed up behind them, roiling in the swirling air of their swift passage only to be gathered up and absorbed into the massive, unliving thing pursuing them.

"Bigger," Ben yelled as he looked back over Clark's shoulder. "It's getting bigger!"

Alex risked another glance behind as he darted between trees, trying to watch his footing. Branches of trees that had long ago fallen, but never decayed back into the earth, littered the forest floor. Nothing in the Dead Forest was alive, but neither could anything fully decay. Everything was suspended in a perpetual state of rot.

Alex leapt across of swallow pool of stagnant, scum-covered water and found himself grinning. He was no longer able to repress the feeling that had been welling up inside him. He had never heard of a Dead-Tree-Monster. Thanks to his father being the town warlock, Alex had heard of nearly all the dangerous creatures of the Rune Valley. That meant it was entirely possible, in fact, more than likely, he and his friends were being chased by something no one in the entire valley had ever seen, much less been hunted by. A part of him found that notion to be unspeakably exciting. Of course, another part of him found it to be ridiculously moronic. The latter part of his mind was the part insisting on running, not the part insisting on grinning.

"Are you smiling?" Rafael asked, incredulous.

"Well," Victoria said, "I'm glad to see someone is enjoying themselves."

"Mom swears she didn't drop him on his head," Nina said, "but I don't believe her."

"Gorping idiot," Daphne growled.

Alex couldn't help it. He grinned wider.

The Dead-Tree-Monster was close now, close enough that twigs and rocks from its body shook loose as it ran, pelting Alex in the back. The growls of Beowulf the beagle grew louder and then suddenly, impossibly loud, as though the small dog had been joined by a mountain-sized mastiff. Then a sound erupted behind them like a thousand trees falling all at once and crashing to the ground.

Alex instinctively looked behind to find the Dead-Tree-Monster was nowhere in sight. He saw no sign of Beowulf, either, although the sound of crashing trees still echoed through the lifeless forest. Alex looked a little too long, his foot catching on a knarred root, sending him sprawling forward head first toward one of the small pools of putrid water scattered throughout the forest. Just as his face was about to dive into the filthy water, he felt himself gliding through the air.

His first, and rather irrational thought, was he had somehow managed to learn to fly as he often did in his astral travels. Then he felt the pressure of his shirt against his chest and realized he was being held in the air. Held by Victoria, who had somehow managed to grab him while he fell. She placed him on his feet, still running. He looked at her and grinned wider than ever.

"Thanks!"

"Not a problem," Victoria said, smiling back. "I'm sure you'd do the same for me."

"He's not big enough," Nina said from behind Victoria.

"He'd think of something," Victoria said. "He's very clever when he wants to be."

"How about giving us some of that clever, now?" Daphne, looking behind for any sign of the Dead-Tree-Monster.

"Keep running," Alex said, still smiling.

"See?" Victoria said, "Very clever."

Even as the sounds of Beowulf's too-loud roars faded and the noise of clashing trees receded, Alex and the Guild kept running. If there was one thing Alex had learned in all of his adventures, it was that when you started running from something evil, it was best to keep running until you knew you were safe or you had to stop. Their arrival into another clearing forced them to halt and seemed safe at first sight.

Alex skidded to a stop as he entered the large clearing, sucking air deeply and quickly, as much from the harried run as from the sight he saw before him. The clearing of short, dead, brown weeds was the size of a football field and roughly the same shape. In the middle of the clearing sat a large pond, its water still and stagnant, a fetid smell hovering in the windless air. A small island of ash-gray grass rose out of the water in the middle of the pond.

In the center of this island stood a solitary tree. A living tree. A wide trunk of healthy black bark and strong, thick branches stretched up toward the sky, bright green leaves opening upward to catch the rays of a single shaft of light breaking through the slate-colored clouds above.

The Rune Tree.

Chapter Two
The Ruin Tree

"Oh, goodness," Victoria panted as Nina and Daphne slid from the back of her horse half.

"Great Zeus' something or other," Daphne said, her mouth hanging open.

"You were right, Brother," Nina said, beaming with excitement. "We found it."

"But how do we get to it?" Rafael asked, wiping the sweat from his forehead.

Alex looked behind and listened, but he could see and hear nothing in the Dead Forest they had run through. No sign of the Dead-Tree-Monster. No hint of Beowulf the beagle. Alex turned back to stare at the tree. Beowulf would catch up with them eventually. A magical tacking-dog should be able to do that much, at least.

"Transportation," Ben said as Clark lowered him to the ground. "There's a raft over there."

Alex looked to where Ben pointed and saw there was, indeed, something that might once have been called a raft, tied with a slender piece of rope to a stump at the edge of the pond.

"Mmmm, are you sure that's a raft?" Clark said, walking toward the assemblage of logs and branches.

"Whatever it is, I'm not setting foot on it," Victoria said, her hooves dancing anxiously. "I'd only end up swimming."

"I don't think you'd want to swim in this pond," Rafael said as he cast a stone into it. There was no ripple along the surface of the water. The stone simply disappeared without a sign or sound.

They all stared at the pond in silence for a moment. Alex peered into the murky black water. There was a film of something slick and oil-like along the surface of the pond, but he could not tell what it was and had no inclination to touch it and find out.

Something moved in the shadowy depths of the water. Something white and swift. Then it was near the surface, near enough to almost see, but not quite. Alex leaned a little farther over the edge of the pond. What was that thing? It reminded him of something. Was it a fish? The surface of the water erupted as a slimy white creature with fins and a gaping mouth of razor-sharp teeth burst from the pond and launched itself at Alex's head.

But, Alex's head was not where the dead fish had thought it would be. Alex's head was several feet away from where it had been a moment before. The hungry dead fish fell back to the water and disappeared, again without a ripple or a noise. Alex blinked and realized he could feel a hand holding the back of his shirt. He turned to see that Victoria had pulled him back to safety at the last second. Again.

"For such a clever boy, you don't seem to learn very fast," Victoria said with a smile.

"I may make a lot of mistakes," Alex said with a grin, "but I never make the same mistake twice." Rafael coughed. "Well, not three times, anyway. Thanks. Again."

"You're welcome," Victoria said. "Again."

"Right," Alex said, turning to the others and trying to let his grin widen into something that would seem like confidence rather than insanity, "nobody fall in the pond."

"I never would have thought of that on my own," Rafael said, rolling his eyes.

"Here's the plan," Alex said, ignoring Rafael's jibe. "First we need to find some long branches to use as poles for the raft. Then we'll take the rope from Clark's backpack and tie it to the raft. Victoria and Clark will stay here. That way if something goes wrong, they can pull the raft back. Fast."

"Finally, you're beginning to plan for things going wrong," Rafael said.

"I always plan for things going wrong," Alex said, "only it's never the things I plan for that go wrong."

"Reassuring as always," Rafael said.

"That's the easy part of the plan," Alex said. "The hard part will be figuring out how to get the Rune Tree to give us the rune we need to finally defeat the Shadow Wraith."

"Something about that tree doesn't feel right," Daphne said, staring across the strange pond.

"How so?" Alex asked. As a half-human and half-dryad wood nymph, Daphne could commune with trees in ways ordinary mages never could.

"It's too quiet," Daphne said. "Normally, I feel something from a tree. Get some impression of it."

"Maybe it's been surrounded by all these dead trees too long, and forgotten how to talk," Nina suggested.

"No," Daphne said. "I feel something alive, but it doesn't feel like a tree should."

"We'll be extra careful then," Alex said.

"Yes, that always helps," Rafael said. "Nothing ever goes wrong when we're *extra* careful."

"You can stay here with Victoria and Clark if you want," Alex said to Rafael with a taunting tone.

"What, and miss all the screaming?" Rafael said. "Don't be silly. The screaming is almost as much fun as the running."

"Both," Ben said with nervous laugh. "It's best when there's screaming and running."

"Were all of you dropped on your heads as babies?" Nina asked.

"Let's get moving," Alex said, ignoring the others. "We don't want to get caught the Dead Forest after dark."

That thought sufficiently motivated them all, and within several minutes, they had scavenged five long and relatively straight branches that looked as if they would remain whole long enough to use as raft poles. Clark rummaged through the oversized backpack of supplies he carried and produced a long length of rope that he tied to the edge of the raft. Shortly after that, Alex, Nina, Ben, Daphne, and Rafael clambered unsteadily onto the raft, holding their poles, as much to steady themselves as to steer the craft.

"Good luck," Victoria said with a small wave as Alex used his pole to push the raft away from the shore.

"Thanks," Alex said, waving back at Victoria. It was an odd moment to think about it, but he wished he had kissed her before starting across the pond toward the Rune Tree. It had been nearly two months since that first kiss on the day they had saved the town from the Shadow Wraith, but somehow there had never been a second.

It was not that Alex didn't want to kiss Victoria. He thought about it all the time. But most of the time they were with the rest of the Guild and it didn't seem right to kiss her in front of everyone else. Again. And every time he did manage to arrange for them to be alone, he could never quite figure out if she wanted him to kiss her or not. Sometimes the look on her face seemed to say she wanted to be kissed, but then she would start talking about something, rambling in that wonderfully endearing way she had, and he couldn't figure out how to kiss her when she was talking. If she was talking, she probably didn't want to be kissed. Right?

So they flirted, or at least they did what Alex hoped was flirting, and they spent most of their time together, although usually surrounded by the rest of the Guild, and Alex tried not to think about the centaur boyfriend she was supposed to have had back in England. She never mentioned him. Was it because she had broken up with him? Or was she still writing him and that was the reason she didn't want to kiss Alex again? He had tried to bring the subject of the boy centaur up several times, but Victoria always turned the conversation elsewhere. What did that mean? Was she interested in Alex or not? Maybe he should ask her. No. That seemed too easy. It couldn't be the right thing to do if it was that easy.

The raft shuddered and Alex lurched forward, catching himself from falling into the dead pond with the poll. He turned to see that they had arrived at the small island. He had daydreamed about Victoria the whole way.

"Glad you could join us," Daphne said, smacking Alex in the back of the head. Alex flinched and frowned.

"Yes, whatever could you have been thinking about?" Rafael said, sarcasm disguised as innocence dripping from his voice.

"Tree," Ben said stepping from the raft to the dry grass of the island. "Think about the tree."

"I was," Alex said, covering his embarrassment by jumping from the raft.

"So what's the plan, Stan?" Nina said, smiling up at him in a way that let him know she knew exactly what he had been thinking about.

"Simple," Alex said, setting the pole down on the raft. "Daphne and I will approach the tree and see if we can talk to it. Or something. And you three will stay here as backup in case that doesn't work so well."

Surprisingly, no one said anything. Alex couldn't decide if that was a good omen or a bad one. He turned and started walking the twenty yards to the Rune Tree, Daphne falling in at his side. The shaft of sunlight breaking through the clouds touched only the leaves of the tree, giving them a vibrant green hue completely incongruous with the rest of the island and the forest.

"Feel anything yet?" Alex asked in a half-whisper.

"Something," Daphne said, squinting at the tree. "It feels like it wants something."

"What could a Rune Tree want?" Alex asked.

"I don't know," Daphne said, staring up at the massive tree and brushing a strand of long, black hair from her face. "Normally trees want simple things like sunlight and water. This tree seems hungry for something else."

"Let's hope we can figure out what it wants and how to get it to give us the rune we need," Alex said.

"Assuming it even knows the rune," Daphne said.

"The Rune Tree is supposed to know all runes," Alex said. "That's why they call it the Rune Tree."

They reached the tree and walked across the edge of its shadow and into its shade. Now that he was closer, Alex could see the tree did not look as healthy as it did from a distance. The bark of the trunk was warped and twisted into shapes that did not resemble runes at all. They almost resembled a face. All of the stories Alex and the Guild had managed of track down spoke of the bark and leaves of the Rune Tree as imprinted with runes. It was said each leaf of the Rune Tree held a different rune. All the runes of the world. If a leaf

13

and its rune were to fall, that rune would cease to function for magic for all time. But, as Alex stared up at the leaves above his head, he saw that, while they were mottled with reddish-brown textures on the undersides, they did not seem to be marked with runes of any kind.

"Maybe this is the wrong tree," Alex mumbled aloud.

"Back away slowly," Daphne said, her eyes suddenly wide. Alex had heard that tone in Daphne's voice before and he didn't need to question it. He stepped backward cautiously, matching Daphne's pace, looking around to see what had spooked her.

"What is it?" Alex whispered.

"You're right," Daphne said, backing away a little faster, her eyes locked on the tree before them. "That is definitely the wrong tree."

Alex was about to ask why, when the shaft of sunlight above winked out of existence and the tangled bark of the tree's trunk began to shift and twist. The impression of a face became clearer and clearer until suddenly two large black eyes snapped open, followed by a gaping massive maw littered with spiked teeth jutting out at irregular angles. The leaves of the tree faded from green to black as Alex gasped and turned to run. Daphne turned with him, but the branches of the tree came alive with motion, reaching out like mangled arms to grasp at them.

Alex and Daphne dove into the dead-dry grass as an enormous gnarled branch swung over their heads. Alex could hear his friends by the raft and across the pond shouting in panic, but the sound was drowned out by the clangorous roar of the tree beast behind them.

The thinner branches were like hands now, clutching at them as they dodged and scrambled to get away. One of the prehensile branches clasped Daphne around the waist and yanked her into the air. Alex had just enough time to see Nina, Rafael, and Ben dashing toward the tree as he ducked a grabbing branch and latched onto Daphne's leg, pulling with all his strength.

"Hades' hairballs," Daphne yelled. "I should have known."

"Known what?" Alex asked as he felt a branch wrap around his waist and pull him up and away from Daphne.

"What it wants," Daphne screamed, pulling at the bone-like branches holding her fast.

14

"What does it want?" Alex shouted, hoping it wasn't going to be the answer he feared it would be.

"Lunch!" Daphne cried as the branches holding her swung her toward the open and still roaring mouth at the center of the tree trunk.

Alex yelled and twisted to see as he struggled against the branches wrapped around his chest and waist. As the tree's limber limbs pulled Daphne toward its monstrous maw, three long, straight branches flew through the air, thrown like javelins by Nina, Ben, and Rafael. The three former raft poles plunged into the mouth of the tree monster. The death-black eyes in the tree trunk went wide as the creature roared even louder, its mouth crashing down on the raft poles, snapping them into kindling pieces.

Branches of the tree creature swept out to clear its jaws even as others sought to capture the new comers. Nina was pulling at Alex's foot as Rafael and Ben wrestled with the branch holding Daphne. A branch slithered out to wrap around Ben's torso and he turned and shouted a rune word.

"No!" Alex yelled, but it was too late. Orange-white fire leapt out of Ben's hand and quickly turned to an inky black smoke that billowed back and engulfed him, clinging to his body and clogging his lungs as he coughed and cursed. Magic didn't work the way it should in the Dead Forest. *Ben's impulse had been right*, Alex thought as he frantically struggled with the wooden arms holding him tight. *We need fire. But we can't create enough fire without magic. And the magic won't work. What we really need is…Wait. Will that work?*

"Rafa!" Alex yelled, yanking himself around to see his friend ducking between two swinging branches and skipping outside their reach.

"Tell me you have a genius idea to get us out of this," Rafael shouted back. The tree creature had cleared its mouth and was now roaring again, preparing to make a meal of its captives.

"Dragon," Alex yelled at Rafael. "We need a dragon."

Rafael stopped and stood still as tree branch swung inches from his face. "I should have thought of that," he said as he pulled his shirt over his head.

The air around Rafael shimmered with a brilliant crimson glow for a moment and when it was gone, a small, but brilliantly blue-scaled dragon flapped its wings in his place. The dragon thrust itself upward into the air and then dove down toward the tree, avoiding the wildly swinging branches with aerial pirouettes. The dragon opened its mouth, belching a jet of azure flame into the mouth of the tree creature. The tree creature unleashed a piercing howl like a million birds trapped in a forest fire. The dragon flapped it wings, gaining altitude again, only to dive toward the branch holding Daphne, blue flame spurting from its mouth to set the tree limb afire.

The tree creature roared louder, its branches going wild with motion even as it released Alex and his companions. They fell to the ground and expertly rolled to their feet. They were members of the Young Sorcerers Guild, after all. They knew how to land from a fall. Rafael, in dragon form, unleashed two more bursts of flame at the tree creature to keep it from grabbing his friends again as they ran for the raft at the edge of the pond. He swooped down and grabbed his clothes from the ground with dragon claws before turning to circle the others as they ran.

Alex looked across the pond to see Victoria and Clark already had the rope attached to the raft in their hands and ready to pull. There was no need to give any orders. This plan was instinctual — get on the raft and get away as fast as possible.

Alex reached the raft first and helped Nina and Ben aboard as Victoria and Clark yanked the flimsy vessel into motion. Daphne jumped the last few feet to land safely beside him. They leaned into the motion of the raft as Clark and Victoria pulled them swiftly to the opposite shore. The raft riders turned in unison to look back at the tree creature they had so narrowly escaped.

The tree was fully on fire now, its leaves crinkling and crackling as the flames leapt over them. The tree creature writhed and wailed, shaking violently from the tops of its flame-ridden branches to its roots. Alex watched those roots wriggle up from the ground as the tree creature lurched forward. The roots of the tree knotted around themselves, forming two thick legs, thrusting the tree creature out of the earth and sending it lumbering toward the pond, its path leading directly toward Alex and his friends on the raft.

"Seriously?" Ben whined. "A tree that can run?"

"That's not fair," Nina moaned. "Not fair at all."

"What kind of tree is that?" Alex said in exasperation as he watched it run toward the pond.

"I think it's an old Colossus Tree," Daphne said.

Alex watched as the burning Colossus Tree jumped into the pond. It sank as swiftly, silently, and completely as the rock and the fish they had seen earlier. The only difference was the steam rising from the water as it quenched the flames tormenting the Colossus Tree's branches.

"Lucky," Ben said. "That was close."

"How deep to do you think that pond is?" Alex asked aloud as he looked at the once again stone-still pond. He didn't have time to ponder the question.

"Look out," Victoria shouted from behind him. Alex and the others on the raft turned as it slammed into the shoreline, sending them sprawling forward. They all managed to catch themselves without falling into the water and quickly jumped from the raft. Alex looked up to see Rafael struggling into his clothes.

"Thanks, Rafa," Alex said to his friend as they all walked briskly away from the edge of the pond and back toward the wall of dead trees surrounding the clearing.

"Thanks for the idea," Rafael said. "I don't know why I never thought of changing into a dragon before."

"Yes, that was some very clever thinking," Victoria said, patting both Alex and Rafael on the backs.

"Well, so much for finding the Rune Tree," Clark said.

"Now what do we do?" Daphne said. "I suppose we'll have to find that gorping useless beagle and start all over again."

"Beowulf was very brave chasing after that Dead Forest-tumbleweed-crab-spider thing that wanted to kill us," Nina said.

"You know we're having fun when we can say two deadly creatures have tried to kill us in one afternoon," Rafael said.

"Maybe we should head back to the Guild House and regroup," Victoria said. "We could dig up some other ancient book that has a hint about where the Rune Tree might be. Or, maybe I can talk to

Daddy and see if there might be a way to create a Rune Tree detector. That's exactly the sort of thing he'd love to invent."

"Maybe," Alex said, looking over his shoulder and frowning. "But before that, I think we should run again."

"What?" Victoria asked, turning to see what had caught Alex's attention.

They all turned to look back at the pond and stopped in their tracks. Charred black branches, dripping slimy water, rose up from the pond and moved toward the outer shore. Moment by moment, more of the massive Colossus Tree emerged from the water until it was standing on land, its root-legs propelling it forward with long strides even as it shook the water from its branches. The creature opened its mouth, emitting a deafening roar, sounding like the simultaneous felling of a thousand trees.

"Again!" Ben yelped. "I take back what I said about screaming and running."

"Mmm, you do the screaming, I'll do the running," Clark said, hefting Ben into his arms.

"Ladies," Victoria said to Nina and Daphne as they ran and she helped them scamper up her hind flanks. Alex and Rafael fell into a run beside her.

"How far do think that thing can chase us?" Victoria asked, glancing behind as the Colossus Tree roared again. "It looks very hungry."

"And mad," Daphne added.

"And mean," Nina said.

"If we're lucky, it'll get tired before we reach the forest edge," Alex said, sprinting to keep pace with Clark and Victoria.

"If we're lucky, it will follow us home and we can keep it for a pet," Rafael said.

"I was not thinking that," Alex said, grinning at Rafael.

"I know you too well to believe that," Rafael said with a worried glance behind.

They ran and ran for what seemed like forever, but it was not the edge of the forest or the length of the pursuit that finally convinced the Colossus Tree to give up its chase. It was something else large and fierce bursting from behind a stand of dead, dry bushes near Alex and the Guild.

"Gaia's gallbladder!" Daphne yelled as they all scattered and jumped from the path of the giant spotted beast charging past them, growling and baring its teeth at the Colossus Tree. The Colossus Tree stopped. The creature facing it growled again. The Colossus Tree shook itself, turned, and began a long lumbering walk back toward the dead pond.

"Beowulf!" Nina said, breathless from the run as much as the excitement of the now-massive beagle's entrance.

"Good boy," Alex said, walking over to Beowulf, who was no longer a tiny beagle, but a dog the size of a large grizzly bear.

Beowulf trotted back to Alex then stopped, shook himself, first slowly, then faster, and then in a whirl of motion, shrank back to his normal size.

"Impressive," Ben said. "A shape-changing, giant beagle."

"I take back every bad thing I said about you, dog," Daphne said. As if in response to her, Beowulf jumped up and licked her hand.

"How does he do that?" Rafael asked. "I can only turn into things the same size as me."

"That giant dog is his real size," Alex said, bending down to scratch Beowulf behind the ears. "He's small now, but has the mass of that big dog. I doubt even Clark could lift him."

"Ahh, that's why he eats so much," Clark said, stooping to try to lift Beowulf in his arms before grunting and giving up.

"I guess you both have that in common," Rafael said with a friendly pat on Clark's arm.

"Mmm, that and nobody can lift us," Clark said with a chuckle.

"There," Ben said, pointing. "What's through those trees?"

"Whatever it is, I hope it can't run," Rafael said as they all turned to see where Ben was pointing.

"Looks like a hut," Alex said, squinting to see through the trees.

"Like a hut something wicked might live in?" Nina asked in weary voice.

"Possibly," Alex said as he started walking toward the ramshackle structure. "Let's go check it out."

"You knew he was going to say that, didn't you?" Rafael said with a smile to Nina.

"Never gorping learns," Daphne said with a slight laugh.

"Clever is as clever does," Victoria said with a wink to Alex.

"Hmm, he's not the one who pointed it out," Clark said frowning down at Ben.

"A hut," Ben said, his voice defensively dropping an octave. "What are the chances a hut can run?"

"Ever heard of Baba Yaga?" Daphne said, and frowned when Ben gave her a quizzical look in response.

"What can go wrong?" Alex said, optimism back in his voice. "We have Beowulf, after all."

"Wuff," Beowulf said and trotted off toward the hut.

"You heard him," Alex said as he set off to follow the beagle. "Wuff."

Chapter Three
Cauldron Conundrum

In the end, nothing went wrong because there was no one in the hut. It looked deserted or at least very poorly maintained. The only credible sign of habitation was the rusted black cauldron hanging on a tripod of tree branches over the remnants of a fire pit that hadn't seen a flame in years. The cauldron was about two feet in diameter with a thick iron handle attached to a chain running up to where the three legs of the wooden tripod intersected.

Alex stuck his head through the doorway of the dilapidated hut and waited a moment for his eyes to adjust. The hut was bare, except for a simple wooden stool with three legs and a small wooden bed with a flat board where a mattress should have been. Although there was a thick layer of dust covering everything, there were no spider webs to collect it in the corners of the roof beams, as would normally have been the case. Spider webs required spiders and there were no spiders in the Dead Forest. Or any other kind of insect or living thing. Alex shook his head and turned back to the others outside the hut.

"Disappointing," Ben said, kicking at a stone. "What a dud."

"Not finding something interesting might be the best thing to happen to us all day," Rafael said.

"Mmm, this pot is interesting," Clark said, bending down to sniff at the cauldron hanging above the ancient fire pit.

"It's a cauldron, not a pot," Nina said.

"And I rather doubt there's been any food in it for quite some time," Victoria added.

"Ahh, I don't think cooking food is what it's usually used for," Clark said, his nose wrinkling as he breathed deeply over the cauldron.

"What do you mean?" Daphne asked, leaning over to smell the cauldron with Clark.

"Well, it smells like magic," Clark said.

"A magic cauldron," Daphne said, a smile spreading on her face.

"Wuff," Beowulf said, sniffing at the bottom of the cauldron.

"Beowulf agrees," Nina said.

"It's definitely a magic cauldron," Daphne said. "Even I can smell it this close up." She looked at the others, but especially Alex. "We should take it with us."

"You want to steal a magic cauldron from the Dead Forest?" Rafael asked as he turned to Alex. "You have officially corrupted her common sense."

"Rafael does have a point," Victoria said. "It may belong to someone."

"This hut is deserted," Nina said. "Probably no one has been here in years. Maybe centuries. Maybe. Probably."

"Heavy," Ben said, giving the cauldron a kick. "It's cast iron."

"Clarke can carry it," Daphne said, smiling up at Clark. Victoria could also probably carry the cast iron cauldron, as she was nearly as strong as Clark, but Alex wasn't about to volunteer her for the job when he knew Clark would be happy to do anything Daphne asked of him.

"Well, I suppose so," Clarke said, eying the cauldron in a new way.

"What do you think, Alex?" Victoria asked.

"What kind of magic is in it?" Alex asked, walking closer to examine the cauldron.

"Mmm, I don't know," Clark said. "All I can smell is a powerful magic. I can't tell what it does."

"A mystery," Alex said, sniffing at the cauldron.

"Exactly," Daphne said, her eyes lighting up.

"As if we don't have enough mystery in our lives," Rafael said with a sigh.

"We should take it back and figure out what it does," Daphne said. "It could be something important."

Everyone was looking at Alex, waiting to see what he would say. If he suggested it was too dangerous or difficult to take the cauldron with them, the others would probably follow his lead. If he told them Daphne was right, that it might be important, then they would begrudgingly agree with him.

He didn't have to debate with himself what he thought. It was a magic cauldron from the Dead Forest, probably abandoned there by some powerful mage years and years ago. There was no telling what magic it might be able to perform. It could also be dangerous beyond anything they could predict. The only way he'd consider leaving it behind was if he really had been dropped on his head as a child. But that's not what he said.

"I think we should vote," Alex said, trying to use his best reasonable-leader voice. "But I think Daphne's right. We should try to figure out what it does. So I vote we take it home." Alex raised his hand. "All those in favor?"

"You bet your butt I'm in favor," Daphne said as her hand shot up.

"Me, too," Nina said, raising her hand. Alex glared at his little sister. Her twelfth birthday was the following Monday, and she would finally be eligible for membership in The Young Sorcerers Guild, but she adamantly believed in participating in official Guild votes even though she knew her vote would not be counted.

"Mmm, I guess it's not that heavy," Clark said, giving the handle of the cauldron a tug with one hand and raising the other. Daphne smiled at him and blinked bashfully.

"Yep," Ben said, grinning, "I never pass up a chance to see Clark carry heavy things."

"I suppose it might prove useful someday if we can figure out what it does," Victoria said, raising her hand. "Daddy has several old magic cauldrons we can examine for clues."

"Being the sole voice of rational caution would be useless at this point, so…" Rafael said, reluctantly putting his hand in the air.

"Wuff," Beowulf said, cocking his leg at one of the tripod branches holding up the cauldron.

"Then it's unanimous," Alex said, smiling widely at his friends.

"Yes!" Daphne said, as she ran her hand along the edge of the cauldron.

Alex cleared his throat and raised his voice. "I officially claim this abandoned cauldron for the purposes of magical research and practical application until such time as its rightful owner may appear to claim it."

"Is that really all that's necessary to claim abandoned property in Runewood?" Victoria asked with a slight tilting of her head.

"Close enough," Alex said with a wink. "Clark, if you grab the cauldron, I'll carry your backpack." He glanced at his watch. "If we make good time, we should be home for dinner."

"Do we even know where we are to know how to get out?" Rafael asked, looking around at the wall of dead trees around them.

"That's the best thing about a magical tracking beagle," Alex said, bending down to pet Beowulf on the head. "He always knows how to find his way home. Isn't that right, boy?"

"Wuff," Beowulf said and trotted off into the forest.

Clark handed his oversized backpack to Alex and hefted the cauldron into his arms. It was heavy, but not too heavy for Clark's half-giant strength. Daphne walked beside him, eying the cauldron and smiling as if she had found a stray puppy her parents had agreed to let her keep.

"What about the Rune Tree?" Victoria asked as they all set out to follow Beowulf through the Dead Forest flora. She walked beside Alex at the rear of the group.

"We'll have to look for it again some other day," Alex said, frowning a bit at the thought of having failed in his search yet again. "If it's in this Dead Forest, we'll find it. We'll find it wherever it is. We don't have any choice."

"Can the Shadow Wraith really break free again?" Victoria asked, her voice dropping down to a whisper as she slowed her pace to give more distance between the others in the lead.

"I don't know," Alex said, feeling the seriousness of the question settle around him as he sought for an answer. "I can still feel it there, touching the world faintly. Like the scent of smoke after a fire. I don't think I would sense it at all if we had sealed its prison completely."

"What if we can't find the Rune Tree?" Victoria asked. "Or what if we find it and it doesn't have the rune we need?"

"Then we'll have to think of something else," Alex said. "Something clever." Victoria smiled and Alex grinned back. This was the first time the two of them had been able to speak in private in days, if not weeks. Alex felt his stomach tighten as he thought about all the things he had been wanting to say to Victoria, or really the one thing. Or was it something he wanted to ask? But could he ask it now? And if he got the answer he was hoping for, would that be of any help right now?

Every time he looked in her eyes, he wanted to kiss her again. Like he was looking in her eyes right now. But could you kiss a girl in the middle of the Dead Forest? Was that romantic? Alex realized he had been looking into Victoria's eyes for far longer than would be sensible for anyone walking through a forest. And she was still looking at him. What was she thinking? What did that look on her face mean?

Then Victoria stumbled, a hoof caught on a tree root, and Alex grasped to steady her, a fruitless endeavor given the disparity in their sizes. Alex stumbled as well, the two of them crashing into the trunk of a dead tree, its broken branches cascading down around them. Victoria scrambled for her footing and Alex tried to keep his feet beneath him, their arms tangled together, as they tried to find a mutual balance. Finally, they both stood upright, holding hands, once again staring into each other's eyes.

"Thank you," Victoria said, "I wasn't looking where I was going."

"It's my fault," Alex said, "I wasn't paying attention."

"You shouldn't try to stop me from falling. You could get hurt."

"You're not that heavy. Besides, I've had Clark fall on me plenty of times."

Victoria giggled and Alex laughed quietly. And they continued to stare into each other's eyes. Alex wasn't sure what Victoria might be thinking, but he knew what he was thinking and he was always one to act on his impulses. He was just about to act when he heard something.

"Wuff."

Alex and Victoria turned their heads in unison to see Beowulf staring at them, his head cocked in curiosity. Behind the beagle stood the rest of the Guild, heads all tipped in silent imitation of their canine companion.

"I, uh, lost my footing," Victoria said, blushing deeply as she and Alex disengaged their hands. "Alex caught me."

"I tried to help," Alex said, feeling an uncomfortable heat welling up in his cheeks. "I wasn't very successful."

Alex and Victoria's friends stared in silence a moment.

"The forest floor can be treacherous," Rafael said, a thin smile spreading across his face.

"Let's get gorping going," Daphne said. "I want to take a look at this cauldron before dinner."

"Wuff," Beowulf said, spinning and trotting back into the trees again. The others turned to follow, Nina turning last and grinning at her brother. Alex coughed, Victoria sighed, and the two of them set off following their friends.

Thoughts of kissing eliminated, mostly, from his head, Alex walked wordlessly with Victoria through the woods of the Dead Forest, staying near the rest of the Guild, unwilling to part, but keeping somewhat separate from the others. It had been a long, exhausting, and largely unsuccessful day and the Guild followed Beowulf through the forest in silence. When they finally emerged from the Dead Forest, the sky above turned blue once again and they found themselves almost exactly where they had entered it.

They were to the northeast of the Silent Swamp, south of the town of Runewood. They crossed the Creaking Creek by way of an old log laid between its banks, hiked up along the edge of Farmer Watson's cornfield, and past the wheat fields of the Kinup family. They retrieved their bicycles from where they had hidden them in the tall grass and at the edge of a field of barley and rode along an old dirt path running between the fields, Victoria trotting beside them. A short time later, they came across the East Road that would lead them into the town of Runewood and saw something that surprised them almost as much as the Colossus Tree had.

Alex wiped the sweat from his brow as he crested the top of a small hill overlooking the well packed dirt road running between fields of tall green corn. On the road, a line of trucks spread back for nearly a mile. Big trucks and small trucks, Studebakers and Fords and Packards and Chevrolets, some piled with boxes and crates, some pulling colorful wagons and trailers, their rolled canvas awnings flapping in the wind of their passing. The sides of the wagons were painted with depictions of various magical creatures and astounding scenes of mystery with bright, bold letters declaring what might be found inside by the brave and adventurous of heart.

Alex breathed in the sweet, warm air of the late midsummer day and exhaled with exhaustion and excitement as he read aloud the single word painted in an alternating rainbow of colors on the wooden side of the lead truck.

"Carnival."

Chapter Four
Carnival Cavalcade

Alex peddled hard, Victoria galloping at his side, the rest of the Guild following close behind. They raced down the slight hill of a dirt path and quickly crossed the East Road. The caravan of carnival trucks had already passed, but the cloud of dust it had kicked up stretched back for nearly a mile.

Alex coughed and wiped the dust from his eyes as he and his friends raced along an old farm path running roughly parallel to the East Road. The caravan was moving far too fast for them to follow, but they had other things to tend to before they could do the one thing they were all looking forward to — finding where the carnival was going to set up.

"Carnival," Ben panted, his short legs pumping furiously at the pedals of his diminutive bicycle. "How could we not have heard about a carnival?"

"It must be for the Founders Festival," Alex said. The Founders Festival was a yearly affair bringing the entire Rune Valley together to celebrate the official founding of the town centuries ago.

"I can't believe Dad didn't tell us," Nina said.

"Neither can I," Alex said.

"I do so love the carnival," Victoria said.

"You been to the gorping carnival?" Daphne said.

"Why, certainly," Victoria said. "They stop in Warwick every spring. They always let Daddy set up a booth where he sells his inventions. His small ones, anyway. I help him, naturally. I wonder if he'll have a booth this year. I can't imagine he knew they were coming. Daddy can never keep secrets. He chatters too much."

"Amazing," Ben said. "I can't believe you get to see the carnival every spring."

"Why ever not?" Victoria asked.

"We've never seen the carnival," Rafael said. "We're too young."

"What do you mean?" Victoria asked. "I was never aware there was an age limit for entry to the carnival."

"Rafa means we're too young to remember the last time the carnival was in town," Alex said.

"It hasn't been here in gorping ages," Daphne said.

"Long before we were born," Nina said.

"Too far," Ben said. "I always heard it was too hard for them to cross the ocean so often."

"That's simply awful," Victoria said. "The carnival is terribly fun. And they are ever such nice people. Daddy and I thought about joining them for a while, but in the end, his inventions were too big to carry with us. I can show you around. I can be your guide. It's the least I can do for all of you guiding me around Runewood."

"Mmmm, where do you think they'll set up?" Clark asked. He was balancing the cauldron on the handlebars of his massive jalopy-like bicycle and having a rough time of it.

"There's only one place near town with enough room," Nina said. "The open field behind the Town Hall."

"Exactly," Alex said. "Which is where we'll meet up."

"After we drop the cauldron off at the Guild House," Daphne said.

"And convince our parents to postpone dinner," Alex said.

"I doubt my aunt will let me fix her dinner any later," Rafael said.

"Maybe she's in the mood for a peanut butter and jelly sandwich," Alex suggested.

"Maybe she is," Rafael said, a smile spreading across his face. "Funny how she forgot how to cook after she took me in. And clean. And do laundry. And feed the animals."

"It sounds as if your aunt needs a memory charm," Victoria said.

"Sounds as if she needs a good, swift…" Curses drowned out Daphne's next words as her bike tire hit a rut and she swerved to avoid a tree. She recovered quickly and barely lost her pace.

A short time later, they coasted into town, raced up Marigold Street, crossed Alex's backyard, and skidded to a stop at the door to the old horse barn that served as the Guild House.

"Mucus Marmalade," Nina said, speaking the secret password that would undo the magical charms protecting the door.

Clark hauled the cauldron through the door and sat it down in the middle of the room. The others crowded in, Nina and Ben collapsing into the cracked depths of the monstrous old leather couch against the wall as Raphael plopped himself into one of the mismatched wooden chairs strewn around a patch-work table assembled from odds and ends and spare pieces.

"Push the cauldron into the corner," Daphne said, pointing to the empty space near the woodstove. In the winter, small magical logs for the fire filled the corner, but in the middle of summer, it was barren. "I have an idea. Give me a hand, Nina."

As Clark moved the cauldron to the corner of the room, Alex and the others watched as Daphne and Nina darted outside. A few moments later, they both retuned, carrying a potted rosebush between them.

"Mom's winter roses?" Alex said as he watched them carry the potted plant across the floor and gently slide it onto the cauldron. Late summer light bathed the small plant as it sat between the two windows at the corner of the room.

"Oh, that's lovely," Victoria said. "That brightens up the room considerably."

"And draws attention away from the cauldron to the flowers," Daphne said.

"Genius," Ben said. "A potted plant in a pot."

"Hmmm, very clever," Clark said, smiling at Daphne.

"Until Mrs. Ravenstar goes looking for her roses," Rafael said.

"Mom won't mind," Nina said. "We'll tell her we needed to decorate."

"You'll tell her," Alex said. "She'll never believe that from me. She'll know something's up."

"Leave it to me, Brother," Nina said with a grin.

Minutes later, the Guild members had dispersed to their various homes seeking permission to postpose their dinners in lieu of watching the assembly of the carnival. As it turned out, Alex and Nina's mother was far less interested in what they had done with the potted winter rosebush than with the arrival of the carnival.

"The carnival!" Alex's mother said with an almost childlike excitement. "The carnival hasn't been to Runewood since I was a girl. I can't believe your father didn't tell me it was coming."

"So what do you think, Mom?" Alex asked.

"I think if my winter rosebush dies, someone is going to find himself grounded," his mother said, surprising Alex by changing the subject.

"That was Nina's idea," Alex said. "I don't even know how to decorate."

"The rosebush is fine, Mom," Nina said. "What about watching the carnival setup?"

"I'd love to watch the carnival set up," their mother said, her eyes glittering with excitement. "Thank you for inviting me."

Alex and Nina stared at their mother in silence.

"That was an invitation, wasn't it?" their mother asked, her eyes going round with innocent curiosity. "To spend some time together as a family?"

"Ah," Alex said.

"Well," Nina added.

"You two are so gullible," their mother said, laughing. "No wonder you both thought the tooth fairy wasn't real until you were ten. Run along. We'll have dinner late. Grab some apples from the root cellar before you go. I'll bring your father something to tide him over. You're not the only ones who want to see the carnival setting up."

Minutes later, an apple apiece in their stomachs and two in their pockets, Alex and Nina stashed their bikes at the side of the Town Hall, quickly chanting rune-spells of warding around them to prevent anyone from tampering with them. It was a precaution that had become second nature after a prank had left the Guild's bicycles with a magnetic desire to crash into each other. Alex and the Guild suspected their rivals, The Mad Mages, but they hadn't been able to prove anything.

Alex swept the hair from his sweat-covered face as he stood up straight. It was oddly warmer now at the end of the day than it had been earlier. He and Nina walked around the centuries-old brick walls and broke into simultaneous smiles as they saw the carnival trucks spread out in the wide field behind the Town Hall.

The field was slowly becoming a carnival ground. Trucks and wagons parked in a large circle, creating a sort of barrier between the outside world and the place where the carnival was slowly coming to life. The carnival workers, *roustabouts*, Alex remembered they were called, unloaded the wagons and trucks in small groups. A brightly-colored carousel was already assembled, a circular parade of magical metal creatures spinning slowly as they rose and fell on brass poles.

The first thing to really catch Alex's eye, even more so than the spectacle of the multitude of mysterious carnival elements slowly being revealed as the wagons and trucks were unpacked, was the composition of the carnival workers themselves. The carnies — Alex was already thinking about them in storybook terms — were an even more diverse group than the citizens of Runewood. People from seemingly every corner of the world labored side-by-side with more magical creatures than Alex had ever hoped to see in one place. Elves, dwarves, giants, nymphs, and others Alex wasn't sure what to call, strode across the growing carnival grounds on various errands.

Alex looked around to see that he and Nina were not the only ones who had decided to watch the carnival come together. A steady stream of people strode from the edge of town to the field. Groups of students off for the summer, running in lazy circles around each other, as adults walked in more restrained, but equally excited, groups of twos or threes or fours.

"Quite a sight," Alex heard a deep and familiar voice say form behind him.

"Dad," Alex said with a startled jump. His father liked sneaking up on him and Nina. He said it kept them on their toes.

"How could you keep it a secret?" Nina said, recovering quickly from the sudden appearance of their father. "Why didn't you tell us the carnival was coming for the Founders Festival?"

"Because I didn't know," their father said with a look of equal parts amusement and annoyance. "I found out when I saw the carnival trucks rolling past the jail house windows. The mayor didn't tell anyone. Says he wanted it to be a surprise. Although, he looked a little surprised himself when he stepped out of the Town Hall to greet them."

"At least he's doing something right," Alex said.

"Mind your words," his father said. "He's a good mayor. Most of the time."

"Right, Dad," Alex said, heading off toward the carnival grounds. "We'll catch up with you later."

"What about dinner?" their father asked.

"Mom is postponing dinner," Alex said.

"Really?" their father said, raising a questioning eyebrow.

"She's bringing you a snack," Nina said.

"Couldn't wait to see it herself, could she?" their father said, a grin beginning to fill his wide jaw. "She always did love the carnival. Nina, keep your brother out of too much trouble."

"Seriously, Dad," Nina said with a mock whine, "I should get a larger allowance if I'm going to be responsible for him all the time."

"How much trouble is too much trouble?" Alex laughed.

"You'll know if I find out about it," their father said with a wave.

Alex and Nina ran along the outskirts of the field, taking in the sights of the still-forming carnival grounds, passing fellow students and older citizens, some just arriving and others staking out the best spots to view the fascinating work in the field. It wasn't long before they came across the rest of the Guild, waiting for them beneath the wide branches of a sycamore tree.

"How'd your aunt like the peanut butter and jelly sandwich?" Alex asked Rafael as he and Nina stepped under the early evening shade of the tree.

"She's wasn't very happy," Rafael said, "until she heard about the carnival and then she couldn't eat it fast enough. She made it here almost as fast as I did, and I came as a panther."

"Seems like the whole gorping town is coming out to see the carnival set up," Daphne said, gesturing to the still growing crowd at the edge of the field.

"Hmm, we should pick a good spot," Clark said.

"Up," Ben said. "We should climb a tree."

"I rather doubt that will work for me," Victoria said. "Why don't I see if the manager will let us take a closer look?"

"That's a much better idea," Alex said.

"Then let's go," Victoria said, trotting toward the carnival grounds. Alex and the rest of the Guild quickly followed.

As they walked toward the circle of carnival vehicles parked in the field, Alex could see a gang of workers pulling at a large canvas tent. Around the tent, carnie workers began to assemble smaller tents and wooden booths, as well as mechanical rides composed of assorted steel arms and legs that gave no clear indication of their eventual form. Alex could only guess from the names attached to some of the parts what the final contraptions might be. *The Whizzing Wonder. The Giant's Wheel. The Flying Carpet. The Trojan Horse. The Flying Dutchman. The Spider's Web. The Dragon's Eggs.*

The names on the sides of the booths and tents were just as exotic and enticing. *The Archer Queen, King Arthur's Sword, Aladdin's Lamp, Davey Jones' Locker, Pandora's Box, Mediterranean Mysteries, The Forbidden Kingdom, Minotaur Mirror Maze,* and so many more that Alex lost count.

As they walked through the entrance between two wagons and along a wide boulevard created by rows of carnival booths on either side, carnie workers began to notice them. Those bent over tasks stood and stared, those walking with burdens came to a halt, those already at rest followed them with their eyes. Victoria waved at those she seemed to know and each waved back, but did not move to greet her. Finally, they came upon a group of a dozen or so carnies blocking the lane.

As they stopped, Alex noticed how oddly quiet it had become. No one moved. No one spoke. Everyone stared at Alex and the Guild. He wondered if maybe Victoria had overstated her acquaintance with the carnival. Maybe they had offended the carnies by entering the grounds before everything was ready. Even Victoria was taken aback and at a loss for words. As the silence dragged on, Alex became less and less sure of what was happening and what he should do about it.

Chapter Five
Celebrity Sighting

"That's him, ain't it?" an impossibly small woman said. As Alex looked more closely, he realized the two foot tall woman with the large pointed ears and wrinkled face was a goblin.

"Him and his band of mighty warriors," a wildly tattooed man beside her said.

"What do they call themselves again?" a dwarfish woman asked.

"The Wild Wizards Club," an elven man said.

"No, it's The Excellent Enchanter's Club," a slender woman with red feathered wings said.

"And our young Victoria right in the middle of them," a bear-like man said.

"It's not a club," Alex said before he could stop himself.

"Actually, it's called the Young Sorcerers Guild," Victoria said, raising her head proudly.

"Of course it is," said a voice from behind them. The man walked around and spread his arms wide before the gathered crowd. He was tall and willow tree-thin with lines of silver-gray streaking his wavy black hair. He wore a red velvet jacket and a black stovepipe hat and held a black-lacquered wooden cane capped with a silver dragon's head.

"Now stop staring like a bunch of rustic rubes," the man said to the crowd, his voice booming. "People are supposed to stop and stare at us, not the other way around. What are you all standing here for? There's work to be done. There's a carnival to create from nothing but sweat and hard work and magic. You can say your hellos to Victoria when the work is done. And you can gawk at young Alex and his Guild all weekend. Now back to work!"

The carnies scattered and ran back to their labors, most of them waving and smiling at Victoria as they hustled past. She waved and smiled back as the man in the red velvet jacket shooed a few straggling carnies away.

"Sorry about that," the man said, gracing them with a dazzling smile and giving Victoria a kiss on the cheek.

"What was that all about, Mr. Apollo?" Victoria asked the man.

"They're not used to seeing anyone more interesting than they are," Mr. Apollo said. "The last time we saw you and your father, you were a coltish young centaur and now you are a member of the famous Young Sorcerers Guild."

"Famous?" Nina said, her voice excited.

"How many people know about us?" Alex asked.

"A young boy and his, shall we say, eccentric friends, save a town from the most ancient of ancient evils?" Mr. Apollo said rhetorically. "That's the kind of story to warm any carnie's heart, and one they are likely to tell again and again as they travel from town to town. Especially if they know one of the heroines of the tale."

"Great," Alex said with a frown.

"There's nothing wrong with a little fame," Mr. Apollo said. "As long as you let it go to your pocketbook and not your head. How rude of me, I have not introduced myself. I am Adolphus Apollo, manager and chief barker of the Conundrum Carnival and Magical Mystery Show."

"And I am his wife," a woman with a gentle British accent said as she stepped up beside Mr. Apollo. She was nearly half a head taller than Mr. Apollo, with long, flame-like hair sitting in an unruly mane around a narrow, porcelain-white face, complimented by a dazzling necklace of nine large sapphires hung along an intricately woven gold chain. The glittering stones seemed to glow from within as they caught and reflected the golden light of early evening.

"My *lovely and enchanting* wife, Esmeralda." Mr. Apollo corrected. "The star of *The Eternal Story* and the woman whose brilliant idea it was to bring the carnival across the ocean once again to see the Americas."

"Oh, posh," Esmeralda said with a wink at her husband. "I haven't been to Runewood since I was a girl. I grew up in the carnival, you know, and left it for some inexplicable reason when I thought I was too grown-up for such things."

"One is never too grown-up for the carnival," Mr. Apollo said, his voice deep and serious.

"Fortunately, I met Mr. Apollo after he bought the carnival, and he showed me the error in my judgment," Esmeralda said.

"The only fault I have ever found," Mr. Apollo said, beaming at his wife.

"You don't have to charm me, Dear," Esmeralda said, her eyes twinkling at her husband's words, "I've already bought a ticket."

"For life, no less," Mr. Apollo said with a laugh as he kissed his wife's cheek.

"Victoria, you are looking as lovely as ever," Esmeralda said, turning from her husband to Victoria, Alex, and the Guild.

"Thank you, Mrs. Apollo," Victoria said, trading triple cheek kisses with Esmeralda. "Allow me to introduce my friends."

"Oh, they hardly need any introduction," Esmeralda said, turning to the others with a wide smile. "A boy of your size, you are clearly Clark, brave young giant. And you must be Ben, the boy who held a dragon's fire. This must be the lovely and talented Daphne, whose fine control of magic is remarkable beyond her age. And you are Rafael, changeling of renowned skill. Which means you must be Nina, young adventuress and sister of this young man, who is, no doubt, Alex Ravenstar, savior of Runewood, and quite possibly, the rest of the world."

The radiance of Esmeralda's smile washed over Alex much as her words had and he felt his face burning with embarrassment. He could see the other members of the Guild were just as enchanted and self-conscious as he was. He never got used to this. Being known for saving the town from the Shadow Wraith had seemed like a great thing for the first day or so. Soon the constant stares and whispers and people stopping to thank him had grown wearisome and altogether annoying. The unwanted attention it brought him from the girls at school might have been enjoyable, if it were not for the fact that they seemed to annoy the one girl, or girl centaur, whose attention he actually desired.

As the months had passed, Anna and the Mad Mages spread rumors suggesting Alex had been less central than he had claimed in the battle to seal the Shadow Wraith back in its prison and the townspeople of Runewood gradually lost interest in him and the Guild. But, everyone still knew what they had done. Now, it seemed the story of their exploits had traveled far beyond the mountain walls of the Rune Valley.

"Esmeralda, you've made them uncomfortable about their uniqueness," Mr. Apollo said.

"They should be proud of being unique," Esmeralda said, staring into Alex's eyes. "It's our specialness that makes us important. Don't let anyone tell you different."

"You don't need to worry about my brother not thinking he's special," Nina said, poking Alex in the ribs.

"I suspect you are all very special," Mr. Apollo said. "Now, if I know Victoria, she is in the mood to get under foot and poke around where she shouldn't be, while the carnival sets up." His eyes twinkled as he teased her.

"I do not poke around," Victoria said, her chin rising with her voice. "I investigate." Mr. Apollo and Esmeralda laughed.

"Then please be our guests and investigate to your heart's content," Esmeralda said.

"And be sure to tell your father we are holding his usual booth under the usual terms, should he wish to have it," Mr. Apollo said. "Now, if you will excuse us, there is a carnival to pull up out of near nothingness before the sun is down."

Mr. Apollo and Esmeralda waved as they walked toward a group of carnies pulling boxes from a wagon. Alex looked around at his friends. Nina smiled at him.

"We're famous," Nina said in an awed voice.

"Around the gorping world," Daphne said with a laugh.

"Yeah," Alex said with a sigh. "Great."

"Well, at least we're famous for doing something good," Clark pointed out.

"Good?" Ben said. "We saved the town from the Shadow Wraith. That's better than good."

"Being famous doesn't feel as fun as I thought it would," Rafael said. "Maybe we should try being rich instead."

"It seems the sensible thing to do is ignore it until it fades away," Victoria said.

"Well, lucky for us," Alex said, looking over at Victoria, "we always do the sensible thing."

Everyone laughed and Alex felt the tension in his shoulders melt away. It was a strain having people know you before you knew them, especially if they knew you for something you had done. Particularly if that something seemed heroic. What most people didn't understand was that Alex didn't think of himself as heroic. He had only done what he felt certain most people would have done in the same situation — what was necessary. Moreover, he knew the others in the Guild felt the same way.

"Time for the tour," Alex said to Victoria. "Show us all the best parts of the carnival."

"Oh, yes," Victoria said, her long hair swishing in time with her tail. "That's exactly what I'll do."

Victoria led them through the grounds as the carnie workers swarmed around them, the carnival slowly taking shape and coming to life with every passing minute. Victoria kept up a running commentary about which ride was which, what games offered the best odds of winning, which sideshow acts were the most interesting, all the while waving to old friends, exchanging hugs and kisses and brief introductions of the Guild before passing on to the next fascinating sight.

"Those two long boxes are coffins. Bernard and Heloise are vampires. They've been married forever. Or at least a couple of centuries. They have an act, but they are also the night guards. Who better to guard the grounds at night than vampires?

"That thing there will become the *Giant's Wheel*. Goliath the giant runs it. That's him there. His real name's not Goliath. It's Horace. But who wants to ride a Ferris wheel manned by a giant named Horace?

"That wagon holds a water tank. A mermaid and a selkie share it. Velma and Paulina. Look, they're waving. Hello. They are terribly nice when they've had a chance to swim a bit, but they can be ever so cranky when they have been cooped up in the tank for too long. I hope they have time to make it to the lake before they leave.

"Over there, that's Nick and Nora, the naga and nagini. They are perfectly wonderful people, but I can never be around them for too long. As soon and their snake half starts moving, I feel an overwhelming urge to stomp on them. Don't tell them I said that, though. They were very nice to me when I was little. And this is…"

Victoria continued her descriptive tour as the as they journeyed through the carnival grounds and the sun slowly sank to meet the horizon. As it did, the carnival gradually filled with shadows. As it grew darker, Alex became more certain someone was following them. A shadowy figure, all in black, would appear at the corner of his eye, but was gone when he tried to look at it directly. It was as if the person melted into the darkness between the tents and wagons and carnival booths. The presence of something, or someone, watching from the shadows brought back unpleasant memories.

"I think someone is following us," Alex whispered to Rafael. He whispered not so much to keep the knowledge from the others, they knew enough not to stare around and give away the advantage, but more to ensure that whoever was in the shadows did not realize Alex had discovered their presence.

"I don't see anyone," Rafael said, risking a quick glance in the direction Alex had indicated. "And I can't smell anything odd, other than all the aromas of a carnival."

"Keep an eye out," Alex said. Being a changeling gave Rafael much better eyesight than a normal human being.

"And this is Melvin," Victoria said as Alex turned his attention back to her voice.

"Which one?" Alex asked.

Even as accustomed as he was to strange creatures and wondrous sights, Alex found his mouth gaping open as he watched a minotaur struggle with a griffin in front of a large open cage with thick black iron bars. The minotaur stood nearly seven feet tall, with muscled arms the size of small tree trunks. His bull face was contorted in a grimace as the griffin's wings whipped about his head and its large beak snapped at his hands.

"Get in there, you dozy beast," the minotaur said in a thick Irish accent. With a great shove, the minotaur knocked the griffin into the cage. Before the griffin could recover, the minotaur slammed the cage door shut. "How many times have I told you, no flying at night. It scares the locals."

"I see Sheila is still giving you trouble," Victoria said to the minotaur, who was obviously Melvin.

"Victoria," Melvin said, his bull face breaking into something resembling a smile as he lumbered forth and wrapped his massive arms around Victoria. She made brief, and largely unnecessary, introductions of Alex and the Guild.

"Ah yes, the heroes of Runewood," Melvin said. "It's a pleasure to meet you. Victoria, it's so good to see you. I was hoping I'd run into you. Is your father here? Will he have his booth again? He still owes me a game of chess."

"I'm sure Daddy will have his booth again," Victoria said. "I can't imagine he could resist. Any more than he could resist a game of chess."

"And a mug of ale," Melvin said with a deep rumbling chuckle. "The only chance I have of beating him is if he has me down two to one in pints of ale."

"You are a bad influence on Daddy," Victoria said with a chiding wave of her finger.

"I'm a bad influence on everyone," Melvin said, laughing again. "These daft creatures most of all. The which, I should attend to. You tell your father I said I'd spot him one pawn and two pints."

"I will inform him of your challenge," Victoria said as Melvin waved and headed off to a row of cages near the wagons, cages containing creatures Alex wasn't sure he could identify.

"Melvin is the creature trainer." Victoria reached through the bars of the cage holding Sheila the griffin and petted her on the head. Sheila rubbed up against Victoria's hand and squawked with pleasure. "All of the creatures have acts. Sheila here does absolutely amazing aerial acrobatics. Although she does have a habit of carrying off local livestock that gets her into trouble." Sheila snapped her beak at Victoria, who simply laughed and pulled her hand away.

41

Alex was more than a little impressed with the fact Victoria had spent so much time with the carnival and knew so many of its most interesting people. He was even more impressed with the fact she seemed so universally well-liked by everyone they encountered. Apparently, he was not the only one swayed by her many charms. Alex was about to compliment Victoria on this when he noticed her attention had turned to a young centaur carrying a stack of wooden crates across the grounds. The crates obscured the centaur's face, but Alex could see a shock of black hair waving behind the boxes.

"Oh, goodness me," Victoria said. "A centaur. I haven't seen another centaur in ages. Hello. Hello there. I wonder if he knows any of my friends in Warwick. I say, are you deaf? Hello."

The centaur lowered his armful of crates to reveal his face. He looked to be about two years older than Victoria. His midnight black hair fell with a gentle curl to the middle of his back. His face was long and angular with high cheekbones and piercing ice-blue eyes. He blinked in surprise and Victoria gasped. She was not the only one to make a noise, as Alex noticed both Nina and Daphne sigh slightly as they gazed up at the somewhat mesmerizing features of the young centaur boy.

"Victoria," the young centaur said in a sharp British accent, his mouth hanging open slightly.

"Nathan," Victoria said, her hands rising to her mouth to cover her shock.

Something about the exchange and the tone of their voices made Alex's stomach flop. He looked between them and could tell immediately by the cast of their eyes exactly who Nathan was.

"Nathan," Victoria said again. "Whatever are you doing here?"

"I work here," Nathan said. "In the carnival."

"You joined the carnival?" Victoria asked. "Whatever for?"

"You always said how much you enjoyed the carnival," Nathan said. "And I wanted to see the world. To travel. And this seemed like the best way. And after your last letter, I thought…"

"I see," Victoria said, her cheeks reddening as she noticed Alex and the Guild intently following every word of her exchange with Nathan.

"So I thought…" Nathan said.

"Yes," Victoria said.

"And here you are."

"And there you are."

"I'm so happy to see you."

"Yes. Happy."

They stared at each other for what felt like an eternity to Alex.

"These must be your friends," Nathan said. "The ones we all hear about."

"Yes," Victoria said, still staring at Nathan as though he were some manner of mirage.

"I'm Alex," Alex said, thrusting his hand toward Nathan.

"A pleasure," Nathan said, effortlessly shifting the crates to one arm and gripping Alex's hand in an iron-firm grasp, though his eyes never left Victoria's. *Does he have to be so strong and handsome*, Alex thought. As Nathan released his hand, Alex made quick introductions of the rest of the Guild. Daphne and Nina sighed again as Nathan shook their hands. Clark frowned and shook Nathan's hand briefly. The spell that had held Victoria's attention captive seemed to have broken. Now she could not seem to look in Nathan's general direction without her hindquarters fidgeting.

"Well, I should get back to my work," Nathan said, a dazzling smile shining for Victoria. "I hope we can spend some time together, while I'm here."

"Ah," Victoria said. "Time together. Yes, well, I'll be at my father's booth, so I'll be very busy."

"I'll stop by," Nathan said as he turned and headed back on his way, glancing several times over his shoulder at Victoria.

"Who in the name of Cupid's cupcakes is that?" Daphne said, still staring after Nathan.

"Mmm, he's just a centaur," Clark said.

"That is my ex-boyfriend," Victoria said with a grimace.

"The one from England?" Nina asked, her head snapping around to Victoria. "The one you haven't seen since you left, the one you had been writing to, the one you were supposed to be engaged to when you turned sixteen, and the one...Oh. Sorry. I got carried away."

"Yes," Victoria said, frowning deeply. "That one."

"Strong," Ben said, smiling at Alex. "He certainly is strong."

"And handsome," Raphael said with a wink to Ben.

Alex scowled at Ben and Rafael. He tried to catch Victoria's eye, but she seemed incapable of looking in his direction. A fluttering piece of paper across the grounds caught his attention. He had seen a paper like it earlier. A flier of some sort. He whispered the rune-word for wind and the flier flittered through the air toward him.

"Oh, look," Alex said, snatching the flier from the air as the wind that blew it suddenly disappeared. It was printed on paper aged to look like old parchment, with letters formed to resemble an old style handbill from the 1800s. He read it aloud, hoping to distract Victoria from thoughts of her ex-boyfriend, Nathan, the impossibly handsome centaur.

"*The Eternal Story* — Told Eternally. Love, Jealously, Murder, Justice, Revenge, Joy, Sorrow, Birth, Death, and all of Life. Never the Same Show Twice."

"Sounds long," Rafael said, looking over Alex's shoulder.

"It's wonderful," Victoria said, her mood becoming lighter with the change of subject. "It's what the carnival is famous for."

"What is it?" Alex asked, hoping to continue the distraction.

"It's a play," Victoria said. "Or it's like a play. It's the main show in the big tent. There are parts that are written and there are parts that are made up by the actors on the spot. There are parts that are performed every night and parts that are hardly ever performed. The actors decide how the story will go and how it will end based on the audience. It's really quite wonderful. Esmeralda plays the lead. A good quarter of the carnival makes an appearance."

"Sounds confusing," Nina said.

"Theatre," Ben said. "Sounds boring."

"It's not," Victoria said, her voice adamant. "There's something for everyone. Kings. Queens. Battles. Love. Romance." With these last words, Victoria fell silent.

It was a silence that fell over the rest of them as well, cloaking them in discomfort. Alex stared, first at Victoria, and then his friends, not knowing what to say or do and hoping for some diversion to arrive that might ease the tension. A disturbance did arrive, but it did not ease the tension, only changed and amplified it.

"Well, mmm," Clark said.

"Mercury's monkey bars," Daphne said

"Them," Ben said. "How did they get in?"

"There was an opening for an act of evil carnies and they came to apply?" Rafael said.

"They probably snuck in," Nina said.

"More likely the mayor arranged it for them," Alex said.

"I'd like to arrange something for them," Victoria said.

Alex and the Guild watched as the Mad Mages walked across the carnival grounds. Anna, Dillon, Koji, Earl, and Mai sauntered across the worn-down grass, heading straight for Alex and the Guild. Although it was not the distraction he would have hoped for, Alex realized he would much rather face a confrontation with the Mad Mages than spend another moment thinking about the look on Victoria's face when she had seen Nathan. What was that look? Was she happy to see him? Was she mad? What did Nathan mean when he had referred to Victoria's last letter? What had been in the letter? And did he have to be so good-looking? No, Anna and the Mad Mages were much easier to deal with than the emotions causing his stomach to churn.

"I told you we'd find them here," Dillon said, flipping his hair back from his long, pale face. "They've probably already joined the circus."

"It's a carnival," Alex said, drawing his attention back from his romantic concerns as he glared up at Dillon.

"It's a show for freaks," Anna said in her usual sweetly sarcastic tone. "It doesn't matter what it's called."

"You must feel right at home," Earl said, a sneering grin on his thin, dark face. "They even have cages for you."

"We saw you with that centaur boy," Koji said, spitting into the grass between the two groups of young mages. "Is he part of your freak family?"

"Maybe he's her boyfriend," Mai said with a giggle. "Maybe they're going to get married."

"Yea," Earl said with a throaty laugh. "And have little horse babies."

"They're called foals, Earl," Anna said, smiling as Victoria's cheeks reddened and her face darkened. "At least if they're horses. In her case they'd have to be called monsters."

"You are the only monsters here," Victoria said, glaring at Anna.

"We should put you creatures in a cage," Dillon said. "To keep the town safe." After his embarrassment at the cave, when the Guild had saved the town, Anna had been able to push Dillon aside and assume command of the Mad Mages Club. It was easy to see how much Dillon resented Anna's new position, and his own, but for the time being, there didn't seem to be anything he could do about it.

"You could try," Alex said, stepping forward to stand between Victoria and the Mad Mages. Dillon thrust his chest out and took a step closer to Alex.

"Oh, I have a much better plan for them than cages," Anna said, stepping in front of Dillon and staring at Alex. "The famous boy loves his fame a little too much."

"And the jealous girl loves herself a little too much," Alex said. Anna's eyes flickered with fire and Alex knew he had struck a nerve. He wanted to strike something else, but he held back. He and the Guild could not be the first ones to start a fight. Not with the Mad Mages. Not with Dillon being the Mayor's son.

"Oi!" a voice shouted from beside them. Alex and Anna continued to stare at each other, unwilling to look aside. "What are you lot doing here?"

The owner of the Scottish accented voice stepped between Anna and Alex and looked at them both. The voice belonged to a tall girl about fifteen years old. Not a human girl, Alex realized. An elf. A mountain elf, he guessed, by the stone gray color of her eyes and the midnight black hair pulled back in a long ponytail that hung to the middle of her back. She carried a long wooden bow in one hand and had a quiver of arrows slung over her shoulder. Another girl stood beside her. This one had the same dark African features as Clark and Earl, and stood as tall as Alex.

"Who let you in?" the elven girl repeated, this time turning and facing Anna and the Mad Mages.

"Who are you?" Anna said, straightening herself slightly.

"I'm the one what's asking you who you are," the elven girl said, her eyes squinting as she stared down at Anna.

"We have permission to be here," Dillon said, stepping forward to stand beside Anna.

"Not from me, you don't," the elven girl said. "So move it along."

"We don't have to listen to you," Anna said. "You're not in charge here."

"That's where you wrong, little miss muffin face," the elven girl said. "I give the orders around here. Want to see one? Kenda, show them why they should leave."

The girl next to her, who Alex assumed must be Kenda, smiled and shook herself. There was a short burst of green light and suddenly Kendra was no more. In her place stood an eight-foot tall hairy beast with large yellow tusk-like teeth and a shaggy coat of black fur. Her clothes, simple pants and a t-shirt, stretched to fit her new impossibly large form. Alex guessed Kendra's clothes must have been enchanted in order to remain whole and untorn. Although Alex had no idea how she had done so, when he looked to the elven girl, he realized she had knocked an arrow and held the bow drawn, aimed at Anna's head.

"You won't shoot me," Anna said, glaring up at the elven girl.

"Victoria," the elven girl said, with a nod of her head in Victoria's direction, "would I shoot her?"

"She is well known for her impetuousness," Victoria said, blinking in surprise at the sudden turn of events.

"She means I tend to do things without thinking about the consequences," the elven girl said.

"I know what it means," Anna said between gritted teeth.

"My father's the mayor," Dillon said, his fists balled in fury.

"And I'm the Queen of England," the elven girl said, still staring at Anna, tilting her head to look down the shaft of the arrow at the smaller girl.

"Let's go," Anna said, sniffing slightly. "There are too many freaks here anyway. They smell bad." Anna turned and started to walk away.

"My father will hear about this," Dillon said as he scowled and followed Anna.

"Just so there's no confusion," the elven girl said, "when you whine like a baby to your daddy, tell him it was Elaeda that spanked you and sent you packing."

Alex watched Anna and Dillon and the rest of the Mad Mages retreat into the growing shadows of the carnival. A burst of green light revealed Kendra standing next to the elven girl Elaeda again, her clothes back to normal size.

"Wow," Ben said, stepping forward and offering Elaeda his hand. "I'm Ben." Alex blinked in surprise. Ben shook Elaeda's hand and grinned up at her.

"I've heard of you," Eleada said. "Heard of all of you. But her we know well." She turned and embraced Victoria. "How have you been, Vic?"

"Better now that I have seen you again," Victoria said, hugging Eleada tightly. "You really didn't need to do that. They're more bark than bite."

"I'm more bite than bark." Elaeda grinned.

"You certainly are," Victoria said with a genuine smile.

"Thank you," Alex said, stepping beside Victoria.

"Not a problem," Elaeda said. "I can't stand kids like that. Thinking they're special because they're born human. Or because they're born the mayor's son. I'd ban them from the carnival completely if it was up to me, but rousting them out tonight will have to do. They don't seem to like you lot much."

"We have a long history together," Alex said. "None of it pleasant."

"That was an impressive transformation," Rafael said as he stepped over to Kendra. "How did you manage to become so large?"

"It's a changeling thing," Kenda said. "It's complicated."

Raphael briefly glowed red, but retained his human form. "I think I can follow the conversation."

"Oh, you're a changeling, too," Kendra said, excited. "It's been so long since I've met another changeling."

"So, what's the secret?" Rafael asked.

"Mass," Kendra said. "It's all about distribution of mass."

48

As he turned away from Rafael and Kendra, something flickered at the edge of Alex's vision. He could have sworn he saw the shadowed figure again. There was someone following them, he was certain of it.

He looked back at his friends. Rafael was quizzing Kendra on the finer points of shape changing while Ben was admiring Elaeda's bow almost as much as he was admiring Eleada. Clark and Daphne were engaged in some kind of conversation together. They seemed to do that a lot lately. Stick their heads together and laugh about things. Alex could only guess at what. Nina was excitedly explaining the relationship between the Guild and the Mad Mages to Elaeda, who laughed. Alex heard Eleada mention Nathan to Victoria as he caught another glimpse of the shadowed figure behind a wagon.

It took Alex only a second to decide he would rather be chasing after some shadow-shrouded pursuer than listen to more about Nathan. He would only chase the person in black for a little bit. Just to prove someone was there. The others wouldn't miss him. He stepped backward around the edge of a wagon in the direction he'd last seen the shadowed figure. He'd only be gone a moment.

Chapter Six
Chasing Shadows

The shadowed figure was elusive, always slipping around a corner, always at the edge of sight, fading into the darkness between tents and wagons and carnival booths. Alex, however, had plenty of experience tracking the elusive. That experience led him to an inescapable conclusion. Whomever he was chasing wasn't trying to lose him. The path through the carnival grounds might have seemed random to someone else, but Alex could tell he was being led somewhere. But where? And for what purpose?

He considered briefly going back and getting the others, but he knew that wasn't really an option. The shadowed figure was interested in *him*. It was leading *him* somewhere. It might not reveal itself at all if the others were with him. Alex weighed the risks, the danger inherent in following a shadowed figure alone through the ever-darkening carnival grounds, and decided curiosity might be his greatest weakness.

Alex stepped around the corner of a wagon and into a row of small tents, each set up to display a particular sideshow act. As he did so, a warm wash of light suddenly illuminated the row of tents. Alex looked around to see magic glow-globes hanging from the edges of the tents, each one casting a pleasant yellow radiance. Alex stopped and stood in the middle of the lane between the tents. The light from the glow-globes eliminated most of the shadows, but also seemed to deepen the darkness in those places where no glow-globes were present.

As Alex looked around, searching for the familiar flash of black cloth signaling the cloaked figure's presence, he noticed the whole of the carnival grounds were now lit up. The setting of the sun must have triggered the magic glow-globes to activate all over the carnival. He sighed. The addition of the lights diminished his chances of following his mysterious prey.

"Looking for something?" a sandpapery voice said. "Maybe someone. Maybe some young girl?"

Alex turned to see an old woman with long gray hair pulled up in a bun setting up a small folding table and chairs within one of the sideshow tents. The painted cloth banner hanging over the edge of the tent read: *"Fortunes Told, Futures Revealed, Fate Uncovered — Madam Fortuna."*

"Maybe you're looking to have your fortune told," the wrinkled woman who Alex took to be Madam Fortuna said.

"No," Alex said with a weary smile as he looked into Madam Fortuna's kind, blue eyes. "I've already seen my destiny."

Madam Fortuna cocked her head in puzzlement a moment and then chuckled to herself quietly. "Yes, I believe you have." She smiled and placed a deck of cards on the small wooden table. "But maybe there are other questions that plague you. Romantic questions, maybe? I could read your cards. Wouldn't take long. I'll give you the first reading for free."

"No thanks," Alex said. Although he was tempted by the possibility of the old soothsayer reading the cards to see what the future might hold for him and Victoria, he had finally caught sight of a black cloak dashing between the tents at the end of the lane. "Maybe some other time," Alex said, running toward the tent where he had seen the shadowed figure make an appearance.

"There's always time," Madam Fortuna said with a sigh. "Only not as much as we think when we are young."

Alex slid around the corner of the tent at the end of the row and caught another glimpse of the shadowed figure. He slipped through a gap between two wagons and followed the evasive black shape through another, even more slender space between two tents. Alex found himself in a dim and narrow channel between the backsides of two rows of medium-sized tents. He looked both ways down the thin, shadow-drenched path between the tents, but saw no sign of his elusive quarry.

He walked silently between the canvas walls, gently stepping over the safety lines crossing the path, each pinned to the ground with an enormous iron spike. Then he heard something. A word. A word spoken by someone in a tent nearby. A word he would not have heard if he had not been accustomed to moving so silently. A word he should never have heard. A word only a handful would know. A word no one should speak. A word whispered and carried by the still night air. A word at the beginning of a sentence as frightening as the word itself.

"Kal'Etrim shall be free within days and all that is required is your courage and my cunning."

Alex froze where he stood, stilling his lungs into long shallow and silent breaths.

Kal'Etrim.

That was not a word he should ever hear, especially not here in Runewood. It was a word known only by a few scholars. Only by those who would have need to know it. Only by two kinds of people — those who studied the history of the Shadow Wraith, of Shan'Kal — or those who were its servants and sought to set it loose upon the world again.

Alex listened closely. There were others in the tent. At least two more. He could discern a difference between their whispered voices, could tell two were women and one a man, but could not determine if he had ever heard them before. He doubted he would be able to identify the owners of the voices even if he heard them speak aloud. It meant only one thing — he'd have to get closer and try to see their faces. Maybe through a loose seam in the tent fabric. Maybe from the gap between the tent wall and the ground.

Alex crept slowly toward the tent where the whispered voices continued to speak.

"Is it really there?"

"Do you question me?"

"I only question your sources."

"It is there."

Was *what* where? Alex slowly lifted his foot over the safety rope at the edge of the tent.

"It will still be risky even with the device."

"If he still has it."

"Are you afraid of risk?"

Device? Alex leaned in toward the tent. There was a dim light inside and it revealed small holes in the canvas wall.

"I am not afraid of risk. I am afraid of failure."

"As well you should be."

"A bank will have more protection than walls."

Bank? Alex slid his eye close to one of the holes in the tent. It was too small to see through properly, but he could make out three shadowed shapes within the tent.

"I have made preparations for…Quiet."

Alex held his breath, locking his limbs into place.

"Someone is nearby."

"Where?"

"Very nearby."

Alex heard motion within the tent. The sound of feet crossing the ground and heading directly toward where he stood.

"Where?"

"Here!"

A knife blade slid through the fabric of the tent, slicing a long, clean gash as the blade flashed past Alex's face.

He thought of running, trying to leap between the safety ropes and through a gap between the tents, but some instinctive part of his mind knew there was no time, he would be seen, would be caught. Before he was even conscious he had spoken, he whispered the rune-words for air and motion and his body thrust upward into the black sky above. There was a reason mages did not try to fly. It was too hard to control the variables of flight with an ever-changing chant of rune-words. But Alex did not need to fly. He only needed to get away. Away from the owner of that knife blade.

Alex landed five tents away in a part of the carnival grounds where the mechanical rides were staged and constructed before being hauled to their final place of assembly. Most of the rides were in wagons of one sort or another, with long metal arms and various cages and cars for passengers to sit in. No one else was around. Alex heard feet behind him and looked around for a place to hide or an avenue of escape. Running a few paces, he picked up a rock and threw it with all his strength to the far side of the clearing. It bounced off the steel sign of a ride, *The Pirate's Revenge*, with a clattering echo.

Alex dodged between two girder-like metal legs of one of the rides and stopped. He crouched down in the middle the metal framework of the ride and hid in the shadows. He heard the feet of three pursuers cross the grounds and head to where the rock had struck the sign. They stopped. Then moved again. Closer. Alex could see nothing. The bulk of the mechanical apparatus around him blocked his view. He thought he heard them getting closer. Then they stopped again.

The metal around him creaked. Alex looked around frantically, afraid the sound would draw the Shadow Wraith's minions to him.

The metal around him creaked again. Then groaned. Then squealed.

Alex looked up to see the metal legs of the contraption he sat in begin to collapse down upon him. There was no way to escape. No time to crawl between the steal arms of the ride. No time to even to call for help. He flattened himself back into the ground and said aloud the first rune-words that came to mind as he focused on the magical energy of the land. The metal machinery of the ride broke apart in unnatural ways, becoming sharp-edged talons plummeting toward Alex's chest.

"Jenu-Ka!"

A wall of air, hard as iron, erupted around Alex as he repeated the rune-words. The metal shards and truss crashed into his protective bubble of air with a clangorous boom. Alex yelled the rune-words as the heavy parts of the machine continued to fall down around him, metal shrieking as it pressed down upon his shield of magical protection, bringing a spear-like shaft of metal closer and closer to his face.

Alex continued to chant the rune-words keeping him from being impaled as the metal mass around him finally settled and ceased its collapse. Alex fell silent and listened. Although the metal pressed down upon him was now more likely to crush than skewer him, it held him as tightly as if he had fallen into a bear trap. That didn't seem like a simple accident. It seemed intentional. It seemed like someone had tried to kill him. If the three minions of the Shadow Wraith were still present, they would finish their work.

He heard one set of footsteps. Or were they feet? He struggled to move and see which direction they were approaching from, but only succeeded in banging his head against a hard steel gear shaft. The feet stopped and Alex thought about the most dangerous and powerful rune-words he knew.

"Are you okay?" a soft female voice said. "Are you hurt?"

The heart-shaped face of a girl with deep green eyes and short cropped brown hair slid into view above his face. She didn't look like an agent of the Shadow Wraith. She actually looked rather concerned. And quite cute. Alex noticed her pointed ears and something about the moment felt altogether too familiar.

"I have a giant mass of crushed metal on top of me," Alex said to the girl, "but other than that, I'm fine." He realized he was being flippant, but it was true. If the girl was there, others would come soon, as well. She looked over her shoulder. Alex could hear other footsteps now. People running toward him. Whatever the identity of the evil carnies, as Alex had already started to think of them, they would not attack again with a crowd. They would know who he was for certain now, but they wouldn't be able to do anything about it. Not yet, at least.

"Can you move?" the girl asked, looking back to Alex. "See if you can slide out."

"I'm stuck," Alex said. "The beam over my chest is too close."

"Don't move, I've got an idea," the girl said and disappeared from view. Alex tried to watch her go, but the movement of his head was restricted. He could hear more people arriving on the scene. Gasps and exclamations filled the night. The sound of more feet moved toward him. A crowd. He could hear the girl saying something, but couldn't make out what it was. Then the girl's smiling face popped into view again.

"I've gathered some people and we're going to lift the beams pinning you down and pull you out," the girl said, her voice a mixture of excitement and worry.

Alex blinked in surprise. Then a thought crossed his mind — the mountain of metal above him being raised and suddenly crashing down again. "You lift the beams, I'll get myself out."

"It's a plan," the girl said as she moved once again from view.

A chorus of rune-words reached Alex's ears, each a little different, but similar enough that he knew what to expect. The thousands of pounds of metal that had fallen down around him suddenly floated upward several feet as though they were momentarily immune to the pull of gravity and might float away.

Alex wasted no time, rolling on his belly and crawling swiftly from beneath the collapsed ride. As he jumped to his feet, he turned and saw the mound of twisted metal settle back to the ground with a bone-shaking thud.

"Are you hurt?" the girl asked again as she stepped before him.

Alex blinked and looked at her. She was half a head shorter than he was and the two furry goat legs she stood upon signaled she was not a girl, but a female faun. She looked concerned, but her eyes were alight with energy. Alex looked up from her and saw he was surrounded by carnie folk. Melvin the minotaur was there. As well as the soothsayer, Madam Fortuna. All of the same people he had met as Victoria showed him around the carnival. Twenty-some people stood around him with more arriving every second.

"I'm fine," Alex said. "Just a few scrapes and bruises."

"I heard the noise and rushed right over," the girl said. "How did it happen?"

"I don't know," Alex lied. "I was looking inside to see how it worked and then the next thing I knew, it was falling down around me."

"Shoddy craftsmanship," Melvin said, stepping up beside them.

"I'm lucky you were all here," Alex said.

"Lucky young Leanna here has a good head on her shoulders," Melvin said with a low chuckle. "I was going to try and lift it. And me with my bad back."

"Thank you," Alex said, extending his hand to Leanna. "I'm Alex."

"I know," Leanna said with a slight smile.

"Saved the hero of Runewood from a metal monster," Melvin said, patting Leanna on the back. "That's a story to tell around the campfire." Leanna blushed and looked as though she were about to say something when another voice cut through the wall of chatter surrounding Alex.

"Alex," Victoria said, galloping to his side. "Are you okay? We were looking for you everywhere. We heard an awful metal crashing sound and feared the worst. We rushed right here."

"I'm fine," Alex said, happy to see Victoria was so concerned.

"Little Leanna here saved him," Melvin said, giving Leanna a slight shove to place her between Alex and Victoria.

"I helped out," Leanna said, embarrassed by the attention. "Hi, Victoria."

"Thank you, Leanna," Victoria said, looking between Alex and Leanna, her tail swishing nervously from side to side. "I don't know what we'd have done if something had happened to Alex." She stared deeply into Alex's eyes, but for the life of him, he wasn't sure what she was thinking.

"Experienced fewer brushes with death ourselves?" Rafael suggested, stepping up beside Victoria.

"Mmm, had weekends free to relax and sleep in," Clark said, looking down at Alex with a mix of amusement and concern.

"Stupid," Ben said, examining the mess of metal behind Alex. "Tell him how stupid he is for going off on his own."

"Gorping stupid," Daphne said and punched Alex in the arm.

"How am I supposed to keep you out of trouble if you go looking for it?" Nina said, frowning at Alex.

"I wasn't looking for it," Alex said, looking around and feeling uncomfortable having so many people staring at him. "It just happened."

"Trouble always seems to happen around you," Rafael said.

"I'm just glad you're safe," Victoria said, stepping closer and raising her hands to examine Alex's bruises. "I can heal these if you want."

"No, thanks," Alex said, remembering the last healing he had received from Victoria. As he said the words, and watched the crestfallen look spreading across Victoria's face, he knew it had been a mistake. "It's not that bad," he said trying to think of a way to keep from hurting Victoria's feeling and letting her know how glad he was she was concerned for him. A flash of black cloak disappearing into the shadows between the tents behind Victoria brought his mind to the reason he was standing there.

Someone had been following him. Possibly one of the Shadow Wraith's minions. And he had followed that person and had overheard part of a plan. A plan that seemed to have many parts, but one goal — the release of the Shadow Wraith. Alex could only say one thing with such a thought in his mind.

"I'm fine," Alex said. "I was chasing shadows and got lost and found this ride and wondered how it worked. Then I must have done something wrong and it fell apart."

Victoria and the other members of the Guild stared at him in silence.

"Well, you're a lucky young lad," Mr. Apollo said, walking up to the crowd with Esmeralda at his side.

"He certainly is," Esmeralda said. "A lesser boy might have been crushed to death in that monstrosity of a machine. I've told you a thousand times we should rely on magic, not mechanics."

"You have, indeed, my dear," Mr. Apollo said. "As always, you have my appreciation for your counsel. I only wish I had heeded it earlier. As for you, young man, you have my sincere apologies. This is not the sort of thing that happens in my carnival. I cannot possibly make it up to you, but please accept free full passes to the carnival and all its attractions for yourself and all of your friends as a token of my sincere regret." Mr. Apollo pulled a handful of large gold tickets from the pocket of his velvet jacket and handed them to Alex.

"Thank you," Alex said, looking up at Mr. Apollo and seeing he looked to be on the verge of tears. He was far more upset than Alex. But then Alex had others things to be upset about.

Esmeralda took the tickets from Mr. Apollo and handed them out to the Guild. Her eyes twinkled with pleasure as she gave each member of the Guild a golden ticket. They said thank you and smiled back.

They seemed pleased, but Alex knew they were only acting. He knew they were not thinking of the tickets or the carnival. They were only thinking of one thing. They had heard Alex use the phrase "chasing shadows" and they knew what that meant. It was a code phrase they had agreed on months ago and hoped they would never have to speak or hear. It meant one of them had discovered evidence that the Shadow Wraith was back.

Alex caught Victoria staring at him and smiled his most confident smile. She returned the smile and Alex was surprised to see it seemed even more confident than his own.

"Alex!" he heard his mother say from behind him. He turned to see his mother and father running to his side. His mother did not wait to hear explanations. She knew her son too well to suspect anyone else had been in danger. She wrapped him in her arms and hugged him tight.

"We heard a loud crash," Alex's mother said.

"And we thought it couldn't possibly be Alex, because Nina was keeping him out of trouble," Alex's father said, ruffling his son's hair.

"I only took my eyes off him for a minute," Nina said. "I think I need a leash and collar if I'm going to be responsible for him. And a raise in my allowance."

The crowd around Alex laughed as his mother released him.

"What happened?" his father asked.

"Oh, the usual," Alex said, looking up at his father and trying to convey with his eyes that while things might have been usual, they had not been good. "I'll explain later."

"A mechanical failure of some kind," Mr. Apollo said. "I take full responsibility. If you wish to inspect the other rides to ensure yourself, and the town, of their safety, I would be happy to escort you through the grounds."

"That might be a good idea," Alex's father said, stepping over to discuss the incident with Mr. Apollo.

"We'll be heading home for dinner," Alex's mother said. "You've had more than enough excitement for one night."

"I'm sure a good night's sleep will wash the whole incident from his mind," Esmeralda said, smiling graciously.

"I'm sure it will," Alex's mother said, her eyes narrowing as she smiled back.

"I'll head straight home, Mom," Alex said. "We have to grab our bikes. We'll meet you and Dad at the house."

"Alright," his mother said, seeing she was not going to be able to escort him safely home herself. "Nina."

"I know," Nina said. "Keep him out of trouble."

Alex walked over to where Leanna stood with Eleada and Kendra. They seemed to be friends. Considering they all lived and worked together, it wasn't terribly surprising.

"I wanted to thank you again," Alex said.

"I only did what anyone would do," Leanna said.

"But you did it first," Alex said, offering his hand. "I appreciate it."

"Is that how you show a girl your appreciation?" Eleada said with a mischievous smile.

"In some cultures, it's customary to show gratitude with a kiss," Kenda said, sounding as though she were quoting from an authoritative encyclopedia on the cultures of the world.

"Ignore them," Leanna said.

"Ignore me at your own peril," Elaeda said.

"Um, I should go," Alex said, looking past Leanna to see Nathan had joined the crowd of people and was moving closer to Victoria. "Thanks again," Alex said, smiling at Leanna.

As he walked away, he heard Elaeda and Kendra laughing.

"Not a brave as I'd heard," Elaeda said.

Alex's face flushed, but he didn't turn around. He caught Victoria's eye and nodded in the direction of the path leading out of the carnival. She nodded back and the rest of the Guild followed with her. Moments later, Alex was walking at Victoria's side. He glanced back and saw Mr. Apollo leading his father and mother in the opposite direction. He saw no sign of Esmeralda.

Minutes later, the Guild stood beneath the same sycamore tree they had watched the carnival from hours earlier and Alex told them what had really happened.

Chapter Seven
Hook and Bait

"Positive?" Ben asked, looking up at Alex. "Are you absolutely positive?"

"He's always positive about things that can get us killed," Rafael said with a sigh as he leaned against the sycamore tree.

"Aphrodite's acne," Daphne said as she spat into the grass.

"Mmm, maybe you misheard them," Clark said, rubbing the sweat from the back of his neck.

"I heard them clear enough," Alex said, pushing his sweat-damp hair back from his face. The heat that had settled over the valley at the end of the day had not dissipated to be replaced by the usually cool night air. It was not only hot, but humid, the kind of weather that felt like being trapped in a wet, and not too particularly clean, sock. It made their conversation under the sycamore tree all the more unpleasant and unnerving.

"Vulcan's vomit," Daphne said.

"Cloak," Ben said. "What about the person in black?"

"Could it have been one of the Shadow Wraith's followers?" Victoria asked, pulling her long, blonde hair back into a ponytail.

"I don't know," Alex said. "I got the feeling the person in black was leading me through the shadows."

"And yet you followed this mysterious person into the shadows alone," Rafael said, his tone slightly incredulous.

"Gorping goon," Daphne said, rolling her eyes.

"He'll be more careful next time," Nina said, scowling up at her brother. "I won't let him out of my sight."

"What were they whispering?" Victoria asked, looking intently down at Alex.

"I couldn't make out everything," Alex said. "But I could hear the name they used. It's a name only the followers of the Shadow Wraith use."

"Don't say it aloud," Rafael said.

"I wasn't going to," Alex said.

"But what about the bank?" Victoria asked. "What do they think will be in the bank? And what did they mean by the device? And how did they hear you? You're usually so very good at sneaking about."

"Thanks," Alex said. "I don't know. One of them seemed to be able to sense I was there."

"Mind Magic?" Daphne suggested.

"Spirit magic," Ben said. "That's more likely."

"That's what I was thinking," Alex said.

"One of them will need to be a Spirit Mage to release the Shadow Wraith," Raphael said.

"Wasn't there a soothsayer at the carnival?" Nina asked.

"Madam Fortuna?" Victoria said. "I can't imagine that. She's such a nice woman. Like a grandmother to everyone. She even nursed me once when I was sick."

"I met her," Alex said, "and while she doesn't seem like someone who would be in league with the Shadow Wraith, we can't assume anything. Whoever they are, they have been hiding in the carnival for a while, at least. They know how to pretend."

"You have to tell Dad this time," Nina said. "This is way too dangerous with at least three followers of the Shadow Wraith running around and planning to rob the bank and who knows what after that and I don't think that ride collapsed on your head by accident, I think whoever heard you tried to kill you."

The conversation fell quiet as Nina and the rest of the Guild all stared at Alex. He had been thinking the same thing ever since the metal legs and arms of the carnival ride had come crashing down around him. It wasn't poor craftsmanship. Alex hadn't unwittingly bumped something that caused the machine to collapse. It was no accident. The Shadow Wraiths followers had known he was there. They had tried to kill him. But there was something else that occurred to him, as well.

"They know who you are," Victoria said. "That's why they tried to kill you. They know you are a Spirit Mage. They know you sealed the Shadow Wraith back in its prison. They would want to kill you for that."

"Exactly," Alex said, unable to resist smiling at Victoria, her face drawn tight with worry. He should have known she'd be the first to see the implications of everything that had happened.

"That also means they probably suspect that you are the Revenant," Victoria said. "No one else seems to have recognized that fact, but if you are the one returned to fight the Shadow Wraith, then you are their prime adversary. That means they'll keep trying to kill you. That might even be one of the very reasons they are here."

"I thought of that, too," Alex said. Even he couldn't keep smiling when confronted with such chilling logic.

"Gorping gobstoppers," Daphne said.

"On the bright side," Rafael began to say. "Oh, wait. There is no bright side."

"Yes, there is," Alex said. "We know the Shadow Wraith's followers are here, we know they're up to something involving the bank, and we know where to find them."

"We're in real trouble if that's the bright side," Rafael said.

"Plan," Ben said. "We need a plan."

"The plan is simple," Alex said. "We find out which carnies are working for the Shadow Wraith, we find out what their plan is, and we stop them."

"Hmmm, that plan could use a few more details," Clark said.

"We'll fill in the details as we go along," Alex said.

"Good idea," Rafael said. "That's always worked so well for us in the past."

"We'll go to the carnival tomorrow and keep our eyes out for anything suspicious," Alex said. "Victoria, is there anyone from the carnival you trust completely? That you know can't be working for the Shadow Wraith?"

"Elaeda," Victoria said. "If she's a follower of the Shadow Wraith, I'm a tea cup. And Kendra and Leanna. They're like sisters. There's no way one could hide something like that from the other.

And, oh…" Victoria frowned slightly. "And Nathan. He's far too upright to ever even consider something so vile."

Alex found he was also frowning at the mention of Victoria's ex-boyfriend. "Well, don't tell them what we know, but tell them to be on the lookout for anything suspicious or out of the ordinary."

"Will you be safe tonight?" Victoria asked. "There are agents of the Shadow Wraith trying to kill you."

"My dad's the town warlock," Alex said. "And you should see the magic my mom can do."

"And he has me," Nina said, standing up a little straighter.

"Right," Alex said, rustling his sister's hair, much to her annoyance. "My own personal lapdog."

"Guard dog," Nina said, knocking Alex's hand away.

"I'll be safe," Alex said, "but all of you should take extra precautions. If the evil carnies know who I am, they'll know who each of you are, as well."

"What a pleasant thought to rock me to sleep with," Rafael said.

"We'll meet here tomorrow morning," Alex said. "Then the hunt begins."

They all insisted on walking Alex home. He thought it was completely unnecessary, but he was touched by his friends' concern for his wellbeing. He had hoped he would have a moment alone with Victoria, but as she and Ben lived close to each other, they departed together. Daphne offered to walk Clark home and Rafael changed into a large eagle, snatched his clothes from the grass, and flew off to his aunt's house.

A short while later, Alex told his father and mother everything over a Spartan meal of cold sandwiches and potato salad. It was still too unseasonably hot to think about eating a warm meal, even if it hadn't been nearly ten o'clock at night. He finished his story and stuffed a large forkful of potato salad into his mouth.

"I don't want you going anywhere near that carnival," Alex's mother said.

"Mom!" Alex mumbled as he chewed.

"Manners," his mother said, frowning at Alex for speaking with his mouth full.

Alex swallowed a chunk of potato that really should have spent more time between his teeth and repeated his exclamation. "Mom!"

"Don't 'Mom' me," his mother said. "You've just told us people at the carnival are working to free the Shadow Wraith and are trying to kill you. How can you possibly think it's a good idea to go back there?"

"I'll keep him out of trouble this time," Nina said. "I just need that leash."

"You're not going, either," his mother said.

"Mom!" Nina said.

"They may have a point," Alex's father said.

"Don't you start being irrational," his mother said, turning to his father and giving him a look that might have frightened a lesser man into a year of abject silence.

"They know who he is and where to find him," his father said, the normally hard lines of his face softening with the tone of his voice. "Locking Alex away until the carnival ends might stop them from killing him now, but who is to say someone else won't arrive in town with the same intent? Or that one of the townspeople won't turn to the Shadow Wraith's side? Or one or more of them haven't turned already?"

"I can't believe anyone in our town would ever willingly side with that creature," his mother said.

"I'm sure everyone at the carnival would say the same thing," his father said. "But maybe you're right. Maybe they aren't willing accomplices. Maybe the seal on the Shadow Wraith's prison isn't as solid as we all hoped." It was a thought that had been worrying Alex, as well.

"So what do you propose we do?" Alex's mother asked with a frown. "Use your own son as bait to draw them out?" That was basically Alex's plan, but it sounded far more ridiculously dangerous coming from his mother.

"Yes," Alex's father said, staring calmly at his wife. It sounded like an even more dangerous plan with his father's agreement to it. "Think like the warlock, not the mother."

Alex's mother squinted at his father, her lips curling into something that might have been a snarl. Then she let out a long breath and turned her gaze to Alex. Alex held her stare, his heart beating strongly as she seemed to examine him from the inside out. It was similar to the look she gave him when he was telling her a wild excuse for some impossible calamity that had befallen him. It was a calculating look, and more so than usual. He shifted in his chair, but held her eyes.

"You're right," his mother finally said. His father let out a long, slow breath, which made Alex realize he had been holding his own breath, as well. He exhaled as his mother reached out and cupped his face with her hand. "We can't risk the safety of the town and the world to try and keep our son safe."

"Not when our son is who he is," his father said, reaching out to hold his mother's free hand.

"No," Alex's mother said, smiling at him. "They don't know what they're up against, do they?" Alex found himself grinning back at his mother, her sideways compliment filling him with a warm confidence he hadn't known he was missing until that moment.

"They watch him," his father said.

"And we watch for them," his mother added.

"And when they show themselves," his father said.

"We do what we do best," his mother said. The smile that spread across her face was both beautiful and frightening. A similar countenance sat upon his father's face. Alex wasn't sure what his parents might do to someone who tried to kill their children, but if the looks on their faces were any indication, it would be extremely unpleasant. It made Alex feel both a little afraid — of what the combined wrath of his parents might be capable of once unleashed — and a fierce sense of love, knowing not only that his parents cared so deeply for him, but what he might do to someone who harmed them would be terrible beyond imagining.

"Does this mean I get the leash?" Nina asked. "Because part of the plan is keeping track of him, and I don't think I can keep track of him without a leash, and I think it's only fair the cost of it come out of Alex's allowance, although I'll chip in for the name tag, in case he chews through the leash and gets lost."

Alex's father and mother burst out laughing and the tension at the table slowly faded away. Alex wasn't sure how serious Nina was about the leash, and part of him suspected she wasn't merely being sarcastic, but he was thankful his sister knew how to manipulate his parent's mood when the need struck.

"We'll see about the leash," his father said, smiling at his children.

"I was certainly tempted to use one when he learned to walk," his mother said with a motherly chuckle.

"What about the bank?" Alex asked. His sister wasn't the only one who knew how to redirect a conversation.

"The bank is as safe as any building can possibly be," Alex's father said with a frown, "but I'll make sure Mr. Osprey, the bank manager, knows to tighten his security."

"Should you tell the mayor what we know?" Alex's mother asked his father.

"If we wanted the whole town to know," his father said. "For now we should keep this to ourselves. And the other parents, of course."

"What other parents?" Alex asked.

"Of your club," Alex's father said.

"It's a guild," Alex said out of reflexive habit.

"Whatever you call it," his mother said, "the parents of your friends deserve to know what kind of danger their children are in."

"I guess that kind of makes sense," Alex said. The worst-case scenario would be that the rest of the Guild would be grounded and kept at home for safety's sake and only he and Nina who would be exposed to any danger. Of course, he doubted any of the Guild members would let a little thing like being grounded keep them from finding a way to join Alex and Nina in the hunt for the Shadow Wraith's followers.

A smile spread across his face as he imagined Daphne's parents trying to keep her safe at home when there was an adventure this deliriously dangerous unfolding.

"I'll talk to the parents," his father said.

"It might be best if someone a little more persuasive spoke to them," his mother said, her face taking on an angelic look of innocence as she turned to his father.

"I am very persuasive," his father said, brows folding together.

"You certainly are," his mother said, "but mostly because people are terrified of you."

"They only think you're the sweet and nice one because they don't really know you," his father said.

"Then they don't really know you, either," his mother said.

"Fine," his father said with a sigh. "You're right. You are more persuasive. You'll have them convinced in five minutes that dangling their children out as bait for the Shadow Wraith's followers is not only a brilliant idea, but was a plan they thought up all on their own."

"Sounds very similar to another proposal I remember hearing years ago," his mother said, her eyes twinkling with mischief.

"I asked you to marry me of my own free will," his father said.

"But whose idea was it?" his mother said, cocking her head to the side with the question.

"Children, I think dinner is over," his father said. "You're mother and I have certain things to discuss."

"Such as...?" his mother asked.

"Such as what magic you use to still look so beautiful after all these years," his father said, taking his mother's hand in his.

"It must be the company I keep," his mother said.

His father and mother laughed and kissed each other.

"Yuck," Nina said as their parents kissed again.

"Your father and I will clean up," his mother said. "You two run along and get ready for bed.

"Come on, Sis," Alex said. "I need your help with something, anyway."

As Alex and Nina headed upstairs, it occurred to him his mother and father were far better at changing the direction of conversations than even he and his sister combined. They'd probably go back to being serious and discussing his likely odds of surviving the weekend as soon as he and Nina were out of earshot, but that was okay with Alex. It would keep them busy. His plan to find the Shadow Wraith's followers was still taking shape in his mind, but one part, the part he hadn't mentioned to anyone yet, was spying on them at night. And, Alex could spy on the carnival in a way almost no one else could.

Chapter Eight
Night School

"How am I supposed to watch you if I can't even see you?" Nina asked, crossing her legs as she perched at the edge of Alex's bed.

"I'll be right here," Alex said, adjusting a pillow behind him as he sat leaning against the headboard. "At least my body will."

"I hate sitting around watching you sleep."

"I'm not really asleep."

"Boring," Nina said, resting her face in her hands as she leaned forward on her elbows. "And what if something happens to you?"

"Wake me up."

"You said you wouldn't be asleep."

"You know what I mean." Alex rolled his eyes in exasperation.

"How will I know if something is wrong?"

"Watch my breathing."

"If you stop breathing, I'm getting Mom."

"No," Alex said. "My physical body and my astral body will still be linked. If something is really wrong, my real body will start to breathe faster like it would if I were awake."

"Should I get a bucket of water?" Nina asked, an innocent look on her face.

"Just shake me," Alex said with a frown.

"Oh, I'll shake you all right," Nina said. "Be careful."

"Aren't I always?" Alex asked as he settled back against the pillow behind him. Nina snorted with derision, but said nothing more.

Alex cupped his hands in his lap and closed his eyes. He had been practicing astral travel and other Spirit Magics with Batami nearly every day or night for the last two months. One result of this study was that he no longer needed to fall asleep to separate his soul-essence from his body and enter the astral realm. He had learned to attain a meditative state where he was able to assume his astral form without fear of falling into slumber.

Alex breathed deeply and focused his mind, quickly finding the inner perspective that allowed him to see beyond the normal physical realm. As he stilled his mind, he felt his astral form as easily as his physical body. Willing himself away from his flesh, he found himself floating in the air beside his sister.

Alex had not only been learning how to easily enter the astral realm, he had also been learning how to use magic while in that otherworldly state. He formed the rune-word for wind clearly in his mind and Nina's hair whipped around her face with a sudden gusty breeze.

"Funny," Nina said and punched his physical body in the arm. Alex felt a slight jarring sensation, but no pain. He would, however, feel the bruise on his arm later that night. Had she punched him harder, it might have caused him to slip from his trance. It occurred to him a bucket of water might be preferable to what his sister might do to his body in order to being him back to his physical senses in the event something did go wrong on his mission.

Alex cleared his mind and willed himself to where he needed to be. The scene around him blurred and he floated outside the carnival grounds. He thought about his decision not to tell his parents about his plan to spy on the evil carnies that night. It would only make them worry and he doubted they could stop him without keeping him awake. But, they would know if he lied about what he did in his astral form, and they might rescind their decision not to keep him locked up until the carnival left town.

He would have to be quick. His parents would only stay in the kitchen for so long before coming upstairs and wondering what Alex and Nina were up to in his room. Worse, they might already suspect what he was doing. He had considered waiting until bedtime and spying on the carnival in astral form without Nina to watch over his body, but had rejected the idea. Everyone might think he was reckless, and they might be right sometimes, but he wasn't an idiot.

Someone in that tent had been able to sense him, and at least one of the evil carnies would need to be a Spirit Mage to try to free the Shadow Wraith.

Alex willed his astral body to drift upward and toward the carnival. He wasn't sure where the evil carnies might be, or if they would even be together, but he had little time to search them out before his parents finished cleaning up from dinner. He also had a lesson with Batami planned for later that night. With so little time, he needed to be quick about his task. A view from above the carnival grounds might help him pick the best spot to begin his search.

The carnival spread out across the old rye field behind the Town Hall in an elliptical circle, the wagons and trucks forming a sort of outer wall around the well-ordered rows of tents and booths and rides arrayed throughout the inner circle, creating a series of curved lanes that all seemed to lead back into each other, as much as toward the large red tent in the center. Alex could see now why it was so easy to get lost in the carnival. It was set up that way. The layout of the rides, games, and sideshow attractions was designed to keep people constantly walking around in circles, continually passing things that might catch their interest, and upon which, they might spend their money.

Alex saw the remains of the ride that had magically collapsed down around him and tried to follow the path he had taken to reach it. His astral eyes could not see through darkness and shadows any better than his physical eyes. Although Batami had taught him to shift his perspective and see the world as it existed in the astral plane, it was such a disorienting whorl of color and light that it would be more of a hindrance than a help in the present situation. After a few moments of concentration, Alex managed to locate the tent where he had heard the evil carnies whispering.

Knowing whoever might be in that tent could possibly sense him in his astral form, Alex decided to move slowly. Rather than willing himself to the interior of the tent, he focused his mind and floated down toward the tent from above. His progress was swift, and much like flying, but it was also short-lived. When Alex came within two hundred feet of the carnival tent, he found his movement suddenly arrested. He focused his mind more clearly, willing himself forward, but some invisible astral barrier separated him from the carnival grounds. He concentrated and willed himself to the outside of the tent, but nothing happened.

Alex moved back and tried from another angle with no success. He floated around the entire encampment, but it was if some invisible dome of astral energy had been erected around the carnival. Whatever the wall of magical energy was, it prevented him from entering the carnival grounds in any way while in astral form.

Alex floated a few feet above the ground at the edge of the field, near where the low grass gave way to the forest north of the town. Clearly, spying on the evil carnies was not going to be as easy as he had hoped. Moreover, at least one of them was a very skilled Spirit Mage to be able to create such a large and effective barrier to astral travel. That left only one option. Alex would need to find the evil carnies in the real world — a much more dangerous task.

Something caught Alex's attention at the edge of the forest. He did not know how long it had been there, but the black cloaked figure stood at the edge of the tree line, staring at the carnival grounds. Alex willed himself forward slowly, trying to get a better glimpse within the cowl of the long black cloak. This was the clearest view Alex had yet obtained of the figure. It was tall, but not exceptionally so. Slender, but not thin. Its hands were hidden in the folds of the sleeves and its face concealed by the hood of the cloak. It was impossible to tell if a man or a woman stood beneath the black fabric.

As Alex came closer, the figure turned and looked at him. The motion so startled Alex that he came to an abrupt stop, only ten feet away from the cloaked figure. The cloaked figure stared at Alex a moment longer, and then stepped backward into the shadows of the forest, disappearing from view. Alex willed himself forward into the forest, but the moonless blackness clinging to the trees was too thick to see through.

Alex focused his mind in the way Batami had taught him and his vision of the world shifted into the astral plane. The forest was suddenly aglow in shades of pearlescent light. The trees looked like they were on fire with a deep green light, the ground between them appearing like a bluish field of cold flame. Alex scanned around, but could see nothing resembling the blue-white light that would indicate a living being. Had the cloaked figure managed to vanish before Alex could look into the astral realm? How was that possible? Or was it not alive in the normal way of things and thus invisible to his astral sight?

That thought, combined with the knowledge that whoever the cloaked figure was, he or she, was powerful in ways Alex did not understand, helped him decide the best place for him might be back in his bedroom. A moment later, his eyes opened to see Nina staring at him intently.

"What's the status, Gladys?" Nina asked, leaning forward.

"Something weird," Alex said, unfolding his legs to stretch them. He quickly told Nina about the twin failures of his reconnaissance mission.

"Is it one of the carnies?" Nina asked, referring to the cloaked figure Alex had encountered.

"I don't know," Alex said. "It was outside the carnival, so I don't think it was one of the carnies. But that doesn't mean it's on our side, whoever it is."

"You should tell Batami about the astral barrier," Nina said, her face serious.

"That's exactly what I plan to do," Alex said.

It was the first thing he mentioned, twenty minutes later, after his parents had come to say their goodnights, when he appeared in astral form in the yard outside Batami's little wooden hut. His parents knew of his nightly astral assignations with Batami, and they encouraged them wholeheartedly. Especially in light of the evening's events at the carnival.

"A barrier to astral travel?" Alex heard Batami say in his mind when he had finished telling her everything that had happened. She was in her astral form, as well, and rested the fingers of one hand against the jawline of her ethereal, but wrinkled face. *"I have seen such things, but I have never heard of a barrier large enough to cover an entire carnival. To cover anything less would reveal the Spirit Mage's location within the carnival grounds, but to maintain such a barrier throughout the night is a considerable magical feat."*

"Could it be more than one Spirit Mage working together?" Alex asked mentally.

"Possibly," Batami said, her face pulling into a frown. She wore her usual white robe, but the folds of it shifted ever so slightly, as though caught in a breeze. Alex recognized it as a sign she was thinking deeply.

"Do you think the figure in black might have something to do with it?" Alex asked.

"It is hard to say," Batami said. *"This mysterious person seems to be with the carnival, but that does not mean he or she is working with the Shadow Wraith. We simply do not know enough. I will examine the barrier."* She turned her gaze to Alex, her voice firm. *"You remain here."*

Batami faded from his sight, leaving Alex alone in the yard. Not entirely alone. Sufina, the bone-white Titan wolf who was Batami's constant companion, lay in the grass near the hut. Sufina could not see into the astral realm, but she did seem to be able to sense an astral presence and she turned her head back and forth for a moment after Batami's disappearance. The massive wolf, bigger than any bear, snorted loudly and laid her head down between her paws. She knew enough not to worry about Batami.

Although endlessly impressed with Batami's skill and power as a Spirit Mage, Alex was not so easily reassured, especially when the Shadow Wraith was involved in events. He floated in the middle of the yard, his mind filled with anxious thoughts. It was odd, not having a body to reflect and amplify those thoughts, but this did not make them any less potent. Alex sought to calm his mind as Batami had taught him, imaging he was breathing deeply and calmly.

Batami appeared once more in the clearing, her astral form glowing a deep cobalt blue. Alex willed himself to move to her and waited in mental silence. He had learned that asking Batami questions when she was considering something did not result in swift answers. The look in Batami's eyes told him she was contemplating something very deeply.

"I could not cross the barrier," Batami said finally. *"I cannot imagine it is the magic of a single Spirit Mage. Such a mage would be far more powerful than myself. While that is not impossible, in and of itself, for such a person to have escaped my attention would be beyond improbable. And I cannot imagine*

there are sufficient Spirit Mages hiding in the Carnival and working in league with the Shadow Wraith to produce such a barrier."

"Then what does that leave?" Alex asked.

"Judging by how very little magic is being drawn from the land," Batami said, "it can only be an artifact from the time of the War of the Shadow."

"It'd have to be thousands of years old," Alex said, trying to imagine how such a magical artifact could survive for so long.

"Before the War of the Shadow burned the magic from most of the land on the earth, such artifacts were common," Batami said. "And they were well-made. But you are correct. Most of those artifacts have been lost or broken in the long years since the war. I suspect it has been kept by secret followers of the Shadow Wraith for all this time. Hidden to await the time when they might need it most."

"How do we break through the barrier?" Alex asked, hoping there was actually an answer to that question.

"I don't know," Batami said. "From the size of the barrier and how little magic is being drained from the land to sustain it, I suspect it either has a reservoir of magical energy or it somehow is able to amplify the magical energy it draws."

Alex had seen objects enchanted to store magical energy to use at a later time. His father had several at the jailhouse. They were useful when mages needed to leave the magic of the Rune Valley behind. Especially if a warlock needed to pursue a suspect into the normal world. Most of these enchanted objects had some particular magical purpose, like creating light, or stunning blasts of energy, but others simply stored the magical energy so the mage who held them could conjure magic for a short time. However, Alex had never heard his father or anyone else mention an enchanted artifact that might be able to amplify magical energy.

"We have to find the artifact," Alex said, already formulating a plan in his head to do just that the next day when the carnival opened for business and he and his friends had the opportunity to use their golden tickets.

"That will help," Batami said, "but do not expect it to be any place easy to find. And it can be in nearly any form. I will continue to examine the barrier from the outside."

"If it's in the carnival, the Guild will find it," Alex said. "We're good at finding things."

"Like the Rune Tree?" Batami asked, a smile briefly crossing her face.

"Well, that's taking a little longer than expected," Alex said, his mental tone a little defensive. Batami was of the opinion the Rune Tree was nothing more than a myth handed down through the ages. A story to tell young mages at bedtime.

"Nothing turned up in the Dead Forest?" Batami asked.

"We found something," Alex said, being vague to avoid mentioning how dangerous the adventure had turned, *"but it wasn't the Rune Tree."* If Batami knew how potentially deadly Alex's quest for the Rune Tree had become, she would probably forbid him from continuing his search. To Batami, it was far more important Alex be alive to face the Shadow Wraith and its demented supporters than hunting for some legendary tree.

"A fruitless endeavor, then?" Batami said.

"We found an old cauldron, so it wasn't a total waste of time," Alex said.

"A cauldron?" Batami said, raising an eyebrow in curiosity.

"It was outside an abandoned hut," Alex said.

"What did you do with the cauldron?" Batami asked.

"We took it back to the Guild House," Alex said. *"Clark said it smells like deep magic."*

"And you thought it wise to take a magic cauldron from the Dead Forest back to your home?" Batami said. The tone of her voice was familiar enough that Alex took a moment and paused to rethink his decision to take cauldron.

"The hut hadn't been used in years," Alex said, bringing to mind the thick layer of dust coating the inside of the thatched roof shelter. *"And the cauldron might be useful someday."*

"You're certain the hut was abandoned?" Batami asked.

"Positive," Alex said.

"Curious," Batami said, glancing off in the direction of the Dead Forest.

"Do you know who it used to belong to?" Alex asked.

"If it belongs to whom I suspect," Batami's said, her eyes narrowing with thought, *"then you should be cautious of that cauldron. On the other hand, if it is the cauldron I know, it would not be abandoned. At least, I hope not. So…caution."*

"Why does everyone think I don't know how to be cautious?" Alex asked. He had intended the thought to be for himself alone, but Batami must have heard it clearly enough in her mind because she laughed.

"It is only those who know you, who question your caution," Batami said with a chuckle. *"Now, since we cannot pursue the matter of the barrier around the carnival, or the agents of the Shadow Wraith hiding within it, any further this night, let us continue with your lessons. See if you can do this."*

Batami turned and stretched her hands out before her, twin molten-blue lightning bolts leaping forth, striking a boulder ten feet away. Sufina, the Titan wolf, raised her head momentarily, but then settled back down to sleep. Few things unnerved her.

"Wow," Alex said, looking at the burn marks on the newly cracked boulder. Batami had been teaching him how to use magic while in astral form, but this had so far been confined to conjuring the wind, starting fires, moving small objects, and other more mundane actions. Creating lightning bolts while in astral form that could pulverize large boulders, and potentially large evil carnies, was exactly the kind of lesson Alex had been patiently, and sometimes not so patiently, waiting for. He smiled.

"I think it's time you begin learning a few more practical magics," Batami said. *"It seems you might have cause to need them."*

Alex had no doubt he would need them. Once he and the Guild found the artifact creating the Spirit Barrier around the carnival and disabled it, someone would have to confront the Shadow Wraith's followers. Alex knew that confrontation was as likely to take place in the astral realm as the real world.

"Try," Batami said, gesturing toward the boulder across the clearing.

Alex smiled his astral-body-smile again.

Chapter Nine
Carnival Confections

Alex woke up hot, exhausted, and starving. The open windows, and the small, magically powered fan blowing on him from the ceiling, did nothing to dissipate the heat and humidity clinging to the valley. At breakfast, his mother and sister both had their hair pulled back in ponytails. His father muttered a rune-spell and the temperature of the room chilled for a time, but it didn't last.

"Unseasonably hot," his father said, buttering a slice of toast.

"Maybelle should do something about it," his mother said, sipping at her coffee. Maybelle Meriwether was the local weather witch.

"Maybe she's saving her weather charms for when it really gets hot," his father said.

"Maybe she's afraid she'll cause another summer blizzard like she did last year," Nina said with a giggle.

Alex was about to say something, but it came out as a yawn. He covered his mouth with one hand and then stuffed a bite of egg into it with the other. Astral travel always left him extra hungry and extra tired. He wasn't really asleep while in his astral form and something about the process left his physical body much depleted.

"Long night with Batami?" his father asked. His parents knew about his training with Batami, but since they never asked for many details, he rarely gave them any. This morning, he decided to tell them about the suspected artifact creating an astral barrier around the carnival.

"After that, she insisted on a longer lesson," Alex concluded a few minutes later.

His mother and father shared a look between themselves before his father spoke. "I've never heard of an artifact like that."

"Neither have I," his mother said. "We can check the books tonight, but I don't remember ever reading of such a thing." Alex's mother loved to collect books and there were thousands of them around the house, overfilling shelves, stacked in corners, and piled on stairs. "Be careful today," she added.

"Careful is my middle name," Alex said.

"You're middle name is Reckless," his mother said.

"I thought it was Stupid," Nina said.

"Your mother and I will be at the carnival, as well," his father said, ignoring the banter. "If something goes wrong, blow these." He took two small whistles from his pocket and handed them to Alex and Nina. He handed one more to their mother and held up a fourth in his hand. "Each one of these is linked to the others. Blow one and all will sound."

"And we'll know you need us and where you are," his mother said.

"The whistles give a tug toward the one that blew," his father said. "So we'll know what direction to run."

"Cool," Nina said, blowing on her whistle and smiling as the other three sounded in response.

"We need to get some of these for the Guild," Alex said, examining the whistle and trying to sense the enchantments upon it.

"Keep them handy," his father said, staring at Alex. "And heed your mother. If you think you see the person in the cloak, or if you recognize one of the voices from the tent, find us or blow the whistle. Don't try to save the town by yourself this time."

"I wasn't by myself," Alex said. "I had Nina and the Guild."

His parents frowned, but said nothing. Nina, meanwhile, grinned, and Alex knew why. It would only be a few more days and she would be old enough to be an official member of the Young Sorcerers Guild.

After breakfast, Alex and Nina stopped by the Guild House in the backyard to collect a few other items Alex thought might be useful. They found Daphne and Clark examining the cauldron from the Dead Forest. Clark held the cauldron upside down while Daphne stood beneath it, her head deep inside its cast-iron shadows.

"Don't drop that," Nina said.

"Hmm, that'd be the last thing I'd do," Clark said with a grimace.

"You're gorping right it'd be the last thing you'd do," Daphne said, her voice made louder by the echo from within the cauldron.

"If you're going to cook her," Alex said, "you have to turn the pot the other way around."

"Hmmm," Clark said with a quizzical look that Alex wasn't sure was a frown of disgust or a hungry smile.

"Very funny," Daphne said, emerging from beneath the cauldron. "We're trying to figure out what it does." Clark took this as his cue to set the cauldron down.

"Good idea," Alex said. "Any luck yet?"

"Mmmm, not really" Clark said. "I can smell the magic, but it doesn't smell like anything in particular. Except maybe onions."

"Even I can smell the gorping onions," Daphne said.

"Onions?" Nina asked.

"Someone used it to cook a soup, I think," Daphne said. "But other than that, I can't tell what it's used for or what the magic is supposed to do. We're going to run some tests on it later."

"Tests?" Alex said.

"You know, light a fire under it and see what happens when we put different things inside," Daphne said.

"Things?" Nina said.

"Nothing dangerous," Daphne said. "Don't worry, I've got a plan."

"Hmmm," Clark said.

"Now I know how people feel when I say that all the time," Alex said with a laugh.

Daphne frowned and punched him in the arm on her way out the door. Alex laughed again and followed her.

"Let's get to the carnival," Daphne said. "We have work to do."

"More than you think," Alex said, feeling the laughter fade away.

A few minutes later, the Guild assembled under the old sycamore tree at the edge of the carnival. Alex's mother had managed to convince their parents they would all be safe enough to attend the carnival in broad daylight. The Guild stood in a circle and listened to Alex explain his attempts to use astral travel to spy on the carnival and the surprising results.

"I can ask Daddy if he's ever heard of such an artifact," Victoria said when Alex had finished. "He's ever-so-knowledgeable about such things."

"We'll check my mom's books tonight," Alex said. "The library will be closed all weekend."

"We could always break in again," Rafael said in a dry tone. "It was so much fun and so successful the last time."

"No," Alex said, frowning at the memory. "We have enough to do today trying to find the followers of the Shadow Wraith and this artifact."

"Mystery person," Ben said. "We also need to find the person in the cloak."

"I'm not so sure it's someone from the carnival," Alex said.

"So what in the name of Theseus's toenails are we waiting for?" Daphne said, stomping off toward the carnival.

The others looked at each other silently for a moment and then followed Daphne toward the carnival and all the dark mysteries it contained. Normally, Alex would have been filled with excitement about spending a day at a carnival, but the feeling that caused his stomach to tighten more with each step toward the colorful tents was not enthusiasm. It was fear. People were trying free the Shadow Wraith again and whoever those people were, they knew who Alex was, and they had no compunction about trying to kill him.

However, it wasn't himself he was so much worried for. His sister, his parents, his friends, and the whole town were in danger. Focusing on that thought helped turn his fear into anger. Anger was an emotion Alex knew could get him into trouble, but a ball of anger in his stomach felt better than a knot of fear.

Alex and the Guild showed the ticket taker at the entrance booth their golden tickets. The ticket taker, an old man with a gray beard and a gray fedora on his head, frowned at the tickets and then at Alex and the Guild. He seemed unhappy to lose so many paying customers, but eventually, he waved them through.

Victoria said her goodbyes and headed off to help staff the booth of magical inventions her father had setup. After their tour of the grounds, and their adventures the night before, Alex and the Guild were very familiar with the carnival, but they were not used to seeing so many people present.

Word must have traveled fast, because it seemed like the whole town and most of the residents of the Rune Valley had descended upon the carnival. Normally, the Founders Festival was a one-day event, held on Saturday in the town center, in front of the statue of the five founders of Runewood. The presence of the carnival had extended the festivities to include Friday and the entire weekend. The carnival would close its gates on Sunday night, pack up and be gone the following morning. This meant the Shadow Wraith's followers had a limited window of time in which to accomplish their dark mischief. It also meant Alex and the Guild had a limited amount of time to stop them.

They wandered through the carnival grounds, pretending to be just a group of local kids out having fun. They used their golden tickets to pay for games, rides, and entrance to the various sideshows. Alex avoided the rides, preferring to leave them to the others.

As they walked, they tried to taste as much of the various carnival food as they could. They ate magical cotton candy that shifted shape as it got smaller, beginning as an elephant, becoming a lion, then a hawk, and ending as a mouse. They consumed cones of ice-cream that changed flavors as it melted, starting off as chocolate, becoming lime, then banana, then coconut, then peppermint, then pistachio, and then finally, strawberry.

They ate breaded corn dogs that barked as they bit into them and drank sodas that fizzed and bubbled and became all the colors of the rainbow, leaving their teeth tinted like a box of crayons, while they rode the colorful metal backs of lions, unicorns, and hippogriffs on the ever-spinning carousel. The carousel never stopped, it only slowed enough for people to hop on and off, before picking up speed once again in a circular cascade of color.

The whole time, they kept their eyes open, talking to as many of the carnies as they could, Alex straining to hear anything in the voices he might recognize as belonging to the three people he had overheard in the tent the night before.

After a while, they came across a game that caught Rafael's attention. Alex and the others followed him over to it. There was a carnie barker at the edge of the brightly-colored open tent, urging the people standing around to pay for a chance to win one of the stuffed animals hanging around the edge of the canvas enclosure. He had long, blond hair trapped under a faded green felt top hat. Alex noticed the stuffed animals were all what Outsiders would call mythical creatures. Hydras, unicorns, dragons, and even a centaur or two. In the middle of the tent sat a circular platform with three empty cages. Alex looked up at the red and blue cloth banner running along the top of the small tent. It read, *Find the Fake.*

"Place your bets, ladies and gents," the carnie barker shouted. "Find the fake and win the prize." At a wide gesture from the barker, the platform with the three small cages rotated to reveal three numbered cages of medium size, each with a large boa constrictor in it.

"One dollar a bet," the barker said, taking bills from the people gathered around. "Which snake is the fake? Is it number one, number two, or number three?"

"Number three," Rafael said, handing the barker a dollar.

"They all look the same," Alex said.

"Trust me," Rafael said.

"Final bets," the barker said, taking money from several people in the crowd. "We have five for number one, six for number two, and one for number three. And the winner is…" the barker made a melodramatic flourish with his arm and the snake in the third cage coiled itself upward, its head looking right at Rafael and winking.

"Told you," Rafael said with the smile. The snake's head briefly glowed blue and Kendra's head, covered in scales, appeared on the snake's body. The crowd burst alive with surprise, some laughing, some gasping in shock, and other cursing their luck. The barker frowned and tossed Rafael a stuffed toy unicorn.

"Wow." Ben said. "How does she do that?"

"I wish I knew," Rafael said as the circular platform with the cages rotated out of view and the barker began coaxing people to gather around for the next round of betting.

"I've never seen you do that," Nina said to Rafael.

"I didn't even know it was possible," Rafael said. As the only changeling in the town of Runewood, Rafael had only himself to rely upon for learning the limits of his shape-shifting abilities. "I think I may stay here a bit. Catch up with you all later."

"So you can learn more," Alex said, his face serious, but his tone amused.

"So you can pick up a few tips," Daphne said, her voice slightly mocking.

"Kendra," Ben said, unable to contain a giggle. "So he can pick up a few tips from Kendra."

"It's a handy skill," Rafael said, refusing to look the others in the eye. "Might come in useful someday."

"Hmmm," Clark said.

"Be careful," Alex said.

"I'll be fine," Rafael said with a laugh. "I'm hardly ever in danger when you're not around."

As Alex and the others left Rafael at the sideshow booth, the circular platform spun again to reveal three cages with three identical foxes in them. Alex chuckled to himself. It was nice to see that look on Rafael's face. The look he so often saw on Clark's face when he was staring surreptitiously at Daphne.

Alex wondered if he always had a look like that on his face when he was around Victoria. This made him wonder how Victoria was fairing at her father's booth and how long it would be before Nathan stopped by to say hello to her. Alex found it was more pleasant to contemplate who among the carnival's staff might be a follower of the Shadow Wraith.

Ben yanked Alex from his thoughts with a single word.

"Archery," Ben said, his low voice booming.

They had wandered to a part of the carnival near the back edge of the field where several archery targets were set up. A banner held aloft by two slender poles declared they had discovered *The Archer*

Queen. Alex was not surprised to see the Archer Queen was, in fact, Elaeda.

"A simple game, because I'm a simple girl," Elaeda said to the small crowd of people gathered nearby. "Best me at any target, and win a prize. One dollar for each arrow. I match you arrow for arrow. Get closer to the bull's-eye than me and you win the silver arrow. We used to have a golden arrow, but I was tired one day. In fact, I'm feeling a little dozy now. It's been long day and my arm is sore. Who wants to try their luck, I'm sorry, I mean skill, who wants to try their skill against a tired girl with a sore arm? Pick a bow and knock your arrow."

"Me," Ben nearly shouted. "I'm your man."

Alex snapped his head around and down to watch Ben step forward and hand Elaeda a dollar bill. Alex smiled at the look on Elaeda's face. Ben had been pestering the Guild to take up archery since shortly after its founding. They had tried a few times, but Alex was miserable at it, Clark broke too many bow strings, Daphne and Nina were offended by the smallness of the bows they were forced to use, and Rafael had been utterly bored by the whole endeavor. Ben had been disappointed. He had saved for two months to buy a small dwarfish bow made of bone with curved arms. He picked up a similar, well-used bow from those stacked on a table near the archery range.

"We have a challenger," Elaeda said in a loud voice. In a quieter voice that only Ben, Alex and the Guild could hear, she said, "Get within an inch of my arrow, Dwarf boy, and I'll buy you a hotdog."

"Ice cream," Ben said. "Any farther than an inch, Elf Girl, and I'll buy you an ice cream. Then I win either way."

Alex noticed what might have been a blush in Elaeda's cheeks, but she whipped around to face the target before he could be certain. Her ponytail flicked back and forth as she shook her head and knocked an arrow. Then she drew back the arrow and let it fly in what seemed like a single motion. The arrow struck the target with an audible *thunk* a second later. Alex was not surprised to see the arrow was dead in the center of the bull's eye. She turned and smiled at Ben. It was a dazzling smile and Alex noticed Ben grinning back at her.

Ben turned and knocked an arrow, drawing the bowstring back to his cheek as Alex had seen his friend do thousands of times. Then the arrow was speeding toward the target some eighty feet away. The arrow struck and Alex found himself cheering aloud with the rest of the crowd. Ben's arrow was well within the bull's eye.

"Well, this may be an interesting day, after all," Elaeda said, slapping Ben on the back.

A young carnie boy ran over to the target, carrying a wooden ruler.

"One inch exactly!" the young carnie boy shouted back from the target, holding up the ruler to show everyone.

"Dutch," Ben said. "We can go dutch. You buy the hotdogs, I'll buy the ice cream."

"How about two out of three?" Eleada said.

"Deal," Ben said, reaching out and shaking Elaeda's hand. Alex saw the look on Ben's face. It was the same look he had seen on Rafael's face. A look he suspected was probably on his own face as he started to think about Victoria again. Ben wasn't going anywhere.

"We'll catch up with you later," Alex said, but Ben's attention was focused entirely on Elaeda.

"First Rafa, and now Ben," Nina said, walking away with the others. "Must be something about the carnival."

"Or the cute carnies," Alex said.

"Romance is for suckers," Daphne said with a flick of her hair.

"Mmm," Clark said, his wide face contorted in almost palpable anxiety. "What's love got to do with lollipops?"

Daphne stared up at Clark for a moment and then burst out laughing and punched him in the arm. Turning to Alex and Nina, she said, "Since we've lost two sets of eyes, maybe we should split up for a while. Clark and I can go around one way and meet you two on the other side. Maybe he can sniff out some ancient magic."

"Good idea," Nina said before Alex could say anything.

"Great," Daphne said, heading toward a carnival ride called *The Widow's Well*. "We'll see you in an hour."

"Ah, if I smell anything, I'll let you know," Clark said, waving as he followed Daphne into the carnival.

"Do you think he'll ever tell her?" Nina asked as they watched Clark and Daphne fade into the crowd.

"Tell her what?" Alex asked.

"Seriously?" Nina asked. "Even you can't be that stupid."

"The question," Alex said, knowing exactly what Nina was talking about, "is what will Daphne do when he tells her?"

"Oooo," Nina said, her eyes going wide with the thought of Daphne's possible reactions to Clark making a declaration of his love. "Maybe we could tie her down first."

"I don't want to be anywhere nearby," Alex said.

"Maybe Clark will get lucky," Nina said, "and Daphne will realize she likes him, too."

"Daphne likes Clark?" Alex said. "Like Clark likes Daphne?"

Nina stopped and looked up at her brother, her face filled with sympathy. "You really are that stupid, aren't you?"

"You've got to be mistaken," Alex said. "Daphne is... and Clark is..." Alex wasn't sure how to finish that thought. He kept walking instead.

"Clearly the problem is not Victoria," Nina said, following beside Alex.

"What about Victoria?" Alex asked.

"Boys," Nina said. "There must be some rule that you all have to be dropped on your heads as babies."

"You're right," Alex said, not really hearing his sister. "We should stop by and see how Victoria is doing."

"That may be the first sensible plan you've ever had," Nina said.

"She may have learned something from her father about the artifact," Alex said.

"Whatever you need to tell yourself to head in the right direction," Nina said.

"Their booth is over this way," Alex said, cutting into the heart of the carnival. Nina laughed and chased after him.

Chapter Ten
Carnival Conversations

Victoria was not, however, conferring with her father about mysterious magical artifacts. Instead, Alex and Nina found her in the middle of some sort of conversation with Nathan, her impossibly handsome centaur ex-boyfriend.

"Ah, maybe we should come back later," Alex said, seeing the flustered look on Victoria's face.

"Don't be silly," Nina said, grabbing Alex's hand and dragging him forward.

Victoria and Nathan stood outside a medium-sized tent, open at the front. A large hand-painted banner draped over the opening read, *Radcliff's Radical Magical Mysteries.* The interior of the tent was lined with folding tables, each piled with various magical contraptions, many of which Alex recognized from Victoria's father's workshop. Unlike in the workshop, each of the inventions was now labeled with a handwritten note giving it a descriptive name suggesting its nature and properties. Alex noticed a bowl of mumbling marbles on one of the tables next to a large rock labeled, *The Floating Stone.* Only Victoria's father would see the need to make a stone that could float.

As Alex and Nina came closer, they could hear Victoria and Nathan.

"But you still haven't explained," Nathan said, his voice strained.

"It's complicated," Victoria said, wringing her hands.

"But there was an agreement," Nathan said.

"Not that I agreed to," Victoria replied.

Nina did not wait to see where the conversation was going to lead, but inserted herself into it the middle of it. "Hi, Victoria."

Victoria and Nathan both jumped a little at the sound of Nina's voice. They had been so engrossed in their discussion they hadn't noticed Alex and Nina walking up to them.

"Oh, hello, Nina," Victoria said, a pink flush filling her face. "Hello, Alex."

"Hi," Alex said. Allowing Nina to drag him into the middle of a conversation between Victoria and Nathan was clearly the worst idea he'd had since…Well, it was hard to tell with so many bad ideas in his past, but he was pretty sure this ranked among the top three.

"Hello, Nina," Nathan said, a coolness filling his deep voice. Alex wondered if his own voice would ever be that deep. "Hello, Alex."

"Nathan was stopping by to see how Daddy's booth was doing," Victoria said.

"Yes, I was checking on Victoria," Nathan said. "She gets bored and loses interest in things so easily."

"Not when they're interesting, I don't," Victoria said, her hooves stamping lightly in the packed earth beneath the tent.

Well, Alex thought, his mood lightening slightly, *I may not be handsome, or have a deep voice, but nobody can say I'm not interesting.*

"We were stopping by to check on Victoria, ourselves," Nina said, looking up at Nathan's long face with a somewhat dreamy cast to her eyes.

"How are sales?" Alex asked, searching for a safe subject.

"They've been a little slow, actually," Victoria said, "but Daddy's enthusiasm is boundless, so he's gone back to his shop to retrieve a few more items he thinks will have more appeal."

"Those self-hammering nails can be tricky," Nathan said. "I know from personal experience."

"I told you not to hold them like that when saying the charm," Victoria said.

"As usual," Nathan said, "your explanation left out some detail."

"I've always found your father's inventions to be very useful," Alex said.

"Thank you, Alex," Victoria said with a slight sigh.

"Nathan," a voice said from behind Alex. A voice Alex immediately recognized and caused him to swallow involuntarily. "I've been looking all over for you," Leanna said.

Alex turned as Leanna walked across the carnival grounds and joined them. She was wearing bright green shorts over her goat legs and a bright green shirt that made her bright green eyes seem to jump out at Alex. "Oh, hi, Alex," she said, bursting into a smile as she stepped up close to him.

Alex found his brain was suddenly having trouble forming words. This was the kind of situation that caused his mind to move like molasses. To have a beautiful girl who had saved his life staring up at him with her enchanting green eyes, in front of the girl who he wanted to be his girlfriend, who had been talking to the far-too-handsome centaur boy who had been her boyfriend, and seemed to still want to be her boyfriend, and all while his sister watched with a look of absolute amusement on her face, made Alex's brain numb. Alex would rather have been back in the cave with the Shadow Wraith. At least there, he knew what he was doing. At least there, he didn't have to worry about what came out of his mouth.

"Oh, hi," Alex finally said, speaking slowly to make sure what was in his head didn't come out of his mouth.

"How are you feeling today?" Leanna asked. "All healed up?"

"I'm feeling great," Alex said, unable to stop himself from smiling back at Leanna. How do you not smile at a pretty girl who is smiling at you, even if the girl you really want to smile at you is standing right beside her?

"Been on any of the rides yet?" Leanna said, a teasing lilt to her voice.

"I've been avoiding them so far," Alex said. "I want to make sure everyone else has a chance to ride them before I bring them crashing down around me."

"That's very generous of you," Leanna said, laughing. Alex stole a glance at Victoria, but she wasn't laughing. *Great.* Alex thought. *Now, I'm charming.*

"You were looking for me?" Nathan asked, drawing Leanna's gaze from Alex's face.

"Oh, right," Leanna said, her eyes lingering on Alex for a moment before turning to Nathan. "I wanted to run lines with you. It's been a while. We don't want to mess up."

"Right," Nathan said, a serious look coming across his face.

"Run lines?" Victoria asked.

"For the show," Leanna said. "*The Eternal Story*. Didn't Nathan tell you? He and I are actors in the show."

"An actor," Victoria said, looking quizzically at Nathan.

"It's the only opening they had in the carnival," Nathan said, his eyes suddenly darting between Victoria and Leanna.

"Don't be so modest," Leanna said. "He's a natural. The crowd loves him. Loves us, actually. All our scenes are together."

"Together?" Victoria asked.

"Naturally," Leanna said. "We play the star-crossed lovers. Destined to be together, separated by fate and misfortune, but tossed into each other arms in the climactic moment of our reunion. People cheer at the final kiss."

"Do they really?" Victoria said, titling her head as she looked to Nathan.

"Didn't Nathan tell you any of this?" Leanna asked, mimicking Victoria's expression as she looked at Nathan.

"I hadn't gotten around to..." Nathan began, flustering as his face flushed. "It was...Well..."

"I can't wait to see it," Nina said, her voice loud and clear as she, too, looked at Nathan.

"Yes, I'll be looking forward to that, as well," Victoria said. Alex realized he wouldn't mind seeing it, either.

"Your golden tickets get you in free," Leanna said to Victoria before turning back to Nathan. "So, do you want to rehearse? I don't want to interrupt if you're busy. I know you haven't seen Victoria in a long time. Maybe I could talk Alex into running lines with me."

"Me?" Alex said, caught completely off-guard by his sudden entry into the conversation. "Acting?"

"It's easy," Leanna said, her attention focused completely on Alex once again. "We simply read through the lines and act out the scene. You'd be great, I'm certain of it."

"I'm sure I have time," Nathan said. "Victoria is busy and we can catch up later."

"Yes, I'm swamped with customers," Victoria said, looking around at the empty tent.

"If you don't mind sparing him," Leanna said, her eyes once again holding on Alex for an extra second before turning to the others. "It probably would be best to rehearse with my actual lover. I mean my actual, make-believe lover."

"Yes, I can see how that would be helpful," Victoria said, her tail flicking as she smiled.

"Maybe some other time, Alex," Leanna said, grabbing Nathan's hand and leading him away. "I know a place where we can have a little privacy. Bye, Alex. Bye, Nina. Bye, Victoria."

"I'll see you later," Nathan said over his shoulder to Victoria.

"I suppose we'll all see the both of you later," Victoria said. "Kissing in front of everyone." Alex doubted Nathan heard that last bit, as Victoria had lowered her voice to a near-whisper.

"I can't wait to see the play," Nina said. "They say it's different every night."

"It seems you've passed up a preview, Alex," Victoria said.

"I'm not much of a thespian," Alex said.

"You pretend you know what you're doing all the time," Nina said, poking Alex in the ribs.

"I do know what I'm doing," Alex said. Nina and Victoria snorted with laughter. "Most of the time. And I'm always pretending to be myself even if I am pretending."

"That does make a difference," Victoria said. "Particularly when we're facing things like you-know-what."

"Did your father know anything about that certain object we're looking for?" Alex asked, happy to be talking about dangerous and life-threatening things again, even if in vague code words.

"I asked him, but he said he'd never heard of anything like it," Victoria said. "And unfortunately, he made me promise to let him examine it if we find it. I tried to convince him destroying it was the only reasonable thing to do, but once his curiosity is aroused, he can be very unreasonable. And speaking of the search, where are the others?"

"Rafael thought Kendra might have some information that could be useful," Alex said, unable to stop himself from grinning.

"And Ben thought the same thing about Elaeda," Nina said, stifling a giggle.

"I see," Victoria said. "The carnival seems to have captured their imaginations."

"Daphne is with Clark seeing if he can smell any magic around," Alex said, lowering his voice as a middle-aged woman in a large, floppy purple hat entered the tent and began examining the inventions.

"It was her idea," Nina added.

"Really?" Victoria. "How interesting."

"Seems everyone's paired off," Nina said. "I'm supposed to guard my brother every second, but I was thinking about getting an ice cream, so maybe you could watch him for a bit."

"I'm not a pet dog," Alex said with an annoyed tone.

"That's true," Nina said. "Dogs are more obedient."

"Well, I..." Victoria said, flustered for a moment as she looked at Alex.

"How much is this?" the woman in the purple hat asked from the tent, holding up something that looked like a cheese grater welded to an eggbeater.

"It seems I have a customer," Victoria said, glancing back at the woman with the florid hat.

"We can come back," Alex said, feeling a little flustered himself. Why shouldn't he want to spend some time with Victoria? "We should keep looking for that thing and those people." That was not at all what he really wanted to do.

"Yes, that's probably a good idea," Victoria said. "I'll catch up with you after Daddy returns." She smiled quickly and then turned to help her solitary customer.

"Let's go get your ice cream," Alex said to Nina, waving to Victoria as he headed back into the maze of carnival tents.

"Wow," Nina said, striding beside her brother, "you are dense."

"What?" Alex said.

"Dense," Nina said. "Like a rock. But that Leanna sure is great."

"She's very nice," Alex said.

"Boy, are you dense," Nina said. "She's not nice, she's brilliant. I'm hope I'm half that good when the time comes."

"What are you talking about?" Alex asked.

"Not like a rock," Nina said. "Like miles of granite."

"Have you developed your own special language?" Alex asked.

"I'm talking about the language of love," Nina said.

"What would you know about the language of love?" Alex said, sarcasm filling his voice.

"Clearly more than everyone else I know," Nina said, exasperated. "Except Leanna. She should write a book."

"What's that?" Alex said, looking over Nina's head.

"A book," Nina said. "She should write a book."

"Quit babbling," Alex said. "I see Anna and the Mad Mages."

"Where?" Nina said, looking around.

"They went behind that orange tent," Alex said, pointing.

"Leave them alone," Nina said. "We have more important things to pay attention to."

"Anna said she had plans," Alex said, turning down an alley between tent rows. "We should see what they're up to. Careful, though, I think Anna saw me."

"You need to learn to focus on one problem at a time." Nina sighed, following Alex through the crowd of carnival goers.

Alex led Nina through the labyrinth-like lanes of carnival tents, trying to keep an eye on Anna and the rest of the Mad Mages without letting them know they were being followed. When the Mad Mages went right around a tent, Alex would turn early to follow them from another direction. He and Nina ran down back paths between tents, skipping over safety ropes, to emerge ahead of Anna and the Mad Mages, slipping behind a crowd of people as they passed and turned down another lane.

Alex and Nina followed Anna and the Mad Mages like this for five more minutes, watching them stop to buy ice cream cones, and finally, sitting gathered around a tree at the edge of the field, but still within the carnival grounds. Alex and Nina hid behind the wheel of the large truck, out of sight, but close enough to hear some of the conversation between the Mad Mages. Alex turned to Nina and placed his finger over his lips to indicate silence. She looked at him as though she wanted to hit him in the head with a rock.

"…Lesson," Alex heard Dillon say.

"I told you," Anna said, licking daintily at her flavor-changing ice cream cone. "I have a plan."

"I have a plan," Koji said, around a mouthful of ice cream. "Let's beat the crap out of them."

"That is why you do not get to make the plans," Anna said. "A plan needs subtlety."

"But what is the plan?" Dillon asked, nearly pouting and completely ignoring his ice cream. "I should be informed if there is a plan."

"We gonna burn down their club house?" Karl said, wiping his face on the back of his sleeve.

"Burn down the barn that belongs to the town warlock?" Anna said, giving Karl a piteous look. "Not even Dillon's father could save us if we were found responsible for that."

"Maybe, if we could find out what they are running all over the valley looking for," Mai said, her lips stained from her ice cream as it changed from blueberry to vanilla. "We could maybe find it first and then maybe hold it for ransom."

"Pointless," Anna said. "Alex may be an arrogant, self-satisfied, lover of low magical creatures, but he is competent. If he can't find what he's looking for, I doubt we'd have any better luck, even if we knew what it was."

"Then what?" Dillon said, finally eating a bite of his melted cone.

"We need to separate him from the thing he loves most," Anna said.

"The horse?" Koji said with an evil grin. "She might get lost one day."

"No," Anna said, "something really important to him."

"What?" Dillon asked.

"I'll explain later tonight," Anna said, standing up. "At the club house, not out here in public where someone might hear us."

Anna led the Mad Mages back into the carnival grounds, Dillon, sullen at being demoted to second-in-command, following last.

"See?" Alex said turning to Nina. "They are up to something."

"But we still don't know what," Nina said.

"We can find out tonight," Alex said, still staring after Anna and the Mad Mages.

Chapter Eleven
Magic Box

A frustrating and fruitless search for both the followers of the Shadow Wraith and the ancient artifact creating the astral barrier consumed the rest of the day. Near sundown, Alex and Nina finally met up with Daphne and Clark, who claimed to have smelled something that might have been ancient magic, and might have had the scent of Spirit Magic, but which seemed to move around too much for them to be able to locate.

Rafael and Ben reluctantly returned to the group after confirming neither Elaeda or Kendra had seen or heard anything suspicious in the previous months, much less the last two days. Whoever the Shadow Wraith's followers were, they were well hidden among the carnies. For his part, Alex felt like he had listened to every voice of every carnie at least twice and had not discovered a single resemblance to the voices he had heard the night before.

He had come across his parents twice, but they had learned nothing helpful. They walked around holding hands and looking like two young lovers, strolling through the crowds, playing carnival games, and sharing an ice cream cone. Both times, it had made Alex jealous in some weird way that also left him feeling uncomfortable. His parents made being in love look so easy, when it seemed to be just the opposite of that.

This thought then led him to wondering when he had decided he was in love and how that decision had slipped past without him even noticing it. Recognizing it in hindsight only seemed to make it that much more important of a realization. Like something he had always known in his heart, but which his heart had not, until recently, told his head. When Victoria eventually arrived at his side, finally free of her familial duty at her father's invention booth, Alex found he was so confounded by his new feelings he didn't know what to say to her.

They held each other's gaze in silence for a moment and Alex found himself lost in Victoria's azure eyes. *No wonder I'm in love with her,* Alex thought.

"No luck?" Victoria asked.

"Nothing," Alex said, unable to keep himself from sounding happy, even though he hoped he was the only one who knew the source of his improved mood.

"Well, I know a smelled something," Clark said. "But it kept moving."

"Had us chasing a gorping hotdog vendor for twenty minutes," Daphne said with a laugh as she elbowed Clark.

"Mmm, a tasty...I mean, honest mistake," Clark said with a rumbling chuckle.

"At least you paid for the hotdog," Daphne said.

"Did you get your hotdog?" Nina asked Ben.

"Two," Ben said, beaming and blushing in equal measure. "She owed me two hotdogs, but I owed her three ice creams. She's really good. I think she let me win the last one."

"I find it hard to imagine Elaeda letting anyone win at anything," Victoria said. "She can be very...competitive, and...territorial."

"What about you, Rafa?" Nina asked. "Did Kendra show you any new tricks?"

"I learned a few things," Rafael said, his face unreadable except for the darkness in his cheeks. Alex wanted to laugh at Ben and Rafael's discomfort under his sister's questioning, but that sort of thing could all too easily be turned in the opposite direction. Best to get everyone thinking about something else entirely.

"We should see *The Eternal Story*," Alex said, catching sight of a flyer in the hands of a townsperson passing by.

"Yes," Victoria said, a question seeming to flit across her face. "I suppose we should."

"That's a great idea," Nina said. "Love and romance and tragedy."

"Adventure," Ben said. "Eleada says it's supposed to be a great adventure."

"With magic woven in," Rafael said. "That's what Kendra said."

"And sword fights," Daphne said, her eyes lighting up with excitement at the thought.

"Mmm, and a really good story," Clark said.

"Actually, I was thinking since at least half the carnies are in the play, I could get a good listen to them," Alex said.

"Especially Leanna," Nina said, trying to contain a giggle.

"Well, I'm sure I didn't hear her in the tent," Alex said, not sure what else to say.

"And Nathan," Nina said.

"I'm sure he didn't hear Nathan in the tent," Victoria said, her tail swishing behind her.

"I'm sure," Alex said. In truth, Alex wasn't discounting anyone as a possible suspect, even if Leanna and Nathan did seem like unlikely followers of the Shadow Wraith. But, he didn't need to say that out loud. "This way. Our golden tickets should get us good seats."

The golden tickets got them great seats. Except Victoria, who obviously couldn't use a seat. A raised stage filled a quarter of the giant tent, thrusting out into the middle the audience. Magic glow bulbs of various sizes and shapes hung throughout the audience and the stage, strung on thin lines between the large wooden support poles of the tent. Chairs for seating surrounded the stage, with benches on risers behind them. Alex and the Guild picked a spot halfway up a bank of raised benches. Alex took the place at the end, next to Victoria, who stood in the aisle, their heads roughly at the same level.

"I can't wait to see what it's like this evening," Victoria said, twirling a finger through her long, blonde hair.

"Is it really different every time?" Alex asked as the glow lights above began to dim.

"Sometimes more than others," Victoria said, lowering her voice, "but it's always the same general story."

As the glow bulbs winked out and the tent fell into darkness, Alex wondered briefly how different the play would seem this time for Victoria with Nathan in a lead role. Then the lights came up on the stage, the play began, and Alex found himself carried away by the story and the spectacle.

The Eternal Story told the tale of a Queen struggling to save her kingdom from an invading army led by an evil wizard who had once been her suitor when they were both young. Esmeralda played the queen and she looked resplendent in her regal raiment. She was mesmerizing every time she appeared on stage. She wore her stunning necklace of nine large sapphires glittering hypnotically in the bright light of the glow bulbs illuminating the stage.

Mr. Apollo played the evil wizard, a man driven mad by lost love and a rage for revenge. It was a tragic story augmented by subplots involving a small host of characters portrayed by various carnies Alex had met over the past two days. Some even played multiple roles, changing costumes and makeup in between scenes with a speed that would have been impossible without the use of magic.

The stagecraft was as impressive as the story and the acting. A long sheet of some sort of fabric stretched across the back of the stage and magically projected the images for the settings of the scenes played by the cast. Around the stage, dozens and dozens of boxes changed shape and color and texture to transform into scenery filling in the setting created by the magical backdrop.

In this way, a castle throne room with towering marble columns almost instantly transformed into a wooded glen with ancient oak trees. A battlefield with siege machines and catapults became, a moment later, a royal library with rows and rows of books. Alex tried to figure out how the magic behind the ever-changing stage set functioned, but he found himself too drawn in by the story and the characters to focus on the question. He made a mental note to ask Victoria how the magic set worked after the show.

The sword fights Daphne had so hoped to see were nothing compared to the magical battles between the evil wizard and the queen. Balls of fire burst above the audience and lightening arced through the tent like living snakes of electricity.

Nathan and Leanna were extremely convincing as the young lovers torn apart by war. Their first appearance was very dramatic, chased by soldiers, and their first kiss drew sighs from the women, and a number of men, in the audience. Alex noticed Victoria was not among the women who sighed. She, instead, was perfectly still and silent. Alex looked at her out of the corner of his eye and wondered what she was thinking. What were her feelings for Nathan? What was she feeling seeing him kissing Leanna?

Then better questions arose in Alex's mind. What were Victoria's feelings for him? Why did it seem so hard to find a time a place to try to kiss her again? Was there some strange and evil magic trying to keep them apart? These thoughts led to Alex doing something he thought was both bold and decisive — he reached out and took Victoria's hand.

Victoria looked at Alex, surprise filling her face. He smiled at her and gave her hand a small squeeze. She smiled back and her whole body seemed to relax as she turned back to watch the stage.

Alex continued to grin, extremely pleased with himself. His smile faded as his eyes saw something in the shadows at the back of the tent behind the seating risers. A figure. In a cloak. A black cloak. Although the depths of the cowl concealed the figure's eyes, Alex could feel them staring at him. Beckoning him. Then the cloaked figure turned and slipped between a gap in the canvas sides of the tent.

Alex looked at Victoria and then down at his hand entwined with hers. He gave it another light squeeze. Victoria turned to him, her eyes bright, but curious, as he released her hand.

Alex glanced at Nina, sitting beside him, and knew she was so engrossed in the story that it would be minutes before she noticed he was gone. Spinning quietly, he slowly lowered himself down to the ground between the risers and Victoria.

"Where are you going?" Victoria whispered.

"I'll be right back," Alex said as he slid away and ducked into the metal support columns beneath the risers across the aisle. He considered, for a moment, as he climbed between the metal struts, whether it was a good idea to follow the cloaked figure alone, but he knew if he asked one member of the Guild to accompany him, they would all want to do so. Every second might be the difference between catching up with the cloaked figure and losing it again.

Alex slipped from beneath the risers and through a space between two canvas walls and out into the night. The first thing he noticed was that the carnival was much more quiet, which only made sense, as half of the staff was involved in the play, and a good third of the townspeople were in the tent watching it. The second thing he noticed was the cloaked figure vanishing around a corner at the back of the tent. Alex dashed to catch up, running around the canvas circumference, always just a moment behind the night-black cloak he chased.

In seconds, he had come to the back of the tent. There was no sign of the cloaked figure, but several wagons sat near the wide entrance at the rear of the tent, acting as a backstage to the production within. Costumes filled one wagon. Another bulged with props. Several others seemed to be waiting areas for the actors. Around and between the wagons were various stage pieces and crates. Several carnies stood around the props, looking as though they were waiting for something. At a signal from a carnie near the entrance, the men picked up several large boxes, painted in various colors, and carried them toward the rear entrance of the main tent.

Alex looked around and saw a flash of black cloth slip around the side of one of the wagons. He ran toward the wagon, staying low to the ground. There were a few people near the back of the tent, and none at the backsides of the wagons, but Alex knew to be cautious. As he slid up behind the wagon, he heard a voice. Quiet and indistinct. Almost a whisper, but not quite. Familiar, but unrecognizable. The voice Alex had heard the night before. The voice of the Shadow Wraith's follower. He still could not tell whom it belonged to. Two other seemingly familiar whispers accompanied it.

"Tomorrow may be too late."

"We cannot act too soon."

"Timing is all."

"But how do we get it from the centaur?"

"Leave that to me."

"What's that?"

"What? Nothing."

"Your entrance. It's time for your entrance."

The door at the end of the wagon opened and the occupants disembarked. Alex knew he had one chance. He ducked under the wagon and crawled on his hands and knees to the other side. He popped out quickly and tried to see who was leaving the wagon and walking toward the tent, but the large crates stacked around him made it impossible. He was about to step around the boxes when he heard someone coming from the opposite direction. Two men talking as they walked. They would see him in seconds.

Frantically, he glanced around and saw one of the colored boxes at his side. It had a handle and hinges on the lid. Not pausing to think, Alex grabbed the handle and pulled the lid of the box up just enough to allow him to swing his leg over the lip and slip inside.

Once the lid of the box closed, the sound of the men's conversation and footsteps vanished. Alex waited for a few seconds and then sat up and placed his hands on the underside of the lid. If he was lucky, the Shadow Wraith's followers would still be outside and he might be able to get out of the box in time to see them before they went on stage. He now knew that at least one of them was an actor in the play. Alex lifted the edge of the lid to peek through and found himself wishing he'd jumped back under the wagon and risked being seen rather than jumping into the colorful box.

Alex looked out, not at the small circle of wagons behind the great tent, but at the audience within the tent, all staring at the stage. He could see his parents, holding hands in the front row, smiling up at the actors on the stage beside him. He let the box lid drop, slowly and silently.

Magic box, Alex thought. Enter one box and exit from another. Like the closets Victoria's father had fashioned at their house. That told Alex where he was, but not how to get out. The box he had climbed into outside the tent must have led to this box on stage, but how could he get back to that first box? He risked another peek from under the lid and confirmed what he suspected. There were boxes all over the stage. He didn't wait long enough to count them because he could see the lid of another box closing. One of the actors was getting into the box. Which box would that actor end up in? Would it be his?

Alex slipped his lucky piece of broken glow-wand from his pocket and whispered the rune-word for light. A dim glow ebbed forth from the broken piece of glow-wand. It wasn't much light, but it was enough to allow Alex to search the interior of the box. He had been carrying the small piece of cracked crystal in his pocket for months for just such an emergency. It wasn't nearly as bright as a full glow-wand, but it was small enough to put in his pocket.

In the dim blue light, Alex saw what he was looking for. A handle on the inner side of the box. He doused the glow-wand with the rune-word for darkness and pulled the handle gently, opening one side of the box. Alex looked through and saw that this side of the box opened into yet another box. He only hesitated a moment before crawling through to the new box and closing the door behind him.

Looking up, Alex saw another box lid above his head. He lifted it slowly and put his eyes to the gap. It was still the audience outside, but this time from twenty feet above the stage. The box he was in must be floating in the air. Not an improvement.

Alex was about to use the sliver of magic glow-wand in his hand when the backside of the box suddenly opened inward toward him. He scrunched his body into a corner as the side door hit him in the nose. The door swung shut, revealing a very startled Leanna.

Leanna opened her mouth in what Alex expected would be a scream and he reached his hand out to cover her lips. He found Leanna had raised a hand, as well. He could feel her fingers around his throat.

"What are you doing in here?" Leanna hissed as he pulled his hand from her face. She yanked her hand away from Alex's neck and he replaced it with his own. Leanna was much stronger than she looked. As he rubbed his throat, he wondered what would have happened if she hadn't recognized him.

"Trying to get out," Alex whispered in near panic. How many other people would try to get into this box? What would happen if the box tipped and they fell onto the stage?

"Do you always do this?" Leanna asked, smiling in the dim light seeping through the crack where the lid of the box met the frame.

"Do what?" Alex asked.

"Climb into things without knowing what will happen?" Leanna said.

"Most of the time," Alex said. "But it usually works out better."

"I suppose I can save you a second time," Leanna said.

"I'll owe you," Alex said.

"Yes, you will," Leanna said. "And I can't wait to collect. Now we have to hurry. This is the part of the show where I get chased by soldiers through the magic boxes. Follow me and don't stand up until I tell you to."

With that, Leanna stood up, throwing the lid of the box wide open. She gasped in surprise and pulled the lid shut behind her. "This way," she said, opening another side of the box and crawling through.

Alex threw himself after her, trying to crawl around the side door of the box and get it closed. They ended up with their arms and legs entangled, their faces pressed against each other, lips almost touching.

"If you really do this sort of thing all the time, I don't know what's wrong with Victoria," Leanna said.

Another side door began to open inward, pushed by a hand in an armored glove. The force of the door knocked Alex forward, his lips smashing roughly into Leanna's.

"Maybe that's the problem," Leanna said, rubbing her lips with one hand and pushing another side door open with her other arm.

"Sorry," Alex whispered as he followed Leanna through the side door of the box, making sure it closed before the actor, dressed as a soldier following her, could see them together.

Alex followed Leanna through three more boxes. Each time she would pop up through the top of the box, make a melodramatic exclamation, and then lead him through a side door and into another magic box. On the fourth box, Leanna threw the lid open and Alex saw stars above his head.

"Finally," Leanna said, grabbing Alex by the hand and pulling him to his feet.

"Thanks," Alex said. "I thought we were going to be lost in there forever."

"You should have more faith in your heroine," Leanna said with a wide grin. "Now get out. I have to be back on stage."

"Right," Alex said, throwing his leg over the edge of the box and climbing out.

"Alex?"

Alex turned to see Victoria staring at him from a few feet away, her head cocked to the side in that way she always did when trying to figure something out.

"Hey, Victoria," Leanna said. "Keep an eye on him. He's trouble. Good trouble, but trouble." Not waiting for a response, Leanna pulled the lid of the magic box closed as she sat down within it.

"I came looking for you when you didn't come back," Victoria said as she stepped up to Alex. "How did you end up in that box with Leanna?"

"It's a longer story than it should be," Alex said, hoping his climb from the box hadn't looked as ridiculous as it felt.

"You have lipstick on you," Victoria said, her finger reaching out toward Alex's mouth, but stopping right before making contact.

"That's just...What happened was...You see," Alex said and then stopped, brought up short by the look in Victoria's eyes. It was a look of sadness.

"I saw the person in the cloak," Alex said, deciding to start from the beginning. His stomach felt suddenly painful and his face felt like it must be glowing in the dark from the heat in his cheeks.

"And you kissed Leanna?"

"That happened later. In the box."

"You kissed her in the box?"

"No, the kiss was an accident, because the solider was coming."

"There were three of you in the box?"

"No. You see, I heard the three people talking again, and then I tried to see who it was and then someone came and I jumped in the box."

"And that's when you kissed Leanna?"

"No, that came later. But it wasn't really a kiss."

"Then where did the lipstick come from?"

"Well, there was a kiss, but it was totally an accident because we got knocked together."

Alex stopped. Talking was definitely not helping. He didn't think any amount of talking would help. Even if he told Victoria she was the only girl he ever wanted to kiss, it wasn't going to sound right with Leanna's lipstick on his lips.

"Okay," Victoria said, breathing out a little sigh and blinking quickly as she turned away from Alex. "What did you hear this time?"

"I'm not sure," Alex said, "but I think they want to steal something from your father." Alex had the satisfaction of knowing from the look on Victoria's face that, at least for a few moments, she had completely forgotten about his accidental kiss with Leanna.

Chapter Twelve
Spy Games

"I'm still not clear," Nina said, popping a French fry into her mouth and trying not to giggle. "How did you end up kissing Leanna?"

"It wasn't really a kiss," Alex said, looking at the burger and fries on the plate before him and feeling his appetite fade. The Guild had regrouped after the play and settled into their usual booth at Uncle Sal's Burger Joint and Soda Shop. The place was empty except for the Guild, and Sal seemed very happy for the business. They were supposed to be listening to Alex's news and making plans. Instead, all they seemed to be doing was talking about his time with Leanna in the magic boxes. "It was more like an accidental bumping of faces."

"Yes, I've heard that happens often," Rafael said, smirking as he sucked down a strawberry milkshake.

"Well, I believe him," Victoria said, straightening her shoulders as she looked at Alex. "Alex would never lie to us." From the tone of her voice, he thought she really meant he would never lie to her. He hoped that was what she meant. And, he hoped she believed it, because it was true. He smiled at her to thank her for her support and she smiled back. It wasn't the dazzling smile he normally received, it was still tinged by an edge of sadness, but it was enough to bolster his mood. *I really need to kiss her*, he thought. *Soon.*

"Cupid's clammy kisses," Daphne said, a French fry waving in her hand. "The followers of the Shadow Wraith are planning to steal something from Victoria's father to help release that evil thing on the world again and we're talking about kisses."

"Daphne's right," Alex said. "We need to focus on the problem."

"Invention," Ben said to Victoria. "They must want one of your father's inventions."

"Daddy has hundreds of inventions around the house," Victoria said. "I can't imagine what could be used to free the Shadow Wraith. Much less, how they could hope to find it. Daddy's workshop is a terrible mess. Although he does have a safe where he locks up the things he thinks might be dangerous."

"Maybe you should tell your father to add some extra charms to that safe," Alex said.

"Hmm, are you sure it was Victoria's father they were talking about?" Clark said, biting into his second burger.

"I don't know," Alex said, realizing it was true. He replayed what little he had heard of the conversation between the Shadow Wraith's followers in his mind. They hadn't actually said anything about Victoria's father, they had only mentioned a centaur.

"Well, I doubt it's me they were talking about," Victoria said.

"Nathan," Ben said. "Is it possible they were talking about Nathan? He's the only other centaur in the carnival." Alex was glad it was Ben who had asked the question he had been about to pose himself.

"I can't imagine why," Victoria said. "Unless Nathan has something they need and he doesn't know about it. He would never willingly help them."

"Did you at least get a better look at the person in the cloak?" Daphne asked.

"No," Alex said, "but I think whoever it is, he or she is trying to help us. That's the second time it led me to overhear a conversation."

"No," Nina said, her eyes glaring with sudden anger. "That's the second time you've been stupid enough to follow it all alone."

"Anyone want to place bets on whether he's stupid a third time?" Rafael asked.

"Okay, I admit, I should have taken someone with me," Alex said.

"I was standing right next to you holding your hand," Victoria said.

"What?" Ben said. "You were holding hands."

"Yes, well..." Victoria started to say and then fell silent, looking unsure how to continue.

"Now, I really don't understand how you ended up kissing Leanna," Rafael said, laughing quietly.

"Gorping goon," Daphne said, shaking her head.

"I've got an idea," Nina said, looking around the table. "Since we don't know what the Shadow Wraith's followers are up to and since we can't spy on them with vampires protecting the grounds, and Alex can't astral travel to spy on them because of the artifact and the barrier, why don't we spy on who we can spy on because we know they are up to something and we know it will be bad for us if they succeed at whatever they are up to?"

The others looked at Nina in mystified silence.

"The Mad Mages," Nina said, sounding slightly exasperated that no one had followed her train of thought.

"Genius idea, Sis," Alex said, his face brightening with the idea. He was happy to have something constructive to do since they seemed stymied in their attempts to learn the plans of the Shadow Wraith's followers. He was even happier knowing it would finally eliminate his time with Leanna in the magic boxes from the conversation.

"You owe me," Nina whispered to Alex as she leaned over and as the others all began discussing exactly how they might go about spying on the Mad Mages' clubhouse. Alex mouthed a silent, "Thank you."

Their eventual plan was not daring, but it did seem to have a higher chance of success than the various plans originally suggested. Fifteen minutes after Alex finished his last bite of hamburger, he and the rest of the Guild, with the exception of Rafael, crouched in the shadows of the alley behind Dillon's house, waiting for the Mad Mages to arrive.

The Mad Mages clubhouse was an old tree house Dillon's father had paid to renovate and expand until it stretched through three large oak trees in the mayor's backyard. Alex and the Guild knew from past experience there were magical wards and booby-traps of all kinds throughout the backyard, the trees, and around the clubhouse itself. They had no hope of getting physically close enough to hear what might be said inside.

On a previous occasion, Nina had tried to charm a bird to settle in nearby branches and relay the conversation within the clubhouse back to her through a psychic link. The bird turned out to be less than responsive and had flown right into one of the windows of the tree house, nearly breaking its neck and leaving Nina with a headache for days. She had suggested the bird trick again, but Alex had convinced her it would be best to save that for when they had more time. In the end, the Guild decided if they could get close enough to see when the Mad Mages arrived at their clubhouse, Alex could use astral travel to eavesdrop on their conversations.

An impossibly large raven landed on the fence in front of them and spoke in Rafael's voice. "They're coming down the street now."

"You should change before they can see your light," Alex said.

"Then I'd only have to change back when the running starts," Rafael said with a cackle. "This way, I can watch from above for anyone who might come down the alley." Rafael, in raven form, leapt into the air, wide wings taking him up into the night sky. Alex had to admit, whatever Kendra had taught Rafael seemed to work. That raven was the largest bird Alex had ever seen Rafael transform into.

"They're coming," Victoria said and ducked her head down behind the fence. Her horse legs were already curled beneath her as she knelt on the thin strip of weeds at the edge of the alley. It was not easy for a centaur to hide, much less behind a common yard fence.

"Mmm, I wonder if they would notice if we magically made this fence taller," Clark said, hunched down next to Victoria, trying to make himself as small as possible. Victoria winked at Clark in sympathy.

"Get ready," Daphne said, peeking through a knothole in the fence. "The slime suckers are calling down the ladder now." One of the reasons the Guild had never been able to break the security of the Mad Mages tree house was because of the enchanted rope ladder that only unfurled with the correct password.

"Careful, Brother," Nina said from beside where Alex sat cross-legged with his back against the fence.

"I'll be fine," Alex said. "They can't see me."

"It's not the Mad Mages I'm worried about," Nina said.

"Hurry," Ben said. "We don't want to miss anything."

"You know what to do," Alex said to Nina and closed his eyes.

He breathed deeply, focusing his mind and quieting his thoughts. After a moment of concentration, he could feel himself slipping into his astral body. Opening what would have been his eyes, Alex found himself floating a few inches above his physical body, Nina watching over him, waiting for some sign of distress.

Alex looked around at his friends, taking an extra moment to gaze at Victoria. Her face was tight with what Alex hoped was worry about him and not memories of seeing him climbing out of that magic box with Leanna standing next to him, her lipstick smeared on his face. He watched as her face shifted to something that might have been admiration and decided he couldn't waste any more time.

His view changed as he willed himself to the edge of the tree house, appearing outside the window. He could see Anna, Dillon, and the other Mad Mages assembled around a well-polished maple table.

With a gentle thought of his mind, Alex eased through the wooden wall of the clubhouse to hover in astral form at the edge of the room. Anna was in the middle of speaking and he caught only the last bit of what she was saying as he took a moment to look around the interior of the tree house. It was lavishly decorated.

Anna and the others sat in sturdy wooden chairs with plush velvet cushions. There were three couches along the walls with well-packed bookshelves standing between them. There was even a sink, a small stove, and a miniature magical cooling box. A doorway led to a small bridge across the branches of the neighboring tree and toward what seemed to Alex like an office. It had a desk and filing cabinets. *The Mad Mages clearly have a larger budget for their clubhouse than the Young Sorcerers Guild,* he thought with a bit of jealously. Alex ignored all he saw for the moment and concentrated on what he was hearing.

"…We go to the museum," Anna said, taking a sip of a Royal Crown Soda. "Everyone else will be at the festival."

"Won't people notice we're gone?" Dillon asked, his face twisted in annoyance.

"We'll be there when you father begins his speech," Anna said. "Then we'll slip away while he talks."

"He'll talk long enough, that's for sure," Koji said with a snort. The mayor was renowned for his longwinded speeches. Dillon frowned and Koji stifled a grin.

"We have plenty of time to get to the museum, accomplish the mission, and then return before anyone has missed us," Anna said.

"And we get them at the museum," Karl said, his face more thuggish than usual.

"We get it," Anna said, casting a sharp look at Karl.

"Right, we get it," Karl said, his eyes darting around the room quickly before settling on Anna again.

"Then what?" Mai said, taking a dainty sip of her soda.

"Then we get to be the heroes," Dillon said, sneering as he reached into a yellow tin and withdrew a handful of Red Dot potato chips.

"Then we act surprised like everyone else," Anna corrected. "We get to be the heroes later. At the appropriate time."

Alex felt his astral vision of the clubhouse fading, as if something was pulling him back into his body. He struggled to remain present in astral form.

"Timing is the key thing," Anna said. "Now let's go over the plan from the start."

Alex heard no more. The next thing he knew he was back in his body, his eyes blinking open, struggling for breath. He saw the look on Nina's face as she pulled her hands away from his nose and mouth.

"Dillon's dad is coming," Nina whispered as Alex gasped for breath. Nina's instructions had been to hold his nose and cover his mouth to force him from his astral form if something seemed wrong — either with his breathing, which might indicate he was in danger — or in the event something in the alley was amiss. Dillon's father showing up was definitely something amiss.

"Where?" Alex asked, quickly crouching on his knees.

"Around that corner," Daphne said, pointing

"Rafael spotted him," Victoria said, pointing up to where a large black crow circled in the night sky.

"Dog," Ben said. "He's walking the dog."

"Ah, we should go now," Clark said, beginning to run in a low crouch down the alley.

"Rafa will be sorry he missed more running," Victoria said, trotting quickly beside Alex, trying to keep in the weeds to muffle the sound of her hooves.

"This is much better," Rafael said, his raven wings letting him swoop down beside the others and then soar up into the darkness.

"Could you hear anything?" Nina said as she ran up beside Alex.

"Enough," Alex said as they dashed around the end of the alleyway and back into the street. They quickly grabbed their bikes from behind the bushes where they had stashed them and rode as fast as they could. Several blocks away, they paused to catch their breaths beneath a chestnut tree outside the home of the local grocers, Mr. and Mrs. DeSoto.

"What did you hear?" Rafael said, still in the form of a crow, sitting on a low hanging branch.

"They're going to rob the museum," Alex said.

"Perseus's pustules," Daphne said. "What are they going to take?"

"I'm not sure," Alex said and proceeded to recount all he had heard and what he thought it meant.

"We have to stop them," Victoria said, the pitch of her voice sharp and firm.

"We will," Alex said.

"Easy," Ben said. "We know their plan, so we can catch them."

"Most of it," Alex said.

"We should tell Dad," Nina said.

"He has enough to worry about with followers of the Shadow Wraith in the carnival," Alex said.

"Don't we have enough to worry about with followers of the Shadow Wraith in the carnival?" Rafael asked.

"We can handle this," Alex said, determination in his voice.

"Mmm, we owe them one, too," Clark said. "Maybe more than one."

"So, we'll meet tomorrow at the Guild House," Alex said. "The festival begins at noon. That gives us the whole morning to search the carnival."

The others could not think of a better course of action, and Nina was eventually convinced to withhold telling their father of the impending break-in at the museum by the Mad Mages. Once Alex pointed out how satisfying it would be to catch them personally, Nina's opinion swiftly changed.

The Guild departed in pairs, Daphne offering to see Clark home. Clark bashfully, but thankfully, accepted. Rafael flew above Ben before taking wing toward home, while Nina and Alex escorted Victoria to her door. Nina managed to find something interesting in a tree down the block, within eyesight of Alex, but out of earshot.

"Thank you for seeing me home," Victoria said, her tail flicking behind her, "but it's not me people are trying to kill."

"Hang around me long enough and I'm sure they'll try," Alex said. He had meant it as a flippant comment. Something humorous to ease the tension. Instead, the frightening truth of the statement left them both in silence. Maybe being around Victoria was dangerous. For her. Maybe he should stay away from her for a while.

"It was an interesting day," Victoria said in a tone giving no indication what she really meant.

"It was," Alex said, not really thinking about what he was saying, but looking up into Victoria's deep blue eyes and forgetting all thoughts of spending less time with her. *Now.* Now was the time to kiss her. He took two steps up the stairs of the front porch and turned to face her. They stood eye to eye. *Now.* Now was the perfect time to kiss her and make her forget all about the lipstick and Leanna and anything else. All he had to do was lean in and...

"Victoria?"

Alex and Victoria turned their heads in unison to see her father standing in the doorway of their house, looking out at them from behind his lopsided spectacles. He adjusted the glasses and smiled.

"Oh, it is you," her father said. "I was wondering if you would be home before dinner. I've made a roast. Or I roasted something. There are potatoes, too. There were carrots, but I ate those. I got a little hungry. Oh, Alex. Have you had dinner? Would you like to stay and join us?"

"Thank you," Alex said, groaning despite all his efforts not to. "I ate. And Nina's waiting for me. I should go."

"Oh, Daddy," Victoria said with sigh as she looked back to Alex. "I'll see you tomorrow, Alex. I have to help Daddy with his invention booth, but I can join you for the festival speeches and…everything else."

"It's a date," Alex said, fumbling over the words. "Or an engagement…or a…I'll see you tomorrow."

Alex waved goodnight to Victoria and her father, grabbed his bike and rode past Nina.

"Her dad has the worst timing," Nina said, riding up beside Alex.

"I don't know what you're talking about," Alex said.

"I hope for your sake that's a lie," Nina said. "Otherwise, I suspect you might be irreparably brain damaged."

"What I am…" Alex began to say and then suddenly stopped. He stopped not because he wanted to, but because he had to. His body was frozen, locked in place, his hands gripping the handlebars, his feet suspended inches above the pedals, his mouth held open, but unable to move.

Alex knew immediately some magic curse was upon him, but he couldn't figure out what it was. And without being able to speak, he didn't know how he could break it. *Who was responsible?* Alex thought as the bicycle began to slow. Maybe the Mad Mages had discovered his spying. As he tried to figure out how not to land on his face when the bike eventually stopped and tipped over, the bicycle shot forward under its own momentum, gaining speed quickly as it tore down the street and around a corner.

Alex heard Nina yell behind him. Alex wanted to yell back. He couldn't. All he could do was watch from within his rigid body as the magically powered bike careened through the streets, first one turn, then another, until it was clear to Alex where he was headed — the river. Someone was planning to drown him and he couldn't even scream.

Chapter Thirteen
River Rescue

Alex heard a small whistle wailing nearby. Then he felt a tug in his pocket. The whistles his father had given to him and Nina. She must be blowing hers. Alex could hear the whistle behind him now, echoed through the one in his pocket. It wasn't close. Not close enough for Nina to save him. There wouldn't be time for his parents to arrive, either. He needed to think of something. And fast.

The bike whipped around another street corner. He could see Mrs. Grumbleson sitting on her porch stroking her albino cat, but he couldn't call out. He doubted if he had, whether Mrs. Grumbleson would have come to his aid. Most of the people in town were used to seeing Alex racing dangerously through the streets on his bike. This would seem like nothing new.

Maybe that was the plan, Alex thought as the bike turned onto Lake Street, the wide road running straight down to the river. Maybe the plan was to make it look like Alex had lost control of his bike and run into the river, drowning when he was unable to swim back to shore. In reality, he would drown because he couldn't move to swim.

He was fast approaching the river and the old docks lining it. It wouldn't be long now. He had to think of something. He had to get off the bike. But how? He couldn't speak to say any of the rune-words he might use to save himself. But did he need to speak? Centaurs could work magic without speaking. Powerful mages could form rune-words in their minds and perform magic as easily as if they had spoken aloud. Isn't that what he did when he practiced with Batami in astral form? Could it really be that different?

The bike raced across the river road, veered away from the bridge, and barreled onto the old main dock, its thin rubber wheels bouncing along the loose, old boards. There was no more time. Alex concentrated, imaging he was in his astral body, forming the rune-word with his mind. The rune-word for metal. Focusing on the word and on the handlebars of the bike. The metal shaft holding the handlebars to the bike frame turned soft and liquid-like. A bump of the bike as it raced toward the dark black waters of the river separated the handlebars from the front shaft.

Alex yelled silently with satisfaction in his mind. There was only a moment or two left. Just a few feet before the bike flew out over the dock and into the river, taking him down with it. He focused his mind on forming the rune-words for air, and wind and gravity, feeling himself float up above the bike as it sailed out from the edge of the dock and crashed into the water, quickly sinking into the swift-moving Azure River.

Alex floated out over the river, propelled by his previous motion. He watched as his bike sank into the water and drifted downstream. Focusing his mind, he mentally formed the rune-word for motion and guided himself back to the edge of the dock. Nina brought her bike to a sliding stop, jumping from it and running to Alex as he dropped to the weatherworn wooden slats of the wharf.

"Alex!" Nina yelled as she grabbed his face. At her touch, he suddenly found he could move and speak again.

"Hey, Sis," Alex said. He tried to grin, but it came out as a terrified grimace. He lowered the handlebars to the dock and opened his hands, flexing his fingers.

"What happened?" Nina said, tears in her eyes as she gave him a shove. "You shot off so fast and your legs weren't moving. I kept calling you. Why didn't you stop?"

"I couldn't," Alex said. "I couldn't move. Someone was trying to kill me."

"Alex!"

Alex looked back up the dock toward the town and saw his parents running to him, each carrying a long wooden staff, his mother's face contorted with fear and anger, his father's face hard and unreadable. Alex knew those looks.

"Alex," his mother said again as she and his father came to a stop and knelt beside him. His mother ran her hands over him, looking for wounds, and then threw her arms around him. His father scanned the surroundings, looking from the docks to the street to the river to the bridge and back to his family.

"Are you all right?" his mother asked, releasing him from the bone-crushing grip of her embrace.

"I'm fine," Alex said, staring at his parents, grateful for their presence. "Now."

"What happened?" his father asked, placing a hand on Alex's shoulder.

"Someone tried to kill him," Nina said, her voice quiet, but filled with anger.

"You'd better tell us everything," his mother said, briefly cupping his face in her hands.

"At home," his father said, his eyes still scanning the dock and the street. "We're in the open here."

"Right," his mother said, hauling Alex to his feet.

"Where's the rest of your bike?" his father asked, picking up the severed handlebars.

"Somewhere down river by now," Alex said, glancing over his shoulder at the rushing water below the dock. His parents and his sister followed his gaze in silence. Out of the corner of his eye, he thought he saw something on the nearby Ravenstone Bridge spanning the river. A black cloak. When he turned to look, it was gone.

A short while later, Alex and his family sat around the kitchen table eating leftover dessert. Apparently, for his mother, nearly getting killed required apple pie and ice cream. *There must be easier ways to get pie and ice cream*, Alex thought. He explained what had happened and how he had managed to save himself at the last moment. His parents ate in silence for a full minute after he had finished, occasionally glancing at each other, but never looking in his direction.

"This is going to require…" his mother began after setting down her spoon.

"Some serious discussion," his father said, wiping his chin with his napkin.

"Your father and I will talk about this."

"And in the morning, we'll let you know what we've decided."

"If someone is trying to kill you…"

"It may be best for you to stay home."

"But your presence makes it easier to find the Shadow Wraith's followers."

"So, we have to decide if we put your safety first…"

"Or the safety of the whole town."

"Knowing if the Shadow Wraith is unleashed on the town…"

"It will be unleashed on you."

Alex's parents fell silent again and Alex looked back and forth between their faces. Both were concerned, angry, and confused in equal measure.

"I'm glad you guys don't do that all the time," Nina said, shaking her head. "Finishing each other's sentences. That's freaky. It's like watching the Kaldon Twins."

"Why don't you two…" his mother began.

"Go to bed…" his father continued.

"And we will see you…"

"In the morning…"

"See?" Nina said. "Freaky."

Alex made no attempt to debate his parents' decision-making process or plead in favor of not being sequestered at home for some indefinite period. Instead, he hugged and kissed them both goodnight and headed off to bed. It would do no good to argue with them and try to influence their thinking on the matter. He knew from experience that was more likely to result in the decision he least desired. He would have to hope they realized hiding him in the house while the Shadow Wraith's followers were planning havoc didn't make much sense. Otherwise, he'd have to find a way to defy them, and he really didn't want to have to do that. Again.

Nina insisted he sleep with the door open, so she could come to his aid if something happened in the night. Alex didn't point out she hadn't been able to do much the last two times someone had tried to kill him. The look on her face and the tightness of the hug she gave him in the hallway before bed were enough to tell him she blamed herself for his near-death debacle at the docks.

"Thanks," Alex said. "For tonight."

"I didn't do anything," Nina said, her lips curling in an angry pout.

"You'd have thought of something to get me out of the river," Alex said. "I have complete faith in you as my guard dog."

"Thanks," Nina said, her face brightening a little. "I suppose I could have found a fishing rod somewhere."

"See?" Alex said. "A brilliant idea."

"A leash would still be easier," Nina said.

"Go to bed," Alex said.

"Say hi to Batami for me," Nina said as she stepped into her room and climbed into bed.

"Night," Alex said.

Once in bed, he pulled the sheets up over his head and used the shard of glow-wand to read by as he thumbed through his copy of *Spirit Magic Revealed*. He had read the slender book dozens of times, but Batami had been correct when she had said it would only reveal its secrets slowly. Alex doubted he understood even a tenth of what the book explored and explained. However, one passage always intrigued him. He suspected it might be of some help in rooting out the Shadow Wraith's followers. He found the passage, and read it again. Then again. It was still cryptic and confusing.

See within and see the sight that only sightlessness can see.

See the inner essence and know the inner nature.

See what is sought, but seek only to see the seeker.

Alex read it again. It might mean what he thought it did. However, it might mean something else entirely. Batami would know. He could ask her when they met for their nightly astral lesson. They were supposed to meet soon. Not long.

He yawned. It had been a long day. And he hadn't had much rest the night before. He would have to rest later. When the Shadow Wraith's followers had been found. When the Mad Mages had been dealt with. But first Batami and his question. He would ask her first thing. First thing. As soon as he...

"Ick."

Alex's eyes fluttered open. He was lying on his stomach in his bed. His mouth felt dry. His sister's face was close to his own. Too close. She looked disgusted.

"You drooled on your pillow," Nina said. "Oh, ick! It's on my hand! I have your drool on my hand!" She wiped her wet fingers on his forehead and wrinkled her nose in revulsion.

"Hey!" Alex said, sitting up in bed. He barely noticed the drool. His forehead was already wet. He was soaked with sweat. It was stiflingly hot. It looked like it was going to be another blistering day.

"You overslept," Nina said. Alex looked at the clock and then back to his sister. It was late. She was already dressed.

"Hurry up," Nina said, walking out the bedroom door. "You'll miss breakfast."

Alex jumped out of bed, hastily pulling on his clothes. Missing breakfast wasn't what concerned him. He had missed something more important — his astral meeting with Batami. He must have dozed off and slept too deeply. Why hadn't Batami come to his dreams? She had before when he had fallen into a deep sleep rather than the light trance of astral travel. Maybe something had happened to her. That didn't seem possible. There was one way to find out.

"I have to go see Batami," Alex said a few minutes later while seated at the kitchen table with his parents. He shoved a spoonful of oatmeal leaden with dried cherries, pieces of walnut, and shredded coconut into his mouth.

"What happened last night?" his father asked before taking a sip from a glass of milk.

"I feel asleep," Alex said after he swallowed.

"You're pushing yourself too hard," his mother said with a frown.

"I can push him for a while, instead, if that helps," Nina said, her face bright and mischievous.

"This brings up the question of your safety," his father said.

"Your father and I..." his mother began.

"Had a long discussion last night..." his father continued.

"About you..."

"And we are in agreement..."

"That your safety..."

"Is the same..."

"As the town's safety."

"You're doing that freaky thing again," Nina said. Alex shot her a warning look while their mother and father frowned at her.

"So we have decided…"

"That as much as we would like to lock you up…"

"To keep you safe…"

"And to keep you out of trouble…"

"It might be better to follow our earlier plan…"

"With some conditions."

"What conditions?" Alex asked, trying to keep his excitement out of his voice.

"Nina is with you at all times," his mother said.

"As well as your club," his father added.

"Guild," Alex and Nina said in unison.

"Whatever," his mother said. "We're willing to let you out our sight only because we know our presence will make it harder to find the Shadow Wraith's followers."

"They're not likely to show their faces with a famous warlock hanging around you," his father said, looking at his mother. "And me being with you won't help, either."

"So stay with the Guild and keep those whistles handy," his mother said, giving his father a smile and taking his hand.

"Everywhere," his father said. "Take Ben and Clark to the restroom with you."

"Yuck," Nina said.

"We were going to make it your job," his mother said.

"Mom, I'm eating," Nina said, her face scrunching up with distaste.

"Thanks," Alex said to his parents.

"Don't make us regret it," his father said.

"And don't do anything reckless," his mother said.

"Seriously, Mom?" Nina said. "Who are we talking about?"

"I'll be extra careful," Alex said, trying to sound responsible as he took another bite of oatmeal. His parents glanced at each other and frowned. Maybe he had sounded excited instead of responsible.

The sun sat just above the treetops when Alex and Nina stepped outside and headed to the Guild House. Clark and Daphne were already there, working hard at deciphering the secrets of the mysterious cauldron. The large, black pot sat on the woodstove with a small fire burning in the iron chamber beneath it.

"Any luck?" Alex asked.

"The gorping thing is driving me crazy," Daphne said, throwing down a wooden spoon in frustration. "Every potion I try to make comes out completely wrong."

"Maybe it's the onions," Nina suggested with a giggle. Daphne glared at her and Nina fell silent.

"Well, the magic of the cauldron is doing something, but it's doing something different every time," Clark said.

"Two exact potions made exactly the same way, and they came out different," Daphne said.

"Ah, and they smelled bad," Clark said.

"I'm sure you'll figure it out," Alex said, patting them both on the shoulder, which required quite a stretch between their respective heights. "But we have something else we need to do this morning."

"What in the name of Hyperion's hernia has happened now?" Daphne asked.

"Somebody tried to kill Alex again last night on the way home," Nina said.

"Hmm, maybe we shouldn't let you out of our sight," Clark said.

"My parents had the same thought," Alex said. He explained what had happened and how his parents had decided to react to it. Then he explained why he needed them all to go with him to see Batami in the White Forest. Then, when Ben, Rafael and Victoria arrived, he explained it all again.

"It seems we have a very busy day ahead of us," Victoria said. "A meeting for you with Batami. Searching the carnival for the Shadow Wraith's followers and the anti-astral artifact. Then foiling the plans of the Mad Mages. I should have packed a lunch."

"Hmm, you're right," Clark said, absent-mindedly rubbing his stomach. "We should take something with us."

"Food," Ben said. "It's always food with you two."

They grabbed some snacks from the Guild House food locker, an old, wooden cabinet stuffed with dried fruit, nuts, candy bars, potato chips, and sodas. Afterward, Alex dug out his old bicycle from the garage and used the hand pump to fill the deflated tires. Half an hour later, everyone except Victoria laid their bikes in the grass outside Batami's hut. She sat on a small wooden bench of unpainted, but bone-white wood, a pitcher of iced lemonade and a glass seated beside her. Sufina, the giant white wolf, lay in the grass at her side.

As they walked up to the hut, Alex noticed Victoria's tail twitching nervously.

"I'm the one who should be nervous," Alex said. "I missed our lesson."

"I know it's irrational," Victoria said, "as she as proven herself to be friendly, but every time I'm near Sufina, I have an overwhelming desire to run. As though she might change her mind and decide to have me for dinner."

"That doesn't sound irrational to me," Rafael said, surreptitiously eying Sufina. "You won't see me changing into a rabbit while we're here."

"Thank you, Rafael," Victoria said. "That was ever-so-comforting."

"She seems nice enough to me," Alex said, unconsciously smiling at Sufina as he approached the hut.

"I missed you last night," Batami said as Alex and the others stepped into the shade of the white-leafed trees beside the hut.

"I feel asleep," Alex said, his eyes darting away in sheepish guilt. "Deeply asleep."

"You must have had a taxing day," Batami said.

"And night," Alex said.

"I see you brought company today," Batami said, looking past Alex to the rest of the Guild.

"We're his bodyguards," Nina said, proudly squaring her shoulders.

"In case someone tries to kill him a third time," Rafael added, frowning at Alex.

"A third time?" Batami said, her eyebrows rising in question. "It seems you've been keeping busy."

"Keeping all of us busy," Daphne said.

"Why don't you tell me about it on a walk through the forest?" Batami said as she stood up. "Your friends can stay here and enjoy the lemonade." She gestured to a long, white wooden table under a tree not far away. The table had two white benches on either side. "There are more glasses in the house. I'm sure Daphne can find them. Don't wander about," she added, catching Daphne's eye. "The house is easy to get lost in." The exterior of Batami's hut magically led to the interior of a house much larger, which Alex suspected was hidden somewhere deep within the White Forest.

"Sufina will make sure you are all safe while I am gone," Batami concluded. Sufina gave a long low growl that seemed to imply some kind of dissatisfaction, but she remained lying in the shade.

Alex waved to his friends and Batami guided him to a slender path behind the hut. The path was worn down, its rich, dark earth a stark contrast to the bleached ivory colors of the forest around them. The path led straight into the forest for as far as Alex could see.

Chapter Fourteen
Soul Sight

"What is this about another attempt on your life?" Batami asked as they walked through the chalk-colored trees.

"It wasn't that bad," Alex said, trying to sound nonchalant. He told her about being trapped on the runaway bicycle and how he had managed to survive. Then he informed her about how he had spent the day searching for the followers of the Shadow Wraith and the artifact preventing astral travel within the carnival. And, he told her about their lack of success.

"I am not surprised you have been unable to find neither the artifact nor its owner," Batami said. "Whoever it is, they have had a long time to practice their deception. An artifact of that nature would be very difficult for anyone to find. If your father and mother cannot sense it, it is no wonder your large friend, Clark, could not sniff it out."

"Maybe there is a way to break through the astral barrier," Alex said, looking up at Batami.

"I have been attempting just that," Batami said, pursing her lips, "with unfortunately frustrating results."

"What happened?" Alex asked.

"Nothing," Batami said, frowning. "Absolutely nothing. No matter what I attempted, the barrier remains intact. It was irritating beyond measure."

"I've been thinking..." Alex said, looking up at the bone-white trees.

"Dangerous words," Batami said, glancing down at Alex.

"I was reading something in the book," Alex said. He didn't need to say which book.

"Now I see why you came," Batami said, leaning over to smell the flowers of a white-leafed jasmine bush.

"I was reading a section that seems to suggest it's possible to see into someone's soul-essence," Alex said. "To see into the nature of it."

"And you think if you can learn to do such a thing, you will be able to ferret out the followers of the Shadow Wraith," Batami said.

"If I look the right way, I can see a person's soul-essence," Alex said. "What you've taught me has helped me get better at it. But the book was talking about something that sounds like reading someone's soul. And I figure the soul-essence of someone trying to free the Shadow Wraith will be different in some way."

"I'm sure it will," Batami said, turning from the flowers to stare at Alex. "But what you speak of, Soul Sight, is not a thing to be done lightly, if at all. Seeing into someone's soul-essence is not like reading a book. When you read the words of a book, you take them with you, in your mind, but they are yours to command. When you look deeply into the soul-essence of another, you are not reading, not seeing with your mind. Your own soul-essence must touch theirs. When you do, something of theirs stays with you. Clings to you. Haunts you."

"But I could find out who the Shadow Wraith's followers are," Alex said, his tone insistent.

"At what cost?" Batami asked. "What will you see? And what will you do once you have seen?"

"I can handle it," Alex said, standing a little straighter.

"Assuming you could," Batami said, "there are other dangers to consider."

"What dangers?" Alex asked.

"That the sight will not leave you once you have called it forth," Batami said.

"I don't understand," Alex said.

"Seeing into a person's soul-essence is a special kind of inner sight," Batami said. "Like when your eyes adjust to a darkened room. Now imagine if your eyes stayed like that when you went back out into the light. That is what can happen with Soul Sight. It can remain forever once called upon."

"But I would only do it once," Alex said.

"Once is enough," Batami said. "I have seen it happen."

Alex contemplated this information in silence. The book had not hinted at this. It was a serious risk. To be forever forced to see the world through his astral eyes and always to know the depths of others soul-essences, to carry parts of them with him always. It would be enough to drive someone mad.

"I have to take the risk," Alex said, having made up his mind. If the worst happened, it would only be worse for him. If the Shadow Wraith was released from its prison, that would be worse for everyone. "I don't see any other way."

"Neither do I," Batami said, weariness filling her voice. "It was not something I could bring myself to suggest. I would risk it myself if I could enter the carnival grounds, but I cannot leave the White Forest in physical form and I cannot break the barrier around the carnival in my astral body. For the first time in many, many years, I feel trapped."

"Does that mean you will help me?" Alex asked. "Teach me how?"

Batami stopped and stood motionless in the middle of the path. "I will show you what I know, but I can only show you so much. It is not a thing I have ever attempted."

"Thank you," Alex said. He looked up into Batami's cloud-gray eyes and saw a deep sadness there. A sadness for him, he knew. There was a deeper sorrow there, as well, but there was no time to question her about it. "I'm sorry, for asking you to do this."

"I expected you would," Batami said with a sigh. "You're too quick to pick things up from that book. I should have prepared myself. But, we are rarely ever prepared for the things we should be, even when we know what they are. Now, stand before me. Open your mind and heart and see with your astral eyes."

Alex did as instructed, breathing deeply, calming his mind, quieting his thoughts, until his vision shifted to see through his astral eyes — the part of his mind that saw without sight. He could have closed his eyes then and seen the same vision, but he kept them open. Batami appeared as all living things did, with a pale blue-white glow. The forest shimmered behind her.

"Now look at my soul-essence," Batami said.

Alex looked at the small sphere of blazing clear-white light resting at the center of Batami's chest where her heart would be. Alex had done this many times before — looked at the world with astral eyes. Seen the soul-essences of others. Nevertheless, he was always amazed at how bright and clear the light of Batami's soul-essence was.

"Now, focus on your own soul-essence," Batami said. "Feel it blazing in its pure light. Feel through it. Feel through it toward my soul-essence. Feel how they are drawn together. How they wish to be together. How they are not really separate things."

Alex felt his soul-essence in a new way as Batami's words settled into his mind. Its pure, clear light. Its infinite stillness and motion all at once. Its connection to the soul-essence within Batami. Even its connection to the trees, the forest, and the sky above. It was as if the same pure light shown out of two windows. Out of a thousand windows.

He felt the light of his soul-essence reaching out to the light shining forth from Batami and discovered the two lights touching, mingling, separate, but inseparable. In that moment of connection, Alex perceived something else, as well. A force that he had no words for, a force he knew was Batami's inner-most spirit, the part of her that determined the nature of her soul-essence. It was like seeing a sunrise for the first time. Or the last time. A universe of love in a teardrop. A symphony of unspeakable beauty compacted into a single note. An ocean of wonder in wave after wave after...

"Don't look too long."

The words came from somewhere. Someone. Himself? The trees? The sky?

"To look too long is like looking at the sun."

Was that why there were tears in his eyes?

Alex blinked and breathed deep, as though he had been holding his breath. Maybe he had. His eyes fluttered and his vision returned to normal. He stepped back and leaned against a birch tree.

"That was…"

"More than you expected," Batami said with a compassionate smile.

"Yes," Alex said, still blinking and breathing deeply. "It was so beautiful."

"It will not be the same when you find who are looking for," Batami said, lending Alex a hand and guiding him forward along the path.

"That will stay with me?" Alex asked, feeling the answer in his heart.

"Hopefully what you carry from me will be a help rather than a hindrance," Batami said. "A counter-balance to what you will find when you discover the ones you seek."

"I don't know how often I can do that," Alex said, feeling a sharp pang of hunger and realizing what the experience had required of him.

"You must only do this for someone you suspect. It is too dangerous to do repeatedly."

"I understand," Alex said. He did understand. To see so deeply into another person was no light matter and he could not imagine what it would be like to be unable to see in any other way.

"I'll send you on your way with some sandwiches," Batami said, placing her hand on Alex's shoulder.

They walked in silence until the path emerged from the forest. Alex was surprised to see his friends gathered around the table, playing a game of Elements. He had been certain they had kept walking straight on the path, away from Batami's hut.

"How?" Alex began to ask.

"The forest and I are deep friends," Batami said. "Our wills are one."

"Fire," Ben said as Alex and Batami crossed the small glade of white grass to the where the others sat. "Fire beats wood."

"Hmm, the wood was wet," Clark said.

"I never could understand the rules of that game," Batami said with a soft laugh as she and Alex reached the table.

"I don't think this game has rules," Victoria said, frowning at Nina.

"That's because you lost five games in a row," Nina said with a smug smirk.

"You have to learn to think of the rules as more like guidelines," Rafael said, leaning back from the table.

"I'll gorping guideline you," Daphne said, banging the table with the palm of her hand. "Since when does fire not beat wood?"

"I see your temper is improving," Batami said, locking eyes with Daphne.

"Sorry," Daphne said, looking down, her face a cross between embarrassment and annoyance.

"Why don't you help me gather some sandwiches from the kitchen while Alex and the others clear the table?" Batami said. Daphne's face fell and, for a moment, it looked like she might object. Then she smiled as sweetly as possible.

"Certainly," Daphne said.

Alex followed Daphne and Batami with his eyes as they walked to the hut. Sufina was still lying in the grass beside the porch. She winked at Alex as his gaze came to rest on her. He winked back. He wondered what he would see in the soul-essence of the giant wolf. It would be beautiful, he was sure.

By the time Alex and the others had cleared the picnic table, Daphne and Batami returned with a large paper bag filled with sandwiches and a second bag filled with white apples.

"Ooo, Daddy loves white apples," Victoria said.

"I'm glad to hear it," Batami said. "Maybe someday I will make a pie."

Alex could not really imagine Batami baking, but the thought of a white apple pie made his stomach rumble.

"Remember what I said," Batami said to Alex as the others mounted their bikes and Victoria followed them.

"I will," Alex said, his voice reflecting the seriousness he felt in his gut.

"You're probably safe until you reach town, but I'll send Sufina with you, just in case," Batami said. The white wolf climbed slowly to her feet at the mention of her name. Alex saw Victoria eye the wolf and trot quickly toward the path leading back toward town.

"Sometimes, I think you send her with us to make sure we leave faster," Alex said.

"Maybe I do," Batami said, a mysterious glint in her eye.

The ride back to town did not take long, as it was mostly downhill. Victoria easily kept pace with the rest of the guild on their bikes. Alex had never seen Victoria get tired from running. She loved it. He suspected she would run everywhere if it didn't seem so indecorous.

They ate their sandwiches and apples while they travelled. There were still a few hours before the beginning of the Founders Festival festivities, so they rode to the carnival, flashing their golden tickets at the gate and proceeding directly to Victoria's father's invention booth. Victoria was supposed to spend the day helping her father hawk his wares, but her presence at Alex's side was one of the conditions his parents had set for him being able to wander around freely while people were trying to kill him. It was the best part of the bargain, as far as he was concerned.

"Daddy," Victoria said as her father looked up from tinkering with some small contraption. "I'm afraid there has been a change of plans."

"Plans?" her father said, looking up from his work. "We had plans?"

"For me to help you with your inventions," Victoria said.

"Ah, yes," her father said, glancing around at Alex and Guild. "I see you have found more interesting company for the day."

"Not at all, Daddy," Victoria said, "but we haven't finished doing that thing we're doing, and Alex and the Guild need my help."

"Thing?" her father said.

"The project," Victoria said.

"Project?" her father said. "You're building something?"

"Looking," Victoria said, lowering her voice.

"Looking where for what project?" her father said, then his eyes went wide in sudden understanding. "Ah, that project Alex's mother mentioned."

"Exactly," Victoria said with a sigh.

"Well, you have fun," her father said, and then dropped his voice to a whisper. "By which I mean, be careful."

133

"Of course, Daddy," Victoria said with a sunny smile. "And look, as a consolation, I brought you white apples." Victoria handed her father the paper bag with the apples. "Unfortunately, there are not as many left as I had hoped. We were a little hungry."

Victoria's father pulled two very small white apples from the paper bag and held them up to the glaring hot sun.

"Hmmm, sorry," Clark mumbled and seemed about to say something else until Ben kicked his leg.

"They will be a perfect complement to lunch," Victoria's father said, smiling and slipping the apples into the deep pockets of his vest. Alex wondered how long the apples would be in those pockets. He had once seen Victoria's father pull a week-old hamburger wrapped in wax paper from a vest pocket.

With her father's blessing, and words of caution, Victoria joined the Guild in the hunt. The first thing Alex and the Guild sought out was not related to the Shadow Wraith at all. They sought relief from the stifling heat that had them soaking wet from their ride back to town. Relief came in the form of flavor-changing ice cream cones that quickly became runny and sticky in the sweltering heat. Alex spent more time licking melted ice cream from his fingers than from the cone.

He tried unsuccessfully to keep his eyes from Victoria's fingers as she delicately licked now chocolate, now strawberry, now banana ice cream from them. He needed to focus his mind on something less distracting. Like finding the Shadow Wraith's followers or the magical artifact preventing him from searching them out.

Alex crunched at the sugar crust of his ice cream cone and looked around the carnival. He had seen most, if not all, of the carnival grounds and passed, if not talked to, most of the carnies yesterday. Where to continue the search? Alex had to admit to himself he was at a loss for a plan to find either the Shadow Wraith's followers or the artifact. For all he knew, he had already met the Shadow Wraith's followers. They could be anyone. And, short of searching every tent and crate and truck, he didn't really have a clue as to how to track down the anti-astral artifact.

"Do we have a plan?" Victoria asked, walking beside him as the group turned and entered a lane of tents and attractions. Alex noted

Victoria was getting as good at guessing what was on his mind as his sister. He wasn't sure if he found that comforting or annoying.

"Nope," Alex said.

"What did you do yesterday?" Victoria asked.

"Wandered around all gorping day getting frustrated," Daphne said, dabbing with a napkin at a spot of ice cream she had managed to get on her shirt.

"Speak for yourself," Rafael said, taking the last bite of his ice cream cone. "I had a perfectly lovely day."

"That's because you were mooning over Kendra," Daphne said.

"I wasn't mooning," Rafael said. "She was teaching me a few tricks about changing shape."

"Mooning," Ben said with a chuckle. "You were mooning."

"And what were you doing all afternoon with Eleada?" Nina asked.

"Archery," Ben said, managing to look almost offended at Nina's accusation. "We were testing each other in a game of skill."

"I suppose no mooning was involved, was there, Cupid?" Daphne said.

"What?" Ben said. "You can't moon over someone while you're shooting arrows. Besides, where were you all afternoon?"

"I was with Clark," Daphne said. "We were looking for what we were supposed to be looking for."

"I suppose there couldn't possibly have been any mooning going on between the two of you," Rafael said.

"Ah, well, we were very busy," Clark said. "There was a lot of looking."

"But who was looking at whom?" Rafael asked.

"What are you gorping taking about?" Daphne asked, looking honestly confused.

"It sounds like you were all very busy looking in your own ways yesterday," Victoria said, loud enough to distract everyone from the direction their discussion had been taking.

"That's very diplomatic," Nina said with a snort of laughter.

"Since we are all supposed to stay together today, maybe we should try to have a plan for our looking," Victoria said.

"Who needs a plan when you have luck like ours?" Rafael said.

"Victoria is right," Alex said, speaking for the first time. He hadn't wanted to insert himself into any discussion about who was mooning over whom, for fear his name might come up in association with a certain centaur girl. "We should make a point of meeting and talking to every carnie we can. With Victoria to make introductions, it should be easy."

"I can certainly introduce you to everyone you haven't met yet," Victoria said. "I'm not sure how that will help us, though."

"It may not help right now," Alex said, "but it might give me an idea of who to follow at night if we can ever find that other thing we're looking for."

No one could think of a better plan of action, so they proceeded to walk through the carnival, stopping at tents and booths and attractions and rides, allowing Victoria to chat briefly with the carnies they had not yet met and make introductions. Alex tried to use each exchange as an opportunity to get a feeling for the person they spoke with. After about the tenth conversation, Alex realized it was largely pointless. All of the people they met seemed to be no more than happy, helpful, harmless carnies.

As Victoria was introducing the Guild to Helga and Roman, a mother and son pair of werewolves, thankfully in human form, Alex felt a hand rest gently on his arm and tug him away from the others. He turned to see Madam Fortuna, a worried look on her face. She pulled him to the side of a tent within sight of the others, but out of earshot.

"I still don't want my future read," Alex said, trying to be polite.

"Can't help that now," Madam Fortuna said, glancing around quickly. "Too late. I've read the cards already. Couldn't stop myself. That's why I came to find you."

"Really, Madam Fortuna," Alex said. "I already know more than I want to about my future."

"Then you'll know you're in danger," Madam Fortuna said, looking at Alex with worry in her pale green eyes.

"What kind of danger?" Alex asked, lowering his voice.

"Not clear," Madam Fortuna said. "The cards were fuzzy on that. Like something was holding them back. But there's danger around you. I felt I should tell you."

136

"There's almost always danger around me," Alex said, suddenly wishing it weren't quite so true. "Any idea who it's from this time?"

Madam Fortuna looked around again and then leaned close as she dropped her voice to a whisper. "The carnival. Someone in the carnival."

While Alex was not surprised, it did give him pause to have his suspicions confirmed by the old carnie soothsayer.

"Who?" Alex asked.

"I don't know," Madam Fortuna said. "I've been with the carnival since I was a girl and something wicked has been eating at it for years now. Eating at it from the inside. Ever since..."

"Ever since what?" Alex asked.

"I've said too much," Madam Fortuna said. "Things happen to people who talk too much. Don't come to my tent. I'm sorry. But things happen to people."

"But…" Alex began to say as Madam Fortuna spun and hurried into the crowd. The look on her face as she fled told Alex more than he wanted to know. She was terrified. Terrified someone would notice her talking to him. Terrified of what might happen to her as a result.

"What did Madam Fortuna have to say?" Victoria asked as she and the rest of the Guild stepped up beside Alex. "Did she offer to read your cards? She is always trying to read people's cards. She comes up with the wildest predictions. She once told me I was going to be a trapeze artist. Can you imagine that? Me, on a trapeze."

"She told me I was in danger from someone in the carnival," Alex said.

The others were quiet a moment.

"I suppose she's gotten rather a bit better at reading the cards," Victoria said.

"Details?" Ben said. "Did she say who?"

"Nope," Alex said. "And she seemed frightened someone might find out she had warned me. She said something has been eating at the carnival for years." He turned to Victoria. "Do you know what might have happened at the carnival in the last few years?"

"I've only been coming to carnival for the past three years," Victoria said. "It could be anything."

"Cassandra's crabapples," Daphne said. "That's not helpful at all."

"Mmm, at least we know Alex is in danger," Clark said.

"As though that were unusual," Rafael said. Alex found it all too similar to his own thoughts about Madam Fortuna's fortune.

"Persistence," Ben said. "We need to keep searching."

"Who are *they*?" Nina said, pointing to an odd group of carnies clustered in conversation back behind the row of tents, away from the main flow of foot traffic.

They were a peculiar group because of their differences. One, clearly a giant, with a large head and bush-like beard. Even kneeling on one knee, he stood above six feet. Craning back to look up at the giant while he spoke was a stout dwarf, wide as a tree stump and not much taller. He, too, had a beard of considerable size.

Standing beside the two men, and talking in an animated fashion, were two of the most beguilingly beautiful women Alex had ever seen. They were twins and wore matching emerald green dresses that gently swayed around them even though there was no breeze in the oven-like heat. They seemed ageless. While they were clearly women, they had faces resembling young girls in the smoothness of their lines. They were so mesmerizing, it took a moment before Alex noticed the slender, black feathered wings folded tightly at their backs. *Sirens*, Alex realized.

"Do you hear that?" Rafael asked, squinting his eyes at the four carnies.

"What?" Ben said. "Hear what?"

"Yes," Victoria said, furrowing her delicate brow.

"Hear what?" Alex asked, looking at his friends. Rafael and Victoria had much better hearing than the others did — Rafael, thanks to being part changeling, and Victoria because of being a centaur.

"They mentioned the bank," Raphael said.

"And said something about a centaur," Victoria added. Then she was suddenly smiling and waving. Alex looked back to the four carnies to see they were all staring at him and the Guild. They had been noticed. Hopefully, the four carnies would not suspect they had been overheard.

"Let me introduce you," Victoria said, trotting toward the four carnies.

Alex and the rest of the Guild followed. As they approached the four carnies, the Giant stood up to his full height of fifteen feet. He, the dwarf, and the two entrancingly attractive women all smiled as Victoria approached.

"Victoria, good to see you again," the giant rumbled, his face breaking into a wide, gap-toothed smile.

"Where have you been hiding?" the dwarf said, smiling through his bushy bearded.

"It's good to see you, as well," Victoria said. "I've been busy helping Daddy, so I haven't had time to catch up with everyone."

"I am glad to see he has let you have some fun today," one of the bewitching twins said, her voice as cheerfully charming as the look on her face.

"Your father is very brilliant, but he works you too hard," the other twin added with a delicate frown. Alex noticed he was not the only one affected by the considerable charms of the twins. Rafael, Ben, and Clark had all acquired a slack-jawed look in the presence of the women.

"A little hard work never hurt anyone," Victoria said. "Allow me to introduce my friends."

"No need for that." The dwarf laughed.

"Yes," the first twin said in a honey-toned voice. "Everyone has heard of Alex Ravenstar."

"And his Guild of Young Sorcerers," the second twin said.

"Then allow me to introduce you," Victoria said, a pleasant smile on her face. Alex was impressed with Victoria's composure, given what she had heard seconds before and what that seemed to imply about the four carnies. It made him admire her even more. Something he hadn't really considered possible.

"This is George," Victoria said, gesturing toward the towering giant. "Or Graceful Giant George, as his act calls him. His brother, Horace, runs the Ferris Wheel."

"I do a juggling and acrobatic act," George said.

"With Oanadin," Victoria said, nodding toward the dwarf.

139

"We juggle things," Oanadin said. "He doesn't juggle me. Except for the grand finale when I get launched into the air from a seesaw."

"Nope," Ben said, glancing up at Clark. "Don't even think about it."

"Hmm, I didn't say anything," Clark said with a chuckle.

"And these are the Siren Sisters," Victoria said. "Elektra and Medea. Or Medea and Elektra. I'm never quite certain which of you is which."

"You had it right the first time," Elektra said.

"We have a sideshow act," Medea said mysteriously as she smiled at Alex and the Guild.

As sirens, the twins had an unnatural magical power to sway the attention and intentions of men, and to a lesser degree, women. Alex wasn't sure what their sideshow act might entail, but he felt certain Victoria would not approve of him finding out.

"It was nice to meet you all, but we should get going," Alex said, keeping his eyes deliberately away from the twin sirens. "There's still a bunch of stuff we want to see before the Founders Festival begins."

"It was a pleasure meeting you," Elektra said.

"Yes," Medea said. "Maybe we will run into you again sometime."

Alex and the Guild waved goodbye to the four carnies as they walked back to the main part of the carnival.

"You were very impressive," Alex said to Victoria when they were far away from the four carnies.

"Cool," Ben said. "As a cucumber."

"Unlike you," Daphne said. "I think there's some drool on your shirt from staring."

"Sirens," Ben said. "How are you not supposed to stare at sirens?"

Clark laughed and Daphne turned to him. "You're no better. Your mouth was so wide-open, I'm surprised a gorping bird didn't nest in it."

"Ah, I wasn't staring," Clark said. "Besides, they weren't any prettier than…than…well, any prettier than usual." Alex had a good idea who Clark thought was prettier than the Siren Sisters.

Unfortunately, for Clark, the prettier person remained unaware of his opinion. Or, maybe, that was fortunate for Clark.

"Who cares how attractive they are when we know who they are working with?" Rafael said.

"Good point," Ben said with a sigh.

"You're sure you heard them mention the bank and a centaur?" Alex asked, looking between Rafael and Victoria.

"Positive" they both said at the said time.

"Jinx," Daphne said and slugged Rafael in the arm.

"One of us is supposed to say it," Rafael said, rubbing his arm.

"Yeah," Daphne said with a grin, "but Victoria is too nice to punch you, so somebody had to do it for her."

"I don't understand," Alex said, ignoring Daphne and Rafael. "I only heard three voices in the tent."

"You never were very good at math," Nina said. "If we found four of you-know-what's friends, then that can only mean there are more than three of them, which means there may be more than four; in fact, it means there may be a whole bunch of them lurking around, and for all we know, half the carnival is in cahoots with you-know-what."

They were all quiet for a moment as they walked and the implications of Nina's mathematics sank in.

"I can't believe half the carnival would be involved," Victoria finally said. "But at least we know four people we can keep an eye on."

"None of them sounded familiar," Alex said. "So I doubt one of them is the leader, but maybe one of them will lead us to the leader behind all this."

"Do you think we should go back and try to follow them?" Victoria asked.

"Maybe later," Alex said. "Maybe tonight. We stand out too much in the daylight. For now, let's see what else we can find. We might get lucky again."

"Only you would think finding out the number of evil carnies had doubled was lucky," Rafael said.

"It'll be twice as much fun," Alex said as the others groaned.

They continued searching through the late morning and, as it drew closer to the time of the Founders Festival, the size of their group began to grow. The first to join them was Eleada. Ben insisted they stop by her archery range and say hello. Just to be polite. Morning was apparently a slow time for archery challenges, and Elaeda put down her bow and announced she would walk with them to the Founders Festival in the center of town.

It seemed most of the carnies planned on attending the festival. With all of the townspeople heading there, the carnival would be empty, anyway. Alex wondered aloud why the Festival wasn't being held at the carnival grounds, only to be informed by Daphne that the local shop owners, like her parents, the town bakers, had insisted on it. Normally, the Founders Festival was a lucrative weekend for the shops in downtown Runewood. With the arrival of the carnival, the shops would see less business than normal, so the local business council had insisted the actual festivities take place in the town center as usual.

Not surprisingly, Rafael somehow managed to steer the group past Kendra's sideshow attraction. A few minutes later, she walked beside Rafael as the group headed for the main entrance. A few minutes after that, the group came across Leanna and Nathan moving boxes beside a tent. By the time the ticket booth at the entrance was in sight, the size of Alex's protective entourage had nearly doubled.

Rafael walked beside Kendra, laughing as the color of their skins changed from red to blue to green to gray, in some sort of competition Kendra seemed to be winning. Ben walked beside Eleada, his neck permanently bent back so he could talk to her. Clark's neck looked a reverse image of Ben's as he stared down to talk with Daphne as they walked side by side.

Nathan had somehow managed to end up walking with Victoria, a feat of maneuvering that both impressed and annoyed Alex. Nina, deviously loyal sister that she was, succeeded in inserting herself between the two centaurs and peppered Nathan with a series of endlessly inane questions that seemed to amuse Victoria as much as they disconcerted Nathan. Alex didn't know how much chocolate his sister's goodwill would cost him, but he was certain it would be worth every bar.

That was how Alex found himself walking beside Leanna.

"Have you been enjoying the carnival so far?" Leanna asked, glancing over at Alex.

"You mean besides having thousands of pounds of a carnival ride collapse on my head and being trapped in moving magical boxes?" Alex asked with a small laugh.

"Right. Beside that."

"I've been having a blast."

"That's good. You don't seem like you're enjoying yourself. You look like you'd rather be doing something else."

This was true, Alex realized. Firstly, he'd rather be walking with Victoria. Not that Leanna wasn't nice. And pretty. And she had saved his life. But then, so had Victoria. And Victoria was…well, she was Victoria. She encompassed so much in Alex's mind and heart that it was sometimes difficult to see past her at all. And then there was the other thing that he would rather be doing — looking for the Shadow Wraith's followers. He knew who four of them might be. And, they might lead him to the others. Or, hopefully, to the artifact prohibiting astral travel within the carnival.

Wait. Was that true? Alex asked himself. Was astral travel impossible inside the carnival? Maybe the barrier only kept an astral traveler from crossing into the carnival. Maybe if his body was in the carnival grounds while he was in astral form, the barrier might not work. Maybe he could hide in the carnival after it closed and spy in astral form. He'd have to know first. He'd have to test it. He'd have to try astral travel from inside the carnival.

The prudent thing to do, he realized, was to wait until after the Founders Festival and return to the carnival and attempt to astral travel while his friends watched over him in some safe and well-hidden place.

Prudent. Him. Alex Ravenstar. He almost laughed aloud at the thought.

"Are you okay?" Leanna said from beside him. "You're kind of quiet."

"I'm not sure," Alex said, a possible plan percolating up within his mind. They were almost to the main entrance. In a few seconds, they would be outside the carnival proper. If he wanted to test the barrier, he would have to do right then.

"I'm not feeling so well," he said to Leanna as he came to a stop. "Catch me."

Alex let his knees buckle and fell to the ground. Leanna reached out to catch him. As he felt her arms lowering him to the ground, he breathed out slowly, relaxing his body and mind and focusing his will on shifting into his astral form. It was not easy. He was used to making the transition while in a quiet place like his bedroom or the White Glade near Batami's hut. Around him were sounds of hurried movement and the concerned voices of his friends. He blocked them all out and grasped at the state of mind right at the edge of his consciousness.

A moment later, Alex hovered in astral form above his friends as they clustered around his apparently unconscious physical body. Alex took a moment to note with an inner swell of emotion how quickly Victoria moved to kneel by his side.

Then he was willing himself to the main entrance of the carnival. Clearly, the magic that prevented him from entering the carnival in astral form did not prevent him from astral travel within the grounds. Or was that true? Appearing at the main entrance, he felt no barrier at all. Willing himself across the threshold of the entrance, he watched people walking toward the town center, some glancing back to see what the disturbance behind them was. Looking to where a boy had fallen to the ground.

Alex willed himself forward toward the town center, flying over the trees and streets. His movement came to a jarring halt so abruptly, he was almost forced back into his physical body. He felt like an insect smashed into a plate glass window. Then the sensation evaporated. Curious, he moved forward. Again, he encountered the barrier, but closer to the town center. The barrier was no longer around the carnival. Was it possible it was moving toward the town? That would mean the artifact creating it was…

Alex sputtered and blinked and coughed. There was water on his face and up his nose. He looked up to see Victoria staring down at him, her face contorted with worry. Behind her, Alex could see Nina and the rest of the Guild, their faces similarly distraught with concern.

"Are you okay?" Victoria asked.

"You just collapsed," Leanna said from beside him.

"It's lucky she caught you in time," Victoria said.

"Thanks," Alex said, turning to Leanna.

"You had me worried there for a minute," Leanna said, gently patting his chest. "You're dehydrated. You need to drink more water in this kind of heat."

"Here," Victoria said, offering Alex her canteen. "Have a sip of water."

"Thanks," Alex said, taking a sip from the canteen Victoria had been carrying on a strap across her shoulder. Centaurs drank a lot of water and Victoria always had a canteen handy. "I think Leanna's right. I got dehydrated."

"This heat is dangerous," Kendra said, bending down to examine Alex. "I've seen camels collapse in heat like this when we were in Egypt."

"Water," Ben said, said taking a sip from his own canteen. "His brain is probably like a dry sponge."

"A very small, dry sponge," Rafael said, snagging the canteen from Ben and taking a gulp.

"Not enough water in his body," Eleada said, frowning down at Alex. "Eat something salty as soon as you can. It'll help you retain the water."

"What does Mom always say about drinking enough water?" Nina asked as she poked him in the arm.

"Something about drinking enough water?" Alex said, trying to act like he had woken from a faint and not as though he had made a significant discovery about the Shadow Wraith's followers and their abilities.

"Stupid," Nina said. "They should have named you Stupid."

"Do you think you can walk, Bonehead?" Daphne said.

"I'll be fine," Alex said, taking another swig from the canteen and climbing to his feet.

"Ah, maybe we should let you rest for a bit," Clark said.

"I could carry you on my back," Nathan said in a helpful tone.

"I'm fine, thanks," Alex said, trying not to show on his face how annoying he found Nathan's seemingly helpful suggestion. "Besides, we don't want to miss the festival.

After what Alex hoped was a convincing performance pretending to recover from a heat-faint and fending off the offers of help from several passersby, he convinced the others to begin heading for the town center again. The bright side of his dramatic faint was that he now found himself walking beside Victoria instead of Leanna, who seemed far happier to be strolling beside Nathan. Alex caught Leanna give him a look that seemed a cross between worry and curiosity, but then she turned to talk with Nathan again, a bright smile on her face.

"What was that all about?" Victoria asked in a low voice as they walked.

"Not enough water," Alex said.

"You're not half that good an actor," Victoria said. "Besides, we all know that look on your face when you aren't in your body. It took all we could do to keep Leanna from shaking you awake. She's the one who poured water on your face in the end."

Alex was a little deflated at the knowledge his performance had not been entirely believed, but at least it had been good enough to fool Leanna and the other carnies.

"I had to check the barrier," Alex said. "It's moving."

"What?" Victoria said. "How?"

"Because the artifact must be small enough to carry," Alex said. "And someone is carrying it toward the center of town."

Chapter Fifteen
Museum Misadventure

"But why?" Victoria asked, looking around to make sure they would not be overheard.

"I'm not sure," Alex said, glancing over his shoulder, "but I have hunch. There is a way I could see who we are looking for, but not with the barrier in place. If the carnies are all going to the festival, the people we're looking for could be exposed."

"So they're taking their protection with them," Victoria said.

"Right," Alex said. "Which means it must be small."

"We should tell the others what to look for," Victoria said.

"Later," Alex said as they neared the center of town. "When we don't have so much company."

Ten minutes later, Alex had to admit to himself the Guild might have the company of Eleada, Kendra, Leanna, and Nathan for the rest of the afternoon. They stood in a loose group at the western side of the town center, near the back of where the townspeople and carnie folk had congregated to hear the opening speech of the festival, listen to music, and partake of the festival activities.

A wide wooden stage had been set up at the end of Lake Street, where it flowed into the circular path around the town center. A local band, the Corn Fed Crooners, played on the stage, singing tunes by Elvis Presley, Fats Domino, and Johnny Cash. They had an odd way of adding a bluegrass twang to every song they played.

The fountain at the very heart of the town center was surrounded with tables where farmers and crafts people from the Rune Valley had come to sell their wares. Flowers decorated the statues of the founders in the middle of the fountain, chains of daisies draped around the necks of the stone man, woman, dwarf, giant, and tree elf.

The shops circling of the town center had all added booths and tables to the sidewalks outside their facades to facilitate the sale of their goods. The Truffaut Café and Uncle Sal's Soda Shop and Burger Joint had cloth-covered tables and chairs set up to accommodate the additional clientele for their lunch specials.

Alex caught sight of his parents and waved, but did not move toward them. Word of his *fainting spell* had apparently not reached them or his mother would have insisted on inspecting him as she always did.

Alex had tried subtle hints, but there was little that could convince Rafael and Ben to leave the sides of Kendra and Eleada. Nathan seemed equally invested in remaining in sight of Victoria, if not right at her side, and Leanna appeared similarly inclined toward Nathan, even when she was talking to Alex. Clark and Daphne were of no help, either. The two had become so engrossed in discussing the cauldron hidden back at the Guild House, Alex suspected they didn't even notice the festival going on around them. Nina was the only one who seemed to understand her brother was trying to convey something to the rest of the Guild.

"What's the scoop, Snoop?" Nina said as she slid up beside Alex and Victoria.

"We have a better idea what we're looking for," Alex said, lowering his voice.

"You mean for the thing that does that thing so you can't do your thing," Nina said, looking out at the festival as though she were talking to herself.

"Yes," Alex said. "It's something small enough to carry and it's here."

"Well, that narrows it down," Nina said with a sigh. "Should I start checking people's pockets?"

"Funny," Alex said.

"Nina has a point," Victoria said, flicking a fly away from her hindquarters with her tail. "We're no closer to finding it simply because we know it's small."

"Closer," Alex said aloud, realizing something. "It must be with someone here in the town center. Now that we're all close together, maybe I can sense it. Put your arm around me."

"I'm sorry?" Victoria said, blinking in surprise. "Put my arm around you?"

"So I don't fall down," Alex said, feeling his face grow a little warmer under Victoria's gaze.

"Ah," Victoria said, sighing a little as she slid her arm around Alex's shoulder.

"Not again," Nina said. "No one is going to believe it twice."

"Believe what?" Alex asked.

"That you're not doing the astral mambo," Nina said.

"Was it really that bad a performance?" Alex asked.

"Only for someone who knows you," Nina said.

"Great," Alex said. "Well, I won't be gone that long this time. Only a few seconds."

"I'll keep an eye out in case anyone notices," Nina said, nonchalantly peering around at the crowd.

"Right," Alex said, leaning against Victoria's horse shoulder and smiling up at her. "I'll only be a second or two."

"I'll make sure you stay on your feet," Victoria said, pulling him tight to her side.

Alex closed his eyes and forced his mind to calm. Oddly, it was harder to subdue the thoughts in his mind than it had been when pretending to faint. All he had to contend with then was the sound of his friends' voices and Leanna setting him down on the ground. Now he needed to avoid thinking about Victoria's arm around his shoulder and how close she was holding him and how much she smelled like honeysuckle. It took more than a few seconds to will his mind to obey his soul-essence and to leap into his astral form. It took less than a second to realize something was pushing him back into his physical body the way one might shove a hand into a glove.

Alex opened his eyes, looking between Victoria and Nina.

"Nothing," Alex said. "It not only creates a barrier from the outside, it creates one from the inside, as well. If I could get close to the person with it in astral form, I could probably see or sense it. But this way, I can't get near them except in the real world."

"Maybe one of the four we saw today has it?" Nina suggested.

"Good idea," Alex said. "We can try and find them and see if they're carrying anything."

"I can see Elektra or Medea now," Victoria said. Alex and Nina followed Victoria's gaze across the plaza to the center of town and saw one of the Siren Sister twins talking with Mr. Apollo.

"Could Mr. Apollo be one of them?" Alex asked aloud.

"I don't know," Victoria said. "I wouldn't think so. He has such a reputation for fairness and honesty. All of the carnies look up to him and I've never heard anyone say a bad word about him."

Alex's thoughts on the matter and his possible response were drowned out by an amplified voice ringing throughout the town plaza. It was a voice Alex knew well and one that sounded enough like its familial counterpart to make his stomach clinch instinctively.

"Welcome to the annual Founders Festival," Mayor McClint said, his voice booming and echoing off the walls of the buildings. Alex looked to the stage and saw Mayor McClint adjusting the ever-present wide-brimmed hat covering his enormous, balding head. The mayor leaned into the magically amplified microphone, his ample belly keeping him from standing too close to the black-lacquered lectern sitting at the center of the stage. "We are privileged today to have with us fellow magical citizens of the world to celebrate the founding of our fair town. Townspeople of Runewood, please join me in welcoming the members of the Conundrum Carnival and Magical Mystery Show!"

Alex raised his hands to join the applause, seeing for the first time a face that reminded him of another mission he and the Guild needed to tend to that day. Dillon stood at the side of the stage, watching his father. Beside him stood Anna, Mei, Koji, and Earl. Alex had been so consumed with ferreting out the Shadow Wraith's followers within the carnival he had completely forgotten about the Mad Mages plan to pull some prank at the town museum. Whatever they were planning, they hadn't done it yet. At least Alex hoped not.

"When we celebrate the founding of our fair town, we do not memorialize a particular date," Mayor McClint said as he continued his speech. "The founding of Runewood did not take place on a single day. No, the town was built up brick by brick, stone by stone, over many days and years by the first families who settled here. It is therefore only right that we celebrate not a year of founding, but the founders themselves."

Alex had heard this speech before. The mayor gave practically the same speech every year and Alex's attention was no longer for the mayor's words, but for the mayor's son.

Dillon was not paying attention to his father's speech, either. Instead, he was bent down in conversation with Anna. They seemed to be having some kind of argument. Whatever the source of the conflict, Anna seemed to obtain the result she desired. Dillon reluctantly nodded his head and Anna gave him one of her sugary sweet smiles. Then she turned to the other Mad Mages, said something briefly, and led them back through the crowd, away from the town center. Dillon glared at their backs for a moment and then turned back to the stage. The look of anger on his face only deepened as he appeared to listen to his father's words.

"We need to go," Alex said to Victoria and Nina.

"Yes, I saw," Victoria said, turning from the stage and the mayor's speech.

"Saw what?" Nina said, bouncing up to get a better view. "I hate being short."

"The Mad Mages are on the move," Alex said.

"We have to follow them," Nina said, hopping up again to try to see above the heads around her.

"Let's get the others first," Alex said. "We know where the Mad Mages are headed."

Gathering the rest of the Guild was not as easy as usual. Extracting Ben and Rafael from the pleasant company of Eleada and Kendra proved time consuming.

"We'll go with you," Eleada said, after Alex had declared he needed to take Rafael and Ben to help with some Guild business.

"We can be helpful," Kendra added, nodding toward Eleada.

"That's a very kind offer, but there are rules," Alex said.

"Guild rules," Victoria said. "The Guild is very strict about the rules."

"What?" Ben said, "We always bend the rules."

"And Nina certainly bends the rules," Rafael added.

"I don't bend the rules," Nina said, raising her chin. "I'm outside the rules."

"What are you planning?" Eleada asked, her eyes probing Alex's with an intensity he found a little disconcerting. "Something dangerous? I haven't done anything dangerous in ages."

"You haven't done anything reckless and life threatening, you mean," Kendra said with a laugh.

"It's nothing dangerous," Alex said. "Just some boring Guild thing we need to deal with."

"Super boring," Nina said. "I'm bored by it already."

"We'll be back before the speeches are over," Alex said, grabbing Rafael and Ben by the arms and tugging them away from the two girls.

"Yes," Victoria said, stepping between the two carnie girls and the rest of the Guild. "Hold our places. We'll be right back."

Alex didn't wait to see if Eleada and Kendra would follow, but pulled Rafael and Ben toward the side. Victoria stopped near where Clark and Daphne stood, spoke to them briefly, and the three were soon right behind Alex. He caught a glimpse of Leanna and Nathan through the crowd, but they seemed to be engrossed in some conversation and didn't appear to notice the Guild's departure.

"Hey?" Ben said, shrugging off Alex's grip on his arm. "What's the rush?"

"The Mad Mages," Alex said, breaking into a run as they left the crowd of townspeople behind.

"Why didn't you say so?" Rafael asked, dashing to catch up with Alex.

"I like Kendra and Eleada and the others, too," Alex said, "but we don't need them following us."

"Backup," Ben said. "It might be nice to have some backup for once."

"Especially since we don't know what the Mad Mages are planning," Rafael said.

"Backup schmack-up," Daphne said. "We can handle this ourselves."

"Besides," Victoria said, the tone of her voice suddenly diplomatic, "as much as I admire Eleada, she can be rather...unpredictable in dangerous situations."

"Hmm, we're unpredictable enough by ourselves," Clark said.

"Keep running," Alex said, turning down Owl Street and seeing the four Doric columns adorning the facade of the Town Museum two blocks away.

They saw no sign of Anna and the Mad Mages when they reached the front of the museum, so they raced around to the back entrance of the large marble building. Alex in the lead, they approached the rear of the building cautiously. They found the back door to the museum ajar, but no one guarding it. *Sloppy*, Alex thought to himself as he slowly pulled the large metal door open and peered inside.

Alex slipped inside the darkened corridor, sliding to the side to allow the rest of the Guild to follow him and let his eyes adjust to the shadows of the windowless hallway. Alex briefly considered slipping into astral form to scout ahead in the museum proper, but decided against it. It would take too much time. Time the Mad Mages might use to slip away.

Alex brought his finger to his lips to indicate silence from his companions and then gestured toward the end of the hall and the light from the main museum chamber. Alex and the Guild walked silently down the short hallway, pausing at its terminus, clustered in the shadows at the edge of the light. Alex felt a tap on his shoulder and looked back to see Victoria reaching into one of her vest pockets to remove a small, round mirror. She handed it to Alex silently and he smiled back at her.

Alex knelt to the ground and slowly slid the small mirror around the corner of the wall. The reflection of the mirror gave him a good, if restricted, view of the main exhibit hall of the museum. He saw no movement and no sign of the Mad Mages. Maybe they had already come and gone in the time that had been wasted convincing Eleada and Kendra to stay at the Founders Festival.

Then Alex caught a glimpse of something in the glass of the mirror that raised his hopes. Something draped over the heads of the old Founders Statue in the center of the museum hall. The original statue, cracked and worn from weather and age, had been placed on permanent display in the museum when the new statue replaced it some fifty years ago. Alex turned back to the others.

"I can't see them, but I think they're still here," Alex said quietly. "They've got something over the old Founders Statue. If we split into two groups, we can circle around the main hall and take them by surprise. Daphne, Raphael, and Ben, you head left, Nina and I will head right. Victoria and Clark, you stay here in case they try to escape."

Everyone nodded their soundless assent and Alex slipped around the corner of the wall, Nina at his side. He and his sister silently snuck behind an exhibit case on one side of the hall as Daphne, Rafael, and Ben took up position behind a similar case on the opposite side of the entrance to the back hall.

Alex stuck his head around the case and scanned the museum hall, searching for signs of the Mad Mages. He could see a large canvas bag opened over the old Founders Statue as though someone thought to wrap it up and carry it away, but he could see no trace of the Mad Mages. Alex gestured to his sister and they moved in synchronized steps to a place behind an exhibit, closer to the center of the room.

The Town Museum had been built nearly a hundred years ago for the express purpose of housing and displaying the magical artifacts and common antiques of historical importance to the town of Runewood. The main room was round, with a tall, domed ceiling. Red- and blue-veined marble walls contrasted the pure white marble of the floors. Exhibits of various sizes and shapes were stationed around the room in a rough circular pattern. Some were simple, white-painted wooden display cases with glass-enclosed antiquities from the past, labeled and explained by small typewritten notes beside them.

Other exhibits were larger and displayed alone on platforms raised up to eye level. There were chairs and tools and swords and suits of armor, pocket watches, wooden wands, crystal balls, and old, leather-bound books of various sizes and subjects.

Alex and Nina snuck around the curved back wall of the room, slipping from exhibit to exhibit, moving quickly and quietly, all the while searching the room for any sight of the Mad Mages. In less than a minute, Alex and Nina had circumnavigated half of the circumference of the main hall. Daphne, Rafael, and Ben joined them a moment later.

"Where the gorp are they?" Daphne whispered.

Alex shook his head and shrugged. He was wondering that very thing.

"Cowards," Ben whispered. "Maybe they chickened out."

"Maybe they heard us coming," Rafael said.

"The only way out is through the front door," Nina said.

"Let's see what they were up to," Alex said. He stood up and walked toward the center of the room and the old Founders Statue. As he walked, he looked around the room again. He had hoped his sudden movement in the open would startle any of the Mad Mages who might be hiding and force them to reveal themselves. Unfortunately, the only motion in the room was that of his friends and sister following behind him.

Alex stopped in front of the old Founders Statue in the center of the room. It was much like the statue currently residing in the middle of the fountain at the center of town, but considerably smaller. The stone-carved founders were half size, although the statue looked larger from its perch upon the three-foot high dais where it rested. The five founders stood with their backs to each other in a tight circle, the large canvas bag hanging down to cover their heads and shoulders.

Alex looked to the back hall and saw Clark and Victoria standing in the open. They both raised their hands and shoulders in a silent question. Alex understood easily enough. *What was going on?* He mimicked their motions to indicate he had no idea and turned back to the statue.

"I don't like this, Lex," Rafael said, glancing around and sniffing at the air. "Something feels wrong."

"Where in the name of Uranus's underwear are they?" Daphne growled. "And what's with the bag on the heads of the statue?"

"Maybe they were going to steal it?" Nina offered.

"Size," Ben said, leaning back to stare up at the half covered statue. "How'd they think it would fit in that bag? It's not nearly big enough, even if they could carry it."

"That's not a normal canvas bag," Alex said looking around and seeing one of the display cases was empty. He jumped up on the dais and examined the bag more closely.

"This is Sylvester's Sack," Alex said, holding the edge of the canvas bag between his fingers. Sylvester's Sack was named after Sylvester Slumphouse, a tinker and trader who had lived and traveled around the valley over two hundred years ago. He had enchanted his bag so he could carry objects of nearly any size and weight within it. It had been passed down through his family for several generations before being bequeathed to the museum as a relic of Runewood's past

"That explains how they planned to move it," Rafael said.

"But not where they ran off to," Daphne said.

"Why?" Ben said. "Doesn't explain why either."

"Or why Dillon stayed behind," Alex said, tugging at the magical bag and trying to pull it free.

"Maybe we should leave it," Nina said. "Let Mr. Whipplewhip find it and deal with it." Mr. Whipplewhip was the curator of the Town Museum.

"Then he'll start asking questions and the Mad Mages might not try again," Alex said as he tugged at the magical canvas bag, its coarse fibers rubbing his fingers raw. "Almost got it." If the Mad Mages were convinced no alarm had been raised over their plan, they might try it again, and Alex and the Guild might have another chance at catching them in the act.

"Caught in the act!"

Startled by the voice suddenly booming and echoing through the marble-walled museum, Alex nearly lost his balance and fell. He clutched at the canvas bag, still caught on the head of the Runewood's ancient elven founder, as his stomach clutched in fear. He had just heard that voice echoing in the town plaza.

Alex got his footing and spun to see where the voice came from. He swallowed and blinked in confusion at what he saw. Mayor McClint stood inside the front entrance of the museum. Beside him stood his son, Dillon, grinning triumphantly. Beside Dillon stood Anna, smiling as peacefully as if she had eaten a large and delicious cake. Beside her stood the rest of the Mad Mages, Mei, Koji, and Earl, looking as though they could barely contain the laughter trying to burst from their chests. Beside them all stood a person who made Alex's stomach clench twice as hard in fear — his father.

CHAPTER SIXTEEN
FEINTED AND FOILED

"I told you they were trying to steal the old town statue," Dillon said, puffing his chest out in satisfaction.

"We overhead their plan to steal the old Founders Statue yesterday and followed them when then left the festival," Anna said, sounding as though she were explaining something to a child. "When we saw them break into the museum, we ran to get you right away."

It was clear Anna was speaking to Dillon's father. It was also clear Alex and the Guild had been set up. Alex let go of Sylvester's Sack and stepped slowly to the floor to stand beside his friends. Victoria and Clark walked up to join him, followed by deputy warlock Kyle Dervis, Alex's father's assistant.

"Arrest them," Mayor McClint bellowed as he strode toward Alex and the Guild.

"We don't arrest children," Alex's father said, his long legs keeping pace beside the mayor.

Alex struggled to control the waves of disparate emotions coursing through his mind and heart as he watched everyone converge in the center of the museum hall. Anger and fear and frustration whirled in his head and fought in his gut. His anger at Dillon and Anna and the Mad Mages felt like a bomb bursting behind his eyes, but it was nothing compared with the anger he felt for allowing himself to be tricked so easily. This must have been Anna's plan all along. The Mad Mages had lured Alex into spying on them and fed him a story that would ensure he followed them to the museum. He had eaten it up like some starving fool. Maybe that's what he was. A fool so starved for revenge he couldn't see how he was being manipulated.

Anna and the Mad Mages led him right into the trap and he followed like some stupid sheep. He should have suspected something when Dillon had stayed behind at the festival stage. The only thing keeping his anger from lashing out and attacking Dillon and Anna was the fear that came from seeing the look on his father's face. His father seemed torn between mastering his own anger and being overwhelmed by disappointment. Seeing his father's frustration elicited another emotion from Alex's heart — shame.

Alex managed to meet his father's eyes and hold them as the Guild squared off to face the Mad Mages and the mayor. Victoria walked away from Deputy Dervis and stood next to Alex. Clark did the same, standing beside Daphne. Alex was thankful none of the Guild spoke. While he assumed their silence was based in the same fear he felt, he was glad for it nonetheless. This was going to be a tricky situation to explain.

"You may not want to arrest them," the Mayor said, "but I will see them punished this time."

"We should put them on trial," Dillon said with a smirk.

"There may very well be a trial," Alex father said, turning his gaze to encompass both Dillon and Anna. "However, I will begin by doing what I always do when I suspect a crime has been committed — I will investigate the incident. When I have all the facts, then I will take action and the offending parties will be punished." Dillon swallowed hard under Alex's father's glare. To her credit, Anna, merely smiled.

"What's to investigate?" the Mayor said. "We caught them red-handed trying to steal the statue."

"We saw Alex pulling Sylvester's Sack from the statue when we walked in," Alex's father said. Alex was not entirely surprised his father had so quickly identified the true nature of the canvas bag still hanging from the stone head of the town's elven founder.

"He was putting it on the statue," Dillon said. "That was the plan. They were going to use the sack and steal the statue and then hide it for a few days so they could pretend to find it and be heroes."

"We heard Alex say it had been too long since they had been heroes," Anna said with a caustic look toward Dillon. "He thought the carnival being in town when he pretended to find the statue would make him even more famous."

Alex literally bit his tongue to keep from speaking. He suspected the other members of the Guild must have been doing something similar to remain quiet.

"A glory hound," the Mayor said, his loud voice echoing through the museum. "Seems like an open and shut case to me."

"We haven't heard what Alex and his friends have to say," Alex's father said, turning toward Alex. "Can you explain what you are doing here, Son?"

This was the moment Alex had been waiting for so patiently. His only chance to save himself and the Guild.

"We saw the Mad Mages, Anna and Dillon, acting weird at the festival. Dillon stayed behind and we followed Anna and the others here. When we found the back door open we came in to investigate and found this sack over the statue."

"Lies," Mayor McClint said. "It's the same story in reverse. If that were true, it would have been you leading us here instead of my son."

"Your son, who conveniently managed to overhear this supposed plan to steal the statue," Alex's father said.

"What are you implying?" Mayor McClint said, his voice rising and his face flushing a deep crimson.

"I'm not implying anything," Alex's father said. "I'm stating the facts. As I said, I will examine the facts and then decide how to proceed."

"I'm not sure you're the right person to examine these facts," Mayor McClint said. "Not when your son stands accused of the theft of town property."

"Are you questioning my loyalty to my oath of office?" Alex's father asked, his eyes stabbing into the mayor.

"Well, no," Mayor McClint mumbled, stepping back a few paces. "No one questions your integrity. Certainly not." The mayor took a deep breath and seemed to gather up some of the courage that had so swiftly departed him. "But I want to see action on this, Ravenstar. This will not be swept under the rug."

"I never sweep anything under the rug," Alex's father said, still holding the mayor's gaze. Then he faced Alex and the Guild. "These children will accompany me back to the Jail House while Deputy Dervis finds their parents so they can be present when we question them about what took place here today. I may want to question Dillon and the Anna and the others as well. I would suggest you return to the festival and let Mr. Whipplewhip know about the break-in. I'm sure he will want to inventory the museum to see if anything has been damaged."

"I will notify the curator as soon as I can find him," Mayor McClint said. He stared at Alex's father for a moment, but when it became clear the town warlock had nothing more to say, the mayor turned and stomped toward the entrance of the museum. "Come along, Dillon."

Dillon took the time to spare a final smirk for Alex before turning to join his father. Alex noticed Anna seemed to be whispering something to herself as she stared at Alex. It might have been a rune-spell. He would have suspected a curse of some kind, but he knew Anna was too smart to try something like that with his father standing nearby. However, she was also smart enough to trick Alex and the Guild into looking like they were stealing a statue from the town museum, so Alex felt he was justified in being suspicious. Whatever she was doing, she suddenly stopped, smiled briefly, and turned to follow Dillon and the other Mad Mages as they trailed behind Mayor McClint. When they were gone, Alex's father turned to him.

"I'm surprised at you, Alex," his father said, squinting through sad eyes.

"We didn't do this, Dad," Alex said, his voice squeaking with emotion. This statement broke the spell of silence holding the rest of the Guild mute.

"We were trying to do the right thing and they were doing the wrong thing and somehow they turned everything around," Nina said.

"It was those maggot mouthed Measly Mages," Daphne said.

"Trap," Ben said. "It was a trap."

"They trapped us with our own worst traits," Rafael said.

161

"Mmm, they tricked us by pretending to be as awful as they usually are," Clark said.

"They convinced us they were going to do something horrid and now we're in trouble for trying to stop them," Victoria said.

"I have no doubt you are all innocent of trying to steal the town statue," Alex's father said. Alex felt a knot in his stomach unclench. "But you are guilty of being gullible enough to be led into this mess like a gaggle of newborn geese. Your first mistake was in not coming to me and reporting what you suspected. I assume you failed to do that because of the manner in which you obtained the information."

The museum was suddenly so quiet Alex could hear himself breathing.

"Right," Alex's father said as he glanced over at Deputy Dervis. "Hopefully that will be a lesson you will all take to heart. Kyle, why don't you head downtown and find these kids' parents. I'll meet you at the jail house."

"Okay, Logan," Deputy Dervis said, sounding almost cheerful. Deputy Dervis had a nearly indefatigable mood. He was almost always smiling and happy, even when things seemed to be completely wrong. "What should I tell the parents?"

"Say their kids are in some trouble and I'll explain when they see me," Alex's father said.

"Good," Deputy Dervis said as he headed for the entrance door. "I hate explaining this kind of thing." When Deputy Dervis was out of the building, Alex's father let out a deep sigh.

"I don't know what got into your heads," Alex's fathers said, "but short of some sort of miracle, I don't see how you're not all going to be punished for this."

"But…" Alex started to say when his father raised a hand for silence.

"But you were seen pulling Sylvester's magic sack over the old town statue by the mayor, the town warlock, and his deputy," Alex's father said.

"I was taking the sack off," Alex mumbled, wishing he had never touched that confounded canvas bag. Maybe Nina was right — maybe he had been dropped on his head as a child.

"Looks like the same thing from where we stood," Alex father said. "If you're lucky, the town council will be lenient with their punishment. Maybe make you paint the museum or pick up trash around town for a month. Unfortunately, I can't speak on your behalf. I'm already going to look bad enough in the eyes of the town council for not recusing myself from this case."

"Don't get in trouble for us, Dad," Alex said, realizing for the first time how much his misadventure would affect his father's standing as the town warlock.

"I couldn't very well let the mayor take charge of the investigation, now could I?" Alex's father said, his tone brittle. "I'm sure that's what he would have done, given the chance. Then who knows what sort of evidence might 'pop up' indicating some new crime you'd be guilty of."

"I'm sorry, Dad," Alex said, hanging his head.

"You should be," his father said, staring down at Alex and Nina. "You have far more important things to be concerning yourself with than what the Mad Mages may or may not be getting up to."

"We did learn something at the carnival," Alex said, raising his head and hoping to redeem himself at least somewhat in his father's eyes.

"There are at least four followers of the Shadow Wraith in the carnival and we're pretty sure we know who they are," Nina blurted out. Alex sighed. Apparently, his sister also wanted redemption.

"And we know the magical artifact is small enough to carry," Alex said. "Someone has it with them down in the town center."

"That's good," Alex's father said, "because none of you are going near that carnival again. You're all grounded until further notice."

Alex and the Guild let out a collective sigh, but no one questioned Alex's father's authority to ground everyone there. As it turned out, the entire Guild was grounded together. After an afternoon spent in the local jailhouse, with the parents of the Guild members arriving to hear the accusations against their children and listening to Alex's father's interpretation of the events, it was collectively decided, at Alex's mother's suggestion, that the Guild be confined during the daylight hours to the Ravenstar family home.

The thinking was, not only would this placate the mayor and the town council, but it would keep Alex and the Guild safely away from the carnival and all the dangers it contained.

Alex realized it was the best possible outcome, given the charges and the evidence arrayed against them, and kept his mouth firmly shut while the adults explained their decision. One advantage of the plan was that it mollified many of the fears of the parents of the other Guild members about possible encounters with the followers of the Shadow Wraith.

With the exception of Victoria's father, most of the parents seemed to think letting their child hang around with Alex, the known nemesis of the Shadow Wraith, was simply too dangerous. However, they all seemed to agree confining the Guild to the Ravenstar home, which was well known to be protected by powerful magic, would be safer than keeping the kids at home individually. This also allowed the parents to follow Alex's father's suggestion — that they all attend the carnival in hopes of building upon the information Alex and the Guild had managed to obtain. The parents of the Guild would begin by making sure George the giant, Oanadin the dwarf, and the Siren Sisters Elektra and Medea, always had someone watching them.

Alex admitted it was a good plan, even if he and his friends had no part in it. Given his extraordinary failure in judgment at the museum, Alex was in no mood to question the judgment of others, especially his parents.

His father had been right. Alex had let his mind become so clouded by anger and dislike of Anna and Dillon and the Mad Mages that he had turned his attention from the danger threatening the whole town. Only an idiot would worry about what the Mad Mages were up to when there were followers of the Shadow Wraith hiding in the carnival and plotting to set the vile creature loose upon the world. Apparently, Alex was an idiot, because that was exactly what he had done. And, in doing so, he had managed to limit his options and his ability to fight back against the Shadow Wraith and its followers.

These thoughts clouded Alex's mood the rest of the day, through dinner, and into the evening. Later that night, Alex and his family sat simmering in silence around the kitchen table as they sipped at root beer floats, trying to stave off the stifling heat still oppressing the valley like some overstoked stove threatening to explode.

"I'm going to talk to Maybelle about this heat," his mother finally said, breaking the quiet as she wiped her forehead with an embroidered handkerchief.

"She can't do anything," his father said, sipping at the straw in his frosted-glass mug. "I spoke to her this morning. Says she has no idea what's wrong with the weather. None of her spells do a thing to change the heat."

"Well…" his mother said and then fell back into silence. They all knew what that information implied — the weather had something to do with the arrival of the carnival and the Shadow Wraith's followers.

Nina loudly slurped the last of her root beer float through her straw and slumped back in her chair. "This is the best grounding we ever had," she said with a sigh.

Alex blinked at his sister and then burst out laughing. She was right. How often would they get root beer floats and not glares from their parents when they were grounded? Alex's parents held back a moment longer, but soon joined the laughter. It helped ease the tension hanging over the table and the family all evening. When they had recovered their composure, Alex's father placed his hands on the table and looked at Alex and Nina.

"This is not an accusation," his father began, "merely a bit of information. It seems something went missing at the museum today. I spoke with Mr. Whipplewhip and he says Grandpa Griffin's twin tracking coins disappeared from their display case."

Alex frowned at the news. The coins had been used by Alex's great-great grandfather to foil a bank robber back in the late 1800s. The coins were magically linked so that if you held one, you could always find the other. His great-great grandfather had gotten wind of the bank robbery and planted one of the coins in the bank's vault.

"I don't know why someone would take such a thing," his father continued. "They aren't that complicated to make. A decent mage could make one with little effort. They're only kept for historical value."

"Maybe we should do that for the children's shoes," Alex mother said. "So we'll know where they are when they're late for dinner again."

"Very funny, Mom," Nina said with a pout.

"We didn't see anything missing at the museum," Alex said, sipping at the last of his root beer float. "And we didn't take anything."

"Like I said, it wasn't an accusation," Alex's father said.

"You're wild and reckless," his mother added, "but you're not a thief."

"Keep an eye out for them," his father said. "Mr. Whipplewhip is in a tizzy about them and I imagine you and your friends will get blamed for them being stolen even if we have a good idea who might have taken them."

"Sure, Dad," Alex said. He knew exactly who had taken the magic coins.

Half an hour later, while striping off his clothes and getting ready to take a shower, he discovered where at least one of the coins was — in his back pocket.

Alex examined the coin in the light from his bedside lamp. It was a simple silver coin, with the Runewood emblem pressed into one face and the date and denomination stamped on the opposite side. A two-dollar coin from 1848, it was definitely worth more than its face value due to its historical significance. Alex knew Anna and Dillon were responsible, but how had the coin come to be in his back pocket?

Then he remembered the look on Anna's face and the whispered words on her lips just before she had left the museum. She must have placed the coin near the statues before she fled the museum the first time, after placing Sylvester's Sack on the statue's heads. Then she waited until Alex was close enough and floated the coin with magic into his pocket. Had his father not mentioned the missing coins, Alex would never have noticed an old coin among the other money in his pockets. He would likely have grabbed it from his dresser the next morning and stuffed it in his pocket the way he did every morning with the previous day's leftover change. And Anna and the Mad Mages would have been able to track him wherever he went, allowing

166

them to follow him and the Guild, or alert Dillon's father, the mayor, if they tried to leave the house and break their confinement.

Alex hated to admit it, but it was another brilliant plan by the new leader of the Mad Mages. But now that he knew, he could give Anna a surprise. Alex probed the coin with his magic sense and grinned. His father had been right. It would be easy to magically link this coin to another and by doing so, allow him to link through this third coin to the coin Anna held. That would allow him to mislead her about where he was and when.

Alex was still grinning when he settled into bed. The grin stayed on his face as he slipped into astral form for his nightly lesson with Batami. As he floated up from his body, he saw something outside the window. Another astral form. At first, he thought it was Batami, come to collect him in person. With a start, he realized it wasn't Batami. But it was someone he knew. Outside his window, a pale ephemeral blue glow outlining its form, floated the figure in black he had been chasing for so many days.

Chapter Seventeen
Beyond the Barrier

Alex was uncertain what to think or what to feel. He floated in astral form above his bed and body, staring out the window in shock at his fellow astral traveler — the figure in black. *The figure in black is a Spirit Mage,* Alex thought.

Should he be afraid? Was the figure there to harm him? It didn't seem so. It simply floated outside his window, staring from behind the cowl of its cloak. Alex could see the soul-essence within its breast, blazing brightly with a pure white light. He doubted a follower of the Shadow Wraith would have such a clear soul-essence. But could he be certain?

The figure had so far only led him toward discovering the influence of the Shadow Wraith in the carnival, but was that merely the way Alex chose to see it? Why was the figure in black leading him toward the Shadow Wraith's followers? Was it to expose them? Or was it to deliver him into their clutches? And what did this mysterious person want with him now?

That question seemed to be answered when the figure reached out a cloaked arm and gestured for Alex to follow. Then the figure floated away from the window. Had he still been in his body, Alex would have instinctively swallowed against the trepidation he felt spreading through his mind. Instead, he ignored the feeling of fear flickering at the edge of his awareness and floated out through the bedroom window and into the dim moonlight.

The astral figure in black did not waste time waiting to see if Alex was following. It flew through the night, gliding above the rooftops, heading toward the carnival grounds in the open field behind the Town Hall. Alex followed closely, but not too closely,

168

keeping what he hoped was a safe distance from the figure as he searched around for signs of anything that might indicate possible betrayal. He had already been led in to a trap once that day and he had no desire to let his curiosity again turn to gullibility.

As they neared the carnival grounds, the cloaked figure slowed and descended to hover a few inches above the earth, outside the main entrance. Alex floated to a stop several feet away. The figure momentarily turned to Alex, possibly to make sure he was paying attention, then it extended its arm toward the carnival and floated forward.

At the point where the cloaked figure encountered the astral barrier, it came to a sudden halt. As it did so, the space around its arm began to shimmer with a pale white light. Alex felt an unexpected excitement rise in his mind as he watched the cloaked figure press its arm into the barrier, the shimmering white light shrouding its arm and then its entire form as it passed through the barrier and into the carnival grounds. Alex stared at the cloaked figure, its bluish astral form encapsulated in a pale and constantly fluctuating white light.

The mysterious figure had broken through the barrier. But how? As the figure floated back to the edge of the barrier with its arm outstretched, Alex realized the mystery mage was going to show him how to do the same himself. Whatever this person's true intentions, Alex knew he had to take whatever risks were necessary to learn how to mimic the magic that could penetrate the astral barrier around the carnival.

Alex raised his hand to meet that of the cloak-covered figure in black. As their hands met at the boundary of the astral barrier, they shimmered with luminescent white light. Alex extended his magic-sense and tried to discern how the figure in black had managed to thwart the ancient magic of the barrier.

Now that he could feel as well as sense the magic at work, Alex thought he knew how to accomplish it. It was a subtle bit of magical manipulation that turned the invisible energies of the barrier inside out. The magical energies of the barrier prevented astral energies from functioning, repelling them from the area within its boundary. The figure in black had deduced how to create the exact same magical energy and wrap it around its own astral form like a suit of armor, shielding it from the effects of the barrier. It was brilliant.

Alex paused for a moment. Whoever the figure in black was, he or she was a very powerful and experienced Spirit Mage. Even Batami had not managed to breach the boundary of the astral barrier. How could there be another Spirit Mage in the Rune valley he had not heard of? If this Spirit Mage was not from the Rune Valley, was it with the carnival? Was the cloaked figure some carnie working against the Shadow Wraith's followers?

Alex knew he had no more time to contemplate such questions. He reached out with his magic-sense until he could feel the magical energy of the astral barrier. Then he spoke with his mind, thinking rune-words of energy manipulation, words similar to those he might have used to tame a flame of fire. The energy of the barrier quavered with iridescent white light. He willed himself forward and into the barrier even as he mentally chanted the rune-words cloaking his own astral form in that same magical energy.

A second later, Alex floated inside the barrier, beside the figure in black.

"Thank you," Alex thought at the figure. The figure only nodded. Then it did something Alex would not have expected. It floated back outside the barrier.

Alex had no time to ask who the figure was or why it had shown him how to cross the astral barrier only to leave him after having done so. The astral form of the figure in black nodded once more, then quickly faded away, like mist evaporating in bright sunlight.

Panic prickled at Alex's consciousness. He was alone within the astral barrier of the carnival. The Shadow Wraith's followers were there. Alex was certain there was at least one Dark Spirit Mage working for the Shadow Wraith within the carnival, but whoever it might be, he or she would not be expecting Alex to be present in astral form to spy on them.

He needed a plan.

Now that he could sense the magical energy of the astral barrier, he might be able to sense where it was coming from. It might be his best chance of locating the magical artifact creating the barrier. And, it might lead him to the follower of the Shadow Wraith who was holding it.

Alex reached out with his magic-sense, trying to feel if the energy of the barrier was stronger in one direction. Did the barrier radiate out equidistantly? Would that mean the artifact was at the very center of the carnival? What was at the center of the carnival grounds? The main tent where *The Eternal Story* played each night. He would start there and see if the energy of the barrier felt any stronger.

Alex was afraid to try willing himself directly to the main tent. Doing so was likely to release the protective field of magical energy sheathing him. He would most likely end up tossed outside the barrier in the attempt. Instead, he floated briskly through the carnival grounds.

While most of the carnies were asleep, not all were. Some did late night chores here and there, some sat outside their tents and sleeping wagons in small groups, talking around tiny piles of glow-globes radiating dimly from old steel drums. Alex caught sight of the husband and wife vampires, Bernard and Heloise, prowling the grounds on their rounds as security guards.

He passed around the peaked roof of a tent and saw two silhouetted shadows seated by the window of a small sleeping wagon. Alex recognized those silhouettes. They were identical in shape and size. Seeing them made Alex realize they might be able to answer a question that had been silently nagging at him the whole day. The answer to that question might make all the difference in finding the Shadow Wraith's followers.

Alex floated down to peer in the window of the wagon and confirmed his suspicions. Illuminated by a magically powered lamp, the Siren Sisters, Elektra and Medea, sat on a small padded bench. They were talking to someone. Alex willed himself forward and through the wall of the small wagon. He had been unsure if it would work while cloaked in the energy of the astral barrier. The wall seemed to offer some kind of resistance at first, but Alex found he could easily push through it. A moment later, he floated in the cramped living section of the tiny wagon, looking at the Siren Sisters as they talked with Oanadin, the dwarf.

"I don't like it," Oanadin said, his face contorted in displeasure.

"We don't have to like it," Elektra said, her voice harsh.

"We only need to follow our orders," Medea said, her tone only a little less icy than her twin.

"I don't like not knowing what the plan is," Oanadin said.

"We know our part of the plan," Elektra said.

"And we know what the ultimate goal is," Medea said.

"It's safer for everyone this way," Elektra said.

"But how does robbing the centaur help?" Oanadin said. "And what's in the bank?"

"These are not things you need to know," Medea said.

"They are not things we need to know," Elektra said.

"Maybe," Oanadin growled. "But I still don't like it."

"Follow your part of the plan," Elektra said as she stood up.

"And make sure George does the same," Medea said, standing to join her sister by the door.

Alex knew he had only seconds to try what he needed to attempt. He floated closer to Elektra and Medea as Oanadin stood to see them out. Alex focused his mind, opening it as he had earlier that day with Batami in the woods of the White Forest. Staring at the three people, he looked at the soul-essence within each of them. Then he focused on his own soul-essence and reached out through it toward the others.

Alex knew he had made a mistake as the first wave of ice cold blackness gripped his mind. Then images flooded his consciousness — Fallen trees dead from flame and rot…Bone and ash under a blood-red sun…Corpses rotting in stagnate water…Cities fallen to ruin…Oceans boiling and skies black with birds of prey bursting into flame…

Alex forced himself to break the connection. It had been too much. Looking into the souls of three at once had been too great. Too easy to lose his own soul-essence within. Too easy for the merging they seemed to long for to actually take place. Had he been in his physical body, he would have vomited. As it was, he struggled to remain in his astral form and resist the overpowering urge to flee this nauseating feeling and this place for the comfort and safety of his body and his bed.

The three minions of the Shadows Wraith, for Alex had not doubt now that was what they were, stood in silence and looked at each other.

"What was that?" Elektra asked, her voice hushed.

"Did you feel that?" Medea whispered.

"I felt something," Oanadin said and coughed to clear his throat.

"Do you think it was...?" Elektra said.

"Why?" Oanadin said.

"Spying on us," Medea said.

"Maybe," Oanadin said. "But I've never felt that before. It felt almost too...bright."

"Should we mention it?" Elektra said.

"We'd be acknowledging we felt it," Medea said.

"Let's keep it to ourselves for now," Oanadin said with a sneer. "Maybe it's good that we know something for once."

Elektra and Medea exchanged a brief glance of silent sisterly consultation and then turned and nodded in unison to Oanadin. They left without saying another word.

Alex still floated at the edge of the wagon wall. Seeing into the soul-essences of the three Shadow Wraith's followers, merging his own soul-essence with them to some degree, had been terrifying and overwhelming. He could feel the imprints of those three soul-essences clinging to his own. He knew they would be with him now forever. He would always carry a small piece of their corrupted soul-essences within him, just as he carried a reflection of Batami's.

As Oanadin made to get ready for bed, Alex noticed something that had escaped him when looking at the dwarf's soul-essence. He could see a faint tendril of twisting smoke-like blackness wafting away from the dwarf's soul-essence, through the wall of the wagon, and out into the carnival. Alex knew it was easier to see because his own soul-essence had touched Oanadin's.

It was not like the thick and oily blackness the Shadow Wraith had used to control the souls of the townspeople when it had attempted to break free of its prison back in the spring. That connection had been easy to see with astral eyes. This one was much more tenuous and, Alex sensed, much less powerful.

Alex had a hunch what this chain of shadow power leashed to the soul-essence of Oanadin meant and where it might lead. He willed himself to float through the wall of the wagon and out into the night, rising up into the sky, looking for the Siren Sisters. He spotted Elektra and Medea a few moments later as they walked up the stairs to what he assumed was their own sleeping wagon. Looking at them closely, as they opened the door and stepped inside, Alex confirmed his suspicion. They, too, had faint and slender tethers of inky blackness trailing away from the soul-essences at their hearts and out across the carnival grounds.

Alex floated forward and followed those twin tendrils of ephemeral ebony energy through the carnival grounds. The tethers of smoky blackness wove through tents and wagons and rides toward the heart of the carnival and disappeared into the back of the large main tent. Alex could see a third connective conduit he knew linked back to Oanadin's soul-essence disappear into the tent beside those of the Siren Sisters.

Alex knew what this was — Dark Spirit Magic. Very dark. The way the Shadow Wraith had taken control of the townspeople back in the spring had been crude and forceful, overwhelming their souls with its power. This was far more subtle and insidious. A Dark Spirit Mage was slowly poisoning the soul-essences of Oanadin, Elektra, and Medea, and probably those of the other followers, as well.

Rather than seeking out people who were already drawn to the Shadow Wraith, this Dark Spirit Mage had set out to gradually convert people into loyal followers by feeding their soul-essences a slow and steady diet of corrupting spirit energy. Oanadin, Elektra, Medea and the others would probably never have followed the Shadow Wraith under their own will, but their wills had been distorted. Alex wondered if it was possible to release them the way he had managed to release his friends from the Shadow Wraith's power in the spring. The better question was, who was this Dark Spirit Mage and Shadow Fiend?

Alex willed himself forward and through the canvas wall of the tent.

That was when he heard the whispered voices. He followed the voices and the thin trails of shadowy Dark Spirit Magic through one wall of canvas and then another. He was in the area behind the main stage within the grand tent, the part used by the actors and crew to prepare for the show. He passed into a small, canvas-walled chamber and found the source of the voices and the emanation of the chains of Dark Spirit Magic.

Two figures stood in the darkened corner of the space, dimly illuminated by a small magical lantern hanging from a wooden post several feet behind them. Alex could not make out the faces of the two people, but thought he recognized at least one of their whispered voices.

One of them, a woman whose long, curly hair fell off her shoulders in waves, stood in the shadows. The three tendrils of Dark Spirit Magic flowed to the woman and disappeared into her heart, melding with the light of her soul-essence. Alex could discern, now that he was close to the source, several other faint lines of blackness stretching out from the woman's soul-essence in various directions, through the walls of the tent, and into the carnival. They were hard to count, but Alex thought he could see at least nine in all. One of them reached out like a creeping black vine to ensnare the soul-essence of the person who stood before the woman.

"You do not need to know how we will find the sword," the woman whispered. "Only that we will."

Alex thought he could recognize the voice and who the woman was. Almost. She did something to her voice when whispering that altered it and concealed its true sound. Alex doubted it was an accident. It was probably some sort of magic.

"People have been searching for the Sword of Silas for thousands of years," the other shadowed voice said. It was male, but Alex didn't recognize it. He floated closer, hoping to get a look at their faces, especially the woman, the Dark Spirit Mage.

"How can you hope to find it in such a short time when so many others have given lifetimes to hunting it and failed?" the man asked.

Alex was close now. He could see the face of the man talking to the Dark Spirit Mage. He was a carnie. The barker who ran the shape-shifter sideshow with Kendra. Alex drifted even closer, moving around them to get a look at the woman's face.

"Do not question..." she said and paused. "Impossible." She flicked her hand and the magical lantern fluttered into darkness as Alex was about to get a glimpse of her face.

"What's the matter?" the man said. Through his astral enhanced eyes, Alex could see the woman, even if he could not make out the details of her face as she turned away from him.

"We are not alone," the woman hissed.

"But you said..." the carnival barker began to protest, but the woman pushed him out the flap of the tent, through another canvas chamber, and into the night. Alex followed them, floating swiftly behind. The carnival barker did not need to be told to flee again, quickly running off into the shadows. The woman pulled the hood of her cloak up over her head as she ran in the opposite direction, dodging behind one of the smaller tents.

Alex rose up into the air. He spotted the woman easily and dove down in pursuit. If he could get in front of her, he could see beneath the hood of her cloak. Then he would know who was behind the Shadow's Wraith's plot. And he wouldn't need to look into her soul-essence to identify her. That thought chilled his mind. If seeing into souls corrupted by the Dark Spirit Mage had been terrifying, seeing into her own might leave his soul-essence eternally wounded.

The woman ducked and dodged as she ran through the carnival, slipping between tents, sliding behind wagons, racing between rides. Unable to will himself to where he wanted to be, Alex was forced to chase after her. Even though he could move faster in astral form than she could on foot, she knew her way around the carnival better than he did.

He was not sure how she had sensed his presence in the tent. He had been certain the shield of energy he cloaked himself with would protect him from even a Spirit Mage's powers of perception. The woman seemed to be able to perceive when he was close. Just as he was about to round on her so he could see her face, she ducked sideways and into a tent. Alex had no time for his mind to register the words painted on the banner over entrance as he followed her inside.

Alex floated into the tent and into darkness. Then, a dim, blue-white glow illuminated the tent, light bouncing from side to side, cutting through the blackness. Alex could see the woman, a glow-wand held in an outstretched arm, standing beside an identical version of herself, who stood beside a copy of her, endless copies surrounding them.

Mirrors, Alex thought.

The woman had led him into the *Minotaur Mirror Maze*. She stood facing him, her features still concealed within the folds of her hooded cloak. It reminded Alex of another figure in a hooded cloak. But why was she standing there? And where was she standing? It was impossible to tell where the real Dark Spirit Mage stood among the many reflections glittering in the darkness of the tent. He should have been able to discern the real woman from the reflections by seeing her soul-essence, but all the images of the woman bore that sign. How could that be?

Alex drifted forward and caught sight of something else reflected to infinity in the mirrors. Something he should not have been able to see — his own face.

Alex stared at his reflections in the maze of mirrors. That made no sense. He could never see his astral form in a mirror. A mirror could only reflect things in the physical world. Unless these were not normal mirrors. If these were magical mirrors…

Alex shot upward even as he sensed the magical energy reaching toward him. He was not certain what that magical energy was, but he knew instinctively it could harm him. He twisted to the side as he shot upward, a bolt of pitch-black lightening searing past him, snaking through the mirrors and the tent wall with no effect.

Then Alex was above the mirrors and invisible again to the physical world. Similar to how Batami had been teaching Alex to affect the physical world while in astral form, the Dark Spirit Mage below him had the power to affect the astral world while in her physical body.

The woman let the glow-wand flutter out and darkness engulfed the tent of mirrors. Alex could see her, like an astral after-image, as she fled the tent. He rose up through the roof of the tent and high into the sky. The near-brush with the Dark Spirit Mage's power left him even more committed to determining her identity.

Alex looked down to see the woman running again, dashing in a straight line for another tent. He willed himself forward, racing after the woman. She whipped the canvas flap of the tent back and leapt inside. As Alex flew through the canvas wall of the small sideshow tent, he had only a moment to register the words painted on its side — *Pandora's Box*.

The woman raced up a narrow aisle between rows of wooden folding chairs as Alex entered the tent. Darkness draped the space, but Alex suddenly had an idea. The woman knew he was there, so there was no reason to hide. And, no reason to let her hide from him. Alex focused his mind and mentally spoke the rune-word for light, directing the magical energy into the glow-wand the woman still held.

The woman gasped in surprise as the glow-wand suddenly blazed in her hand. In that moment, Alex saw many things — he saw the woman standing on a small stage in the back of the tent. He saw her hand on the lid of a large, black-lacquered chest. He saw the ancient runes engraved in the dented and battered wood of the box like a single flowing letter. He saw something in those runes that sparked a fear within him borne out of some deep-seated soul-memory welling up into his consciousness. And he saw within the folds of the woman's cloak. He saw something glittering in the light of the glow-wand. Something beautiful. Something he could sense the power from now that he paused to notice it. And he saw the woman's face.

She laughed.

And opened the lid of the chest.

Chapter Eighteen
Pandora's Box

Blackness.

Blacker then any earthly darkness.

More than a mere absence of light.

An absence of everything.

That was what was inside the ancient lacquered box. That blackness pulled at Alex like a siphoning whirlpool sucking down a trapped ship. The pull of the darkness within the box was overpowering. Alex struggled against it, but each second drew him closer and closer to the lip of the lid and the empty-nothingness beyond it.

Alex could hear the woman laughing as he was drawn to the very edge of the blackness. He tried to force himself back into his physical body, to escape his astral form, but the darkness held him somehow. It sucked at astral energy. Alex could feel himself weakening as he fought to draw back from the box of blackness. That blackness extracted something else from him, as well. He could feel it leaching the power from his soul-essence. The blackness, whatever it was, and whatever it might look like in the physical world, was trying to devour his soul-essence.

Alex was on the verge of collapsing into the ever-endless night within the box when he noticed a flickering around him. As the blackness drained his power, it also drained his ability to maintain the shield of magical energy around his astral body preventing the astral barrier from expelling him. He risked a look toward the woman and stared at the thing around her neck, the artifact that had originally prevented him from reaching her. In the final desperate moment before the blackness within Pandora's Box consumed him, Alex released the cloak of magical energy he had been using to circumvent the astral barrier created by the magical necklace around the woman's neck.

Instantly, Alex felt himself thrust from the edge of the box and the tent and the presence of the laughing woman and back into his physical body in his bed.

Alex sat up, coughing and gasping for air. His mind was a whirlwind of thoughts and emotions.

Curiosity — What was that box?

Fear — It had almost consumed his soul-essence.

Anger — That was the third time he had been tricked and trapped that day.

Satisfaction — He had managed to escape. Escape with no time to spare before what he knew would have been his death, and a death that would have trapped his soul-essence in some eternal purgatory.

Curiosity — What was the Sword of Silas? And how could the Dark Spirit Mage use it to free the Shadow Wraith?

Satisfaction — He knew who the Dark Spirit Mage was and he knew the necklace she wore was the magical artifact that prevented astral travel.

Fear — Esmeralda. She was a far more dangerous and devious Dark Spirit Mage than he had expected. What was her plan? She obviously kept parts of the plan secret even from her followers — followers whose souls she had slowly poisoned over time to turn their minds and hearts to her will and the service of the Shadow Wraith. Only she would know the full plan and what it entailed. Or was that true? Could her husband, Mr. Apollo, be oblivious to her true nature? Was he part of the plan, as well? Was he her fellow mastermind?

Alex wanted to spring from his bed and wake his parents and tell them all that had happened and all he had learned, but he could feel his exhaustion pulling him toward sleep. He knew there was someone else he needed to speak to first. Someone who had been waiting for him.

Alex closed his eyes and willed himself into his astral form, resisting the temptation to let his mind drift off into slumber. He badly wanted to sleep. Astral travel was exhausting under normal circumstances, but the events of night had been doubly fatiguing.

A moment later, Alex hovered above his body again in astral form. Then he willed himself to where he needed to be and floated outside Batami's hut in the middle of the White Forest.

Batami was waiting for him. She floated in astral form several feet above the ground, her legs drawn up and crossed beneath her body, eyes closed. Alex knew she was engaged in a meditative practice allowing her to extend her time in astral form. As a result of the practice, Batami could prolong her presence in astral form for days, if she needed. Until the needs of her physical body demanded her return. Batami had taught him the basics of the practice, but there was so much to learn, and never enough time for training.

"You are very late," Batami thought into his mind as she opened her eyes.

"I managed to get inside the carnival," Alex thought back to Batami. *"I know who is trying to free the Shadow Wraith."*

Her surprise was evident in the look clouding her face. *"Tell me everything."*

Alex slowly recounted each of the events of the past few hours. When he was done, Batami did something that surprised Alex — She smiled.

"I should admonish you," Batami said, *"for not immediately coming to me and seeking my vast experience and skill to investigate the carnival. However, I feel certain such a thought never entered your mind."*

"Wow," Alex said, suddenly shocked by Batami's perceptiveness and all it implied. *"I don't know why I didn't think of that."*

"Because you are reckless, headstrong, and have a dangerous appetite for adventure," Batami said. *"While these are all great weaknesses, your most debilitating fault is your inability to ask for help when you need it. There is no weakness in asking for assistance."*

"I'll try to remember that," Alex said, actually meaning it.

"Please do," Batami said, placing the words forcefully within his mind.

"What do we do now?" Alex asked.

"First, you will inform your parents of what you have discovered," Batami said. "Your father may be able to arrest Esmeralda and the others based on your testimony."

"I'm afraid my word isn't worth much these days," Alex said, unable to look at Batami while he spoke.

"Why not?" Batami asked, a frown filling her face.

Alex explained, as quickly as he could, how he and the Guild had been tricked by Anna and the Mad Mages into looking like they were stealing the old Founders Statue from the town museum and how they were all now grounded.

"I am afraid my earlier assessment of your character flaws was not critical enough," Batami said, disappointment on her face. "You allowed your pride and anger to cloud your judgment. If that can get you grounded when facing a bunch of scheming children, imagine the result when facing the Shadow Wraith and its minions."

Alex said nothing. Batami words were pointed and powerful. He could not afford to be so foolish again. Too much was at stake.

"While your father may not be able to arrest them, at least he will be able to keep an eye Esmeralda and the others," Batami said.

"Maybe if we could find all the people under Esmeralda's influence, we could figure out the plan," Alex said. "What do they need a sword for? I've never even heard of the Sword of Silas."

"Neither have I," Batami said. "But it might be known under a different name if it is some ancient magical artifact. Esmeralda seems to have a knack for finding magical relics. If I'm not mistaken, her necklace was once called The Necklace of Niarha. It is very, very old."

"What about Pandora's Box?" Alex asked. "I was almost trapped forever in that black box."

"I'm not certain," Batami said. "I think it might be The Box of Internment. It was used to imprison Dark Spirit Mages a thousand years ago. It will appear empty to normal eyes, but it will ensnare anyone in astral form until the box is destroyed."

"Like the prison that holds the Shadow Wraith," Alex said.

"A much weaker prison, but similar," Batami said. "It would never hold a creature as powerful as the Shadow Wraith."

"Who is the figure in black who helped me?" Alex asked, finally coming to a question that he been on his mind for days.

"Someone very clever, but not clever enough to heed my warnings," Batami said, a hint of sadness flickering across her face.

"You know this person?" Alex asked, more curious than ever about the identity of the figure in black.

"Yes," Batami said. *"However, we have a great many other things to concern ourselves with. First, before you fade back into your physical body from fatigue, I need to show you a little of how to use the magic of astral energy to protect yourself. Unfortunately, there is never enough time to teach you all you need to know."*

Alex spent the next hour learning how to manipulate the energy of the astral plane the way energy could be magically controlled in the physical world. Batami made him practice creating a shield of astral energy alternating with learning how to focus that same energy into blue-white bolts of power that could affect other beings in the astral world. Alex practiced until he looked down at himself and saw his astral form fading into ether. He tried to remain alert, but he could feel himself slipping back into his physical body.

"Too tired," was all Alex managed to say before fading away from Batami's side.

"Don't forget…" he heard her say as sleep took hold of his ragged mind and he collapsed into unconsciousness.

Chapter Nineteen
Cauldron Cooking

Flames grasped like clutching hands as he ran. A wall of fire roared up before him, the air feeling like a furnace. Trees around him collapsed and exploded, spewing glowing embers skyward like miniature volcanoes. The flames were all around now, no relief and no escape as his clothes combusted into a fire that seared and surrounded him.

Alex woke up blinking and breathing heavily as he wiped the sweat from his eyes. He was hot. As hot as he had been in his dream.

He sat up in bed. His bedcovers lie on the floor and his pajama shirt was unbuttoned to his belly. The windows were wide open, but only to allow a stiff, hot breeze to circulate through the room like a stove box. Alex saw clouds outside the window and slipped out of bed to investigate.

Dark storm clouds filled the sky, threatening to shatter with rain at any moment, but offering no relief from the sweltering heat blanketing the town. Alex shook his head in puzzlement and caught sight of himself in the mirror. He tried to straighten his sweat-plastered hair with his fingers, but it was hopeless. Then he saw the clock on his nightstand.

"Oh no," Alex sighed.

It was nearly eleven o'clock in the morning. He had forgotten to set the alarm and overslept by hours. His plan had been to wake his parents and tell them what he had discovered as soon as he returned from his astral travel with Batami. However, the lure of sleep had been too strong. At the very least, he could have told them over breakfast.

Why hadn't his parents tried to wake him? Had something happened? Was something wrong?

Alex ran from his room, racing down the hallway and jumping down the stairs two at a time. His bare feet skidded against the hardwood floor of the kitchen as he came to a stop.

"Alex," his mother said, turning from the stove where she was making pancakes on a hot griddle. "You're up in time for breakfast."

"The second breakfast," Nina said from where she sat at the table, fork filled with a syrup-drenched pancake. "Sleepy head."

"Mmm, third breakfast, in my case," Clark said, sitting next to Nina, who sat next to where Victoria knelt at the end of the table. Beside her, Daphne, Ben, and Raphael sat eating pancakes. Alex had forgotten the Guild was collectively grounded and confined to his house.

"Very nice pajamas," Victoria said with a smile as she took a sip of orange juice. Alex looked down and felt his face flush with even more heat than the weather was providing. He began to button up his pajama shirt.

"Morning," Ben said, pointing to the unruly mop on Alex's head. "Great hair."

"Use a little less spit next time you comb it," Rafael said, plopping a bite of pancake into his mouth.

"Morpheus' mud pies," Daphne said, with her mouth full. "Did you forget to sleep while you were in bed?"

"Language," his mother admonished Daphne. "We don't curse in this house. Or speak with our mouths full."

"Sorry, Mrs. Ravenstar," Daphne said, her eyes flicking down to her plate.

Alex's mother frowned at Alex as she placed a plate of pancakes before the open seat beside Victoria. "Batami should know better than to wear you out like this. Have a seat and eat something."

Alex shook his head to clear it and recover from the disparity between what he imagined he might find downstairs and the sight before his eyes. Then he looked at his mother and spoke.

"I know who's trying to free the Shadow Wraith."

The smell of the pancakes wafted up invitingly to Alex's nostrils as the cacophonous questions from his mother and the Guild

185

assaulted his ears. His stomach rumbled as a sharp pain of hunger shot through it. He honestly couldn't decide if it was more important to eat first or tell his mother and the Guild what he had seen and done the night before. He decided he could do both at the same time.

Alex sat at the table and began shoveling pancakes into his mouth at a preposterous pace as he recounted to his mother, sister, and friends all that had happened the night before. His mother's frowns at speaking with his mouth full were quickly replaced by gasps as he got to the more dangerous details of his midnight adventure.

It took four pancakes, two sausages, three scrambled eggs, and a piece of toast smothered in strawberry jam for Alex to finish his story and begin to feel full. He knew from his experiences of astral travel he would be hungry again in less than an hour, but at least for the moment, his hunger felt satiated and his willpower fortified. His last bite, and last words, were met with indecipherable stares from his table companions and a look from his mother that he steadfastly refused to interpret. The way she was wringing the apron at her waist while she stood beside him was enough indication of what she thought. She let the apron fall and smoothed it out before placing her hands on either side of Alex's head and tilting it back so she could stare down into his eyes.

"Why must you always put yourself at the center of every awful thing that happens in this town?" she asked as she sniffed back tears brimming at the edges of her eyes.

"I know it's a bad habit, Mom," Alex said, trying to smile against the tears threatening to well up within his own eyes, "but at least I'm not smoking."

His mother laughed and bent down to kiss him on the head. "I might prefer you tried something that would only kill you slowly." She frowned. "Forget I said that."

"We have to tell Dad," Nina said, her eyes still wide from the recitation of Alex's adventures.

"Yes," his mother said, turning to include Nina and the rest of the table in her words as she removed the apron and stepped over to where the family shoes lined the wall beside the back door. She slid off her slippers and pulled on a pair of leather boots. "I will go immediately and tell your father what has happened. Alex is right, based on the fact the mayor thinks you all tried to rob the town museum, Logan may not be able to make any arrests. But, we can keep them all under observation.

"In the meantime, Alex, I want you to go to the top of the attic stairs. Three steps up on the right you will find a book on ancient magical armaments. I could swear I've heard the phrase Sword of Silas before. That book may have some clue as to what it is and what it can do. I'll be back, but while I'm gone, you are all to remain here. And I will know if you have tried to leave." She locked eyes with Alex and Nina for a moment, then kissed them each quickly on the forehead and strode to the door. She paused and looked back over her shoulder, directly at Alex.

"Don't do anything stupid or reckless or heroic," his mother said, holding his eyes with hers.

Victoria burst out laughing, throwing her hands to her mouth to stifle her giggles as she blushed. "I'm sorry, Mrs. Ravenstar. That simply sounded so ridiculous when you said it."

"You can't ask him not to be stupid," Nina said as the others joined in at laughing at Alex. "It's what he does best."

"It'd be like asking him not to fart," Daphne said.

"Impossible," Ben said. "He can't not fart. He'd explode."

"He'd probably explode if he didn't do something stupid," Rafael said.

"Hmm, we'll keep an eye on him, Mrs. Ravenstar," Clark said.

"Right," Daphne said. "If it looks like he's going to be reckless or heroic or stupid, we'll stop him."

"Yes, I'm sure you will," his mother said with a sarcastic sigh. "You're all so good at discouraging his wild ideas. I can't decide who's the fox and who's the hen." She sighed again. "Take care of each other. I'll be back soon."

As Alex's mother closed the door, Alex turned to look thoughtfully at Nina and his friends. "What eats a fox?"

"A wolf?" Victoria suggested, raising her eyebrows.

"Then I'm a wolf," Alex said, with a sly grin. "I think we're all wolves. And we know who the foxes are."

"Then who are the hens?" Nina asked, looking puzzled.

"The whole gorping town," Daphne said, sounding exasperated.

"So what are we really going to do?" Victoria asked, looking at Alex expectantly.

"Plan?" Ben said, sitting up taller in his chair. "Do we have one this time?"

"For now, exactly what Mom said," Alex replied, looking around the table at the others. "I'll find the book on magical weapons and we'll see if we can figure out what Esmeralda and the others are up to."

"For once, being a wolf might not be so bad," Rafael said, taking the last sip of his orange juice.

"Hmm, Daphne and I have something else to do," Clark said, looking down where Daphne sat beside him. "Out in the Guild House."

"What's more important than figuring out what Esmeralda is up to?" Alex asked.

"Clark has a hunch about what the cauldron might do," Daphne said with a mysterious smile. "I and I have a hunch we might need it to stop the evil carnies."

"What hunch?" Alex said, his voice cracking slightly. He suddenly realized how annoying it must be when he made cryptic statements about plans that might affect the Guild in their adventures. It was very annoying.

"It's only a hunch for now," Daphne said. "We'll work on the cauldron while you research the sword."

"Me too," Ben said. "I'll help Clark and Daphne."

"That will leave the four of us to read the book," Rafael said.

"We can do the dishes," Victoria replied. "I'm sure Alex and Nina's mother would appreciate coming home to find a clean kitchen."

"You know, in your own way, you're as crazy as my brother," Nina said, frowning at Victoria.

Alex changed into his clothes and retrieved the book his mother had mentioned while Victoria enlisted Nina and Rafael to help with the dishes and Daphne, Clark, and Ben headed out to the Guild House in the backyard to continue the examination of the magic cauldron.

Alex was surprised to discover the book was only two steps up on the attic stairs from where his mother has said it would be. His mother had a very peculiar system of organization for the thousands books stacked around the house and it was a methodology that eluded the rest of the family. Alex was impressed she had known where it would be.

The dishes proved a much easier task to accomplish than finding any hint of who Silas might have been and why Esmeralda might want his sword. Nearly an hour after his mother's departure, Alex sat at the kitchen table, Rafa on one side, Nina on the other, and Victoria looking over their shoulders as they slowly flipped through page after page of the book, hunting for any hint of the information they sought. Finally, near the end of the book, they came across something that raised Alex's hopes. Victoria spotted it first.

"There, in the last paragraph," Victoria said, leaning down over Alex's shoulder. He only found her breath on his neck mildly distracting. *"Lord Elvodar claimed Silas's sword and wielded it against the mighty Stone Mountain Monster, shattering the creature into vapor and ash. The Sword of Destruction so frightened Lord Elvodar with its power that he ordered his most trusted vassal to bear it to a far land and hide it forever from human hands. Hammered with blows of magic in a forge of dragon fire by Silas of Abeldeen, the Sword of Destruction was said to annihilate anything it touched, except its own sheath. Lord Elvodar's vassal hid the sword well, for it has never been found in over three thousand years."*

"A sword that can destroy anything it touches," Rafael said, leaning back from the table. "That sounds bad."

"What do they want it for?" Nina asked, running her finger over the passage on the book Victoria has just read aloud.

"To destroy the rune keeping the Shadow Wraith in its prison," Alex said with a sigh.

"But how could they get into the cave without the whole town knowing?" Victoria asked. "It's buried under half a mountain of rubble. She isn't planning on using the sword to excavate, is she?"

"I don't know," Alex said. "At least we know what they want it for."

"But how do they plan to find it?" Nina asked.

Just then, Ben burst through the door, his eyes alight with excitement and his face drenched with sweat.

"Cauldron," Ben practically shouted. "You have to come see what Daphne and Clark discovered about the cauldron."

"I'll catch up," Alex said as the others all made for the door. "I'll leave a note to let Mom know where we are." It would not be good for her to come home and find them all missing.

"What's taking her so long?" Nina asked as she reached the door.

"Probably helping Dad keep track of evil carnies," Alex said, snatching a note pad from the kitchen counter and scribbling out a quick message to his mother explaining where they were.

When Alex stepped into the Guild House a minute later, he instinctively leaned back from the wall of heat that hit him in the face. The air in the small Guild House felt twice as stifling as the heat that had been oppressing the town for days. Alex immediately saw the source of the heat. A large fire blazed in the belly of the cast-iron woodstove. In top of the stove sat the cauldron. Clark and Daphne stood beside the stove, dripping wet with sweat. Daphne stood on a chair so she could see into the bowl of the black cauldron.

"We figured it out," Daphne said, barely able to contain her excitement.

"Hmm, mostly Daphne figured it out," Clark said, nodding toward her.

"We couldn't have done it without your nose," Daphne said, grinning at Clark. "And your stomach."

"Fire," Ben said, stepping up to the stove and cauldron. "I started the fire."

"Fire is part of it," Daphne said, "but the wishing is the important part."

"What does it do, already?" Rafael said, wiping his forehead with back of his arm.

"It's a gorping cauldron of transformation," Daphne said, beaming. "I was thinking we could examine the cauldron by starting a fire under it and testing things we put inside. We started with water, but the water only boiled."

"Ah, then we tried different rune-words," Clark said. "But nothing worked."

"Rumble," Ben said. "Then Clark's stomach started making noise."

"Mmm, I should have had another pancake," Clark said.

"And then the water in the cauldron started to change," Daphne said.

"Soup," Ben said. "The water changed into soup."

"Beef barley soup with carrots and peas," Daphne said with a laugh.

"Well, I was hungry," Clark said, his face serious. Clark was always serious about food. "Soup sounded good."

"Are you telling us that the cauldron transformed water into soup because Clark was thinking about it?" Victoria asked, stepping closer to examine the cauldron. "Daddy would love to know how that works."

"It works for more than gorping soup, too," Daphne said.

"Yeah, we tried a stick from the yard that Daphne turned into a flower," Clark said. "And Ben turned that old baseball that's always rolling around into a pile of poop."

"My lucky baseball?" Rafael said with a yelp.

"Concentration," Ben said, pointedly avoiding Rafael's eyes. "You have to concentrate. I lost focus. I needed to go."

"But it only works for things that aren't alive," Daphne said, wrinkling her nose.

"Mouse," Ben said. "The mouse was a bad idea. My fault."

"Hmm, never had to heal a mouse before," Clark said.

"Daphne, Clark, Ben," Alex said, grinning at his friends, "this is great. You were right, Daph. We can use the cauldron. If we can find the Sword of Silas before Esmeralda and the evil carnies, maybe we can destroy it." Alex quickly told Daphne, Clark, and Ben what he and the others had learned about the Sword of Silas.

"Dionysus' diarrhea," Daphne said. "How are we supposed to find the sword?"

"Don't even think about suggesting that crazy dog," Rafael said. "It couldn't find a bone it hid in its own bed."

"Beowulf is better with people than things," Nina said, her tone a little defensive.

"Maybe Daddy could think of a way to find it," Victoria suggested. "Magic that destructive must leave a trace somehow."

"Jail," Ben said. "Your dad needs to lock them all up before they can find the sword."

"Yeah, you should tell your mom and dad about the sword," Clark said.

"As soon as..." Alex began to say and then jumped as something sharp poked into his chest. Alex looked around, but his friends were all too far away to have been responsible. His first thought was that the Mad Mages were nearby and pulling a prank. Then the poke came again.

"What's the matter?" Nina asked, looking at Alex with sudden concern.

"I'm not sure," Alex said, taking a seat on the nearby couch. "I think Batami is trying to make contact. Keep an eye on me."

Alex leaned back into the deep cushions of the couch and closed his eyes as his friends watched with apprehension. Alex took a deep breath and willed himself into his astral form. As he did so, he saw Batami floating before him, a hint of anxiety on her face.

"I have some news," Batami said.

"What's happened?" Alex asked.

"I've been at the carnival since our meeting last night," Batami said. *"I used the method you described to get past the astral barrier. I had hoped to search out the followers of the Shadow Wraith you were unable to uncover. Instead, I found the necklace, hanging on a mannequin, but there is no sign of Esmeralda or any of the carnival folk you described."*

"Are you sure?" Alex asked.

"I think it would be hard to miss a fifteen foot giant," Batami said with a frown.

"Maybe they fled town when they realized I could identify them," Alex said, knowing such hopeful thoughts never turned out to reflect reality.

"More likely, they have moved up the timetable for their plans," Batami said. *"And left the necklace behind, with the astral barrier intact, so we would think Esmeralda was still in the carnival grounds."*

192

The world outside the Guild House lit up with a blinding bolt of lightning. The thunder that followed was so loud it shook the walls of the old horse stable. Alex saw his friends dash to the door and swing it open as a wall of rain began to pound the ground.

"That does not seem like…" Batami said and then paused, her face twisting as though in pain.

"What is it?" Alex asked, floating closer at Batami's astral form.

"I must go," Batami said, her concern and pain seeping directly into Alex's mind with the words she thought to him. *"The White Forest is on fire."*

Chapter Twenty
Bank Robbery

"But it's raining," Alex said, glancing out the window of the Guild House. *"How can the White Forest be on fire?"*

"It seems this was part of their plan," Batami said. *"To keep me from helping you."* She winced in pain and her astral form flickered. *"I must go. I will come to you again when I can. Take care."*

"Batami..." Alex began to think to his mentor, but she faded from sight. Alex knew Batami and the White Forest were magically entwined in ways that allowed her to live much longer than normal, but that this magical bond also tied her to the life of the forest. If the White Forest were on fire, it was as though Batami herself was aflame. He had to help her if he could. Alex let himself slip back into his physical body and sat up.

"It was Batami," Alex said to the others as they turned from watching the rain to the sound of his voice. Only Victoria and Nina had maintained their vigil over his seemingly sleeping form. "The White Forest is on fire."

"In this gorping rain?" Daphne said, her voice nearly squeaking.

"The weather and the fire must be the work of Esmeralda," Alex said as he sat up. "If the forest is on fire, Batami can't help us."

"Rain," Ben said, looking out the window again. "Then why all the rain?"

"To drown the rest of us?" Rafael suggested with a shrug his shoulders.

The piercing sound of a ringing bell filled their ears and Victoria jumped, her hooves clattering along the wooden floor in her surprise. She reached into the leather satchel she always carried and withdrew a large alarm clock, its little hammer swinging wildly between the two metal bells atop its round clock face. Victoria silenced the bell and looked at Alex and the others.

"Someone is breaking into my house," Victoria said, her eyes wide with worry.

"Esmeralda," Alex said, jumping to his feet. "She must think one of your father's inventions will help her find the Sword of Silas."

"I have to go," Victoria said, slipping the clock back into her satchel.

"You're not going anywhere without the rest of us," Alex said. He looked around the room at the others. Events were happening far more quickly than he had anticipated and he knew too little of Esmeralda's plans and how they might unfold. They needed to act, but they also needed to be prepared. The last thing Alex was going do was lead his friends into another trap. The concern on the faces of the Guild paradoxically increased his confidence and resolve. It was times like these, when someone needed to lead, that Alex felt closest to being the person he imagined himself to be in his dreams.

"Okay, here's the plan," Alex said, clapping his hands together. "We can't leave unprepared. Nina, Daphne, and Rafael, head to the house. Nina, show them where the raincoats are. Daphne and Raphael, gather up anything you think might keep us dry. Nina, write Mom a note and tell her where we went and why, and leave it on the kitchen table. She'll know from her magic that we've left the house, but this way she'll know why. Victoria and Clark, douse the fire in the woodstove and empty the cauldron. Then help Ben pack up everything you think we might need from the storage locker. Rope, canteens for water, compass, flares, glow-wands, smoke bombs, firecrackers, anything you can think of. We meet back here in two minutes."

"What are you going to do?" Daphne asked as she headed to the door with Nina and Rafael.

"I have some magic to work," Alex said, pulling three coins from his pocket. "I'll explain later."

The others quickly ran to their tasks as Alex placed the three coins on the table at the side of the room. One of the coins tugged slightly against his finger in the direction of the carnival grounds. That must be where Anna was with the coin's enchanted companion.

He focused his mind and opened his magic-sense to his great-great grandfather's tracking coin, probing the magic that linked it to its twin. Alex's father had been right. While the enchantments were subtle, they were not complex.

Alex whispered the rune-words he knew would mimic the magic of the older coin as he placed one of the common coins from his pocket on top of it. After a few seconds, he pulled them apart. He could sense the magical link between the new coin and the older coin, and through it, to the one Anna had stolen. Alex then spoke another series of rune-words and felt the connection between the older coin and the other two disappear. Now, only the new coin was linked to the one Anna held.

Alex glanced up from his work. Victoria, Clark, and Ben had nearly finished packing the gear. He saw Nina, Rafael, and Daphne running across the yard, each wearing a rain poncho. Alex quickly placed the second, newer coin, on top of the one he had just enchanted and spoke the rune-words again, but with a minor alteration. This third coin was linked to the others, but not strongly enough to reveal its location.

"What did you make?" Victoria asked as Nina, Rafael, and Daphne ran in from the downpour, quickly distributing raincoats and ponchos. As he took a poncho, Alex silently thanked his parents for never throwing old coats away.

"Anna snuck one of my great-great grandfather's tracking coins into my pocket at the museum," Alex said as Victoria shrugged into a poncho to cover her human half. "I made a copy so she will think we're still here in the Guild House, when she checks the coin she has. But I made a third coin I can use to tell where she is with her coin."

"Very sneaky," Victoria said with an appreciative pat on Alex's shoulder.

"The Mad Mages aren't the only ones who can be sneaky," Alex said, winking at Victoria. "Is everyone ready?" he asked, looking around the room. They all nodded. "Then let's go. They won't be expecting anyone. Hopefully, we can catch Esmeralda in the act."

Alex and the Guild raced their bikes through the rain toward Victoria's house as she galloped beside them, water falling around them by the bucketsful as strong winds blew stinging drops into their faces and threatened to knock them over or lift them into the air. Alex had never seen so much rain. Torrents of water swamped the streets, forcing them to ride their bikes along the sidewalks. The streets were empty, the townspeople likely all still gathered at the carnivals grounds or hiding in their homes from the unnatural downpour.

Alex wiped the water from his eyes and turned the corner onto Raven Street. The storm clouds above blocked out the sun and left the street in near-night blackness. Alex could barely see Victoria's house at the end of the block through the gloom and sheets of rain. Even the magically-powered street lamps glowing in the sudden darkness provided barely enough light to navigate.

A bolt of lightning shattered the sky, briefly illuminating the town and giving Alex the opportunity to gather his bearings. Then the accompanying thunderclap shook the ground and nearly caused him to lose control of his bike.

Alex slid to a halt at the end of the sidewalk outside Victoria's house. He tossed his bike in the grass as the others behind him did the same. He looked at the house. The front door was closed, the windows dark. Waterfalls poured from the rain awnings, flooding down into the lawn. It looked empty, like all the houses around it.

"Rafael, you watch the front in case someone comes out," Alex said. "The rest of us will circle around. Nina and Victoria with me. Everyone else around the other side."

Alex dashed off around the right side of the house, Nina and Victoria close behind. He peeked through the windows as he ran around the house, but it was dark inside and he could not tell if someone was lurking within. He suspected any attempt to burglarize the property would focus on Victoria's father's workshop at the back. That was where most of his inventions resided.

Alex paused at the back wall of the house, cautiously poking his head around the corner. He saw Daphne doing the same on the opposite side of the house. A dim yellow light struggled against the darkness and rain to shine past the two wide open wooden doors of the workshop.

Alex glanced at Victoria for a moment. She nodded and Alex signaled to Daphne. A second later, they all rushed toward workshop doors, relying on the deafening sound of the rain to conceal their approach. They hesitated a moment at the edge of the door and then burst into the room as one massive body of wet arms and legs.

As they ran into the warm magical light of the workshop glow bulbs and out of the pounding rain, the first thing to capture Alex's attention was Victoria's father standing in the middle of the room, shaking his head and attempting to wipe the water from his spectacles with the edge of a waterlogged shirt.

"Victoria?" her father said as he slipped his glasses on.

"Daddy!" Victoria said, rushing to embrace her father. "Are you all right? The alarm went off and we came as soon as we could."

"I'm fine, I'm fine," her father said, gently brushing water from his daughter's face. "I've only been here a moment. I ran over when the alarm went off and found the place like this."

Victoria's father gestured around the workshop and Alex noticed, for the first time, it seemed even more disorganized than usual.

"Have we been robbed?" Victoria asked, shaking water from her hindquarters.

"Ransacked more than robbed," her father said. "They made a bloody mess of the place, but once they located the safe, they seemed to have found what they wanted. I still don't know how they managed to get past the enchantments on the safe door."

"What did they take?" Victoria asked as she walked over and examined a large metal safe partially hidden beneath a pile of boxes. Scorch marks blackened the open door of the safe. Alex could see several small boxes and a stack of papers still inside.

"That's the oddest thing," Victoria's father said. "They left all of the money and valuables and only took my Wall Walking Belt."

"What is a Wall Walking Belt, Sir?" Alex asked, stepping up to Victoria and her father. The older centaur blinked in surprise and looked around the room as if suddenly realizing Alex and the rest of the Guild were present.

"Ah, Alex," Victoria's father said. "I've sent for your father. He should be here soon. I thought you were all supposed to be confined to your house."

"We couldn't let her come alone," Alex said, nodding toward Victoria.

"Yes, good friends," Victoria's father said with a slight smile. "Well, the belt is a simple device, really. But, not the sort of thing one leaves lying about where someone might find it by chance. It does exactly what it says it does. It allows the person wearing it to walk through walls. Can't imagine how they knew about it."

"You're always talking about your inventions, Daddy" Victoria said to her father.

"Yes, I suppose," her father muttered. "But I'd swear I only even mentioned it to Melvin over a game of ale and pint of chess. I mean a game of chess and a pint of ale."

Alex felt a cold certainty filling his body, amplified by being soddenly soaked to the bone. "Does the belt allow you to carry something with you while you walk through walls?" Alex asked.

"Naturally," Victoria's father said. "That's why I had it in the safe. Too tempting for some people who might want to run off with their neighbors' things."

"The bank," Alex and Victoria said as they looked at each other and spoke in unison.

"What about the bank?" Victoria's father asked, looking between Alex and his daughter.

"It's a long story, Mr. Radcliff, but we have to go to the bank," Alex said as he headed toward the open workshop door and the wall of rain outside. "When my dad gets here, please tell him about the belt and that I said he should go the bank right away. He'll know what it means."

"Yes, of course, but I don't know what it means," Victoria's father protested.

"I promise I'll explain everything," Victoria said, kissing her father quickly on the cheek before following Alex out into the rain.

"Well, take care of yourself," her father shouted after her.

Alex and the Guild gathered up their bikes at the front of the house and explained to Rafael what they had learned as they rode toward the bank and the center of town.

"So what do you think they're trying to steal from the bank?" Rafael shouted through the roar of the pounding rain.

"Sword," Ben shouted over the constant drumming of the rain. "Maybe that's where the sword is. The bank has a room with personal vaults. My dad has one."

"How in the name of Poseidon's Pustules could the Sword of Silas be in a bank in Runewood?" Daphne yelled.

"Hmm, how did it end up in Runewood at all?" Clark rumbled.

Alex didn't know what to answer and he was having enough trouble staying on his bike in the ever-increasing and ever-shifting wind. The rain became like a fire hose constantly aimed at his head from different directions, the wind threatening to sweep his bicycle from the sidewalk and into the air at any moment. They rode into the town center and took shelter under the wide awning of the local movie theater marquee. Alex was thankful for the respite from the rain as he looked across the street at the tall pillars of stone holding up the roof of the bank.

"Empty," Ben said, climbing off his bike. "It looks deserted."

"Hmm, all the shops look empty," Clark said, peering through the cascade of rain at the shops across the street.

"I don't think the bank was even supposed to be open today," Rafael said, pulling the hood of his poncho back so he could shake the water from his thick, black hair.

"Maybe they are already gone," Victoria said as she edged her horse half under the awning and out of the rain.

"Or they went in through the back," Daphne offered, wringing water from her long hair.

"You should check it out, Brother," Nina said, turning to Alex.

"Right," Alex said, looking back over his shoulder at the others.

"I've got you," Victoria said, reaching out to place her arms around Alex and hold him to her side so he could not fall down.

"Thanks," Alex said, looking up at Victoria. Water still ran in small rivulets from Victoria's horse flanks, but her embrace was warm, even through the plastic poncho, and somehow, she still smelled like honeysuckle. As Alex closed his eyes and breathed deeply to focus his mind, he noted that even given the rain and the wind and the smothering humidity, being in Victoria's arms was the best way to astral travel.

Then Alex was in his astral form, hovering outside his body, and watching as Victoria held his physical form upright. Alex floated out into the rain, the water passing through him with no effect, as he glided over the street and toward the bank. A moment later, he passed through the thick front doors of the bank and into the main lobby.

The lobby of the bank was old and ornate, carved granite columns supporting a peaked ceiling with skylights allowing flashes of lightening to bounce off the polished marble floor and briefly illuminate the large space. Alex floated over the black marble banking counter running along the back wall and toward the large round metal door of the bank vault. He saw no evidence of Esmeralda or the other carnies and no sign anyone had been in the bank all day. It was Sunday, after all.

Alex noted the geared workings of the vault door's multiple locks as he passed through its thick steel frame. The vault inside was black and lightless. Alex shifted his vision to see more thoroughly in the astral realm and could perceive the ghostly blue outlines of the shelves along the vault walls, lined with stacks of paper money and large sacks of what Alex assumed were coins. He would have been impressed with the amount of wealth held within the small room if he hadn't been so much more concerned with what might have been stolen from it.

Alex drifted back through the vault door and into the bank. There was another steel door, beside the main vault, and Alex slipped through it as easily as he had the first. This vault was smaller, but just as dark. Alex again shifted his vision into the astral realm.

The chamber was composed of a hundred or more lockboxes of various sizes built into the walls. A good half of the lockboxes were blasted open, their charred doors hanging at odd angles. Only one small box, the size of a loaf of bread, was empty.

Alex released his astral presence.

His first thought when he opened his eyes was how pleasant Victoria's warm breath felt on his cheek. He stood up a little straighter and Victoria released him.

"Thanks," Alex said, reluctantly stepping away from Victoria. "The private vault has been robbed. They're gone already."

"What did they take?" Daphne asked, staring up at Alex.

"It's hard to tell," Alex said. "There was only one box that looked empty. Whatever they took was small."

"Something to lead them to the sword, most likely," Victoria said, a worried look on her face.

"Hmm, so how do we find them now?" Clark asked, looking out at the rain as though hoping to catch sight Esmeralda and her cohorts.

"Beowulf," Nina said, almost bouncing with the word.

"That mutt can't find its own tail," Rafael said with a grimace.

"Beowulf can find them," Alex said. "We just need to give him something to get the right scent."

"What did you give the dog to smell for hunting the Rune Tree?" Victoria asked.

"I showed him a picture," Alex said as he climbed onto his bike.

"How in the name of Cerberus' canker sores did you think that was going to work?" Daphne asked.

"It was worth shot," Alex said, pushing down on the bike pedal and shooting off into the torrential rain. "Beowulf is much better with something to smell."

"Should we use the whistle Mom and Dad gave us?" Nina shouted as she and the others followed Alex back into the rain.

"Once we track down Esmeralda and the others," Alex yelled back. "We're going to need some help when we find them."

The town jailhouse was only a few blocks away and they fought to ride against the wind the entire distance. The jailhouse was locked, but a small, hinged flap cut into the bottom of the front door whipped wildly in the wind. Nina jumped off her bike and bent down on both knees. She grabbed the small flap as it flipped violently and thrust her head inside the tiny doorway.

"Beowulf," Nina called out. "Here boy. We need you to find someone." Nina rocked back as the little beagle dashed through the doggie door and licked her face. "So where do we find something for him to track them with?" she asked, looking up at Alex as she petted Beowulf's head.

"I know exactly what we need," Alex said, his eyes narrowing as much in determination as to keep the rain out. "It's at the carnival."

Chapter Twenty-One
Finding the Scent

It took Alex and the Guild much longer to reach the carnival grounds than he had hoped. The wind from the storm grew so strong it forced them to abandon their bikes in an alley between two houses and continue on foot. Daphne and Nina chose to cling to Victoria's horse half rather than continue risking being sucked up into the air by the buffeting winds.

The main carnival gate was empty, the attendant apparently having abandoned his post to seek shelter. It looked as though nearly everyone in the carnival had done the same. Townspeople and carnies huddled together, crammed into tents and wagons, peeking out at the storm. The lanes between the tents were empty as Alex and the Guild marched toward the center of the carnival and the grand tent at its heart. As they turned around the corner of a small row of wagons, they all skidded to a slippery stop on the muddy ground. Before them, three others slid to a stop, as well.

"What are you all doing out in weather like this?" Elaeda shouted from beneath an oiled, leather cowboy hat. She wore a long, well-waxed leather coat reaching down past the tops of her boots.

"It would take too long to explain," Alex yelled above the roar of the storm.

"Have you seen Leanna?" Kendra said, her scaly skin glistening in the lightning as the rain flowed off it in sheets. She had changed her skin to make it impervious to the water.

"Why didn't I think of that?" Rafael mumbled beneath a rumble of thunder.

"She's gone missing," Nathan said. He wore only a dark blue shirt, now plastered to his well-muscled form. "Nearly a dozen carnies were missing this morning. We've been looking all over for them. Esmeralda and Mr. Apollo are gone, as well."

Alex glanced at the other members of the Guild. Leanna. The fact she was missing wasn't likely to be a coincidence. Alex turned back to the three carnies. "We don't have time to tell you everything, so you need to trust us. Esmeralda and Mr. Apollo are trying to free the Shadow Wraith. Esmeralda is a Spirit Mage. She's got Leanna and the others under her control."

"Are you out of your mind?" Nathan yelled. "Leanna would never work to free the Shadow Wraith."

"She's not herself," Victoria said, fruitlessly wiping water from her face.

"We're going to track them down," Nina said, raising her hand to shield her eyes from the rain.

"Woof," Beowulf barked from beside Nina, as through making clear exactly who was going to be doing the tracking. The little beagle wagged his tail, his magically compressed mass pulling him down into the mud so he appeared to be all belly and no legs.

"We'll go with you," Eleada said, stepping forward.

"I'm not sure…" Alex began to say when something behind the three carnies caught his eye. The carousel spun wildly, flinging water in a wide arc as the rain cascaded off its pointed, multicolored canvas roof. Why was the carousel still running? In the middle of a sky-shattering storm? Now that he thought about it, every time he had seen the carousel, it had been spinning. Even the first day the carnival had arrived.

Alex walked past Eleada, Kendra, and Nathan as though they didn't exist, his entire focus suddenly on the carousel.

"Hey," Nathan said, shouting at Alex as he strode past. "We said we'll go with you."

"Does that carousel ever shut down?" Alex asked, still staring at the spinning metal unicorns, griffins, and dragons.

"It's broken," Elaeda said. "Melvin says if he lets it stop, he won't be able to get it going again."

"And does it always spin that fast?" Alex said, still walking toward the carousel, the others following behind. "Clark, can you smell any magic from the carousel?"

Clark stretched his legs to catch up with Alex. "Hmm, I can't smell anything at this distance. Not with all this rain. Let me get closer." Clark broke into a puddle-splashing jog and ran to the carousel.

"What does this have to do with Leanna and the others?" Nathan asked, placing a hand on Alex's shoulder to get his attention.

"It'll make finding them easier," Alex said, staring up at Nathan.

"Oh, yes," Victoria said as she walked up beside Alex. "I see what you're thinking."

"Ah, definitely some kind of magic working in the carousel," Clark said, still sniffing at the whirling metal ride. "The rotation creates some kind of magical cloak. I never would have noticed if I wasn't looking for it."

"We're wasting time," Nathan said, stamping a hoof into the mud.

"If what you said is true, we need to be tracking Esmeralda," Eleada said, stepping over to stand beside Nathan. "Not playing with a carnival ride."

"The carousel is what's been causing the weather to be so strange," Victoria said, turning to face Nathan.

"That's insane," Nathan said with a shake of his head.

"No more insane than the things we usually see happen," Rafael said, leaning to sniff at the spinning carousel.

"We have to shut it down," Alex said, shrugging off Nathan's grip on his shoulder and walking toward the large, metal control lever at the side of the rotating ride.

"Can't let you do that," Melvin the minotaur said as he stepped from the rain-filled shadows at the back of the carousel to stand between Alex and the control lever.

"Get out of the way, you bullheaded bully," Daphne said, stomping through the mud to stand in front of Alex.

"Melvin," Eleada said, looking up at the big, bull-man beast. "What are you doing?"

"What I need to do," Melvin said, glaring down at Alex and the others. "Now run along, children. I don't want to have to hurt you." Melvin growled menacingly as lighting filled the sky. Beowulf snarled and stepped between the minotaur and the others.

"You won't hurt us," Nina said as she calmly walked past Alex to stand next to Beowulf. "You're more bull than man, and animals like me, and because you're mostly an animal, you like me, too, and you won't hurt us because you're feeling like you want to take a nap, because that's what bulls do in the rain, they takes naps, because the sound of the water is so soothing, and it makes them so sleepy, like its making you so sleepy, your eyelids are drooping and your head is nodding and you just want to lie down right now and take a nap, right there under that awning out of the rain because it's so nice and dry and such a nice place to take a nap."

Melvin the minotaur blinked as though mesmerized by Nina's words and stumbled back under the tent awning beside the carousel, slowly sitting down and leaning on his side, curling up to sleep with one massive hand beneath his head.

"We should probably tie him up before that wears off," Nina said, turning around to the others.

"Hmm, good idea," Clark said, grabbing a long rope from the back of the small tent.

"Knots," Ben said, jumping to help Clark bind Melvin. "I'm good at knots. I'll give you a hand."

"That, Little Sister, was stupidly dangerous and impressive," Alex said, throwing his arm around Nina and grinning. He had never seen her use her magical affinity with animals so effectively.

"Do I get to count that as my test for membership to the Guild?" Nina asked, her eyes bright and mischievous.

"As long as you promise never use that magic on me while I'm in animal form," Rafael said with a laugh.

"What is the point of all this?" Nathan asked, frowning as he stepped up beside Alex.

"Watch," Alex said, reaching over and yanking at the large lever beside the carousel control panel. The lever wobbled, but otherwise did not move.

Victoria placed her hand around Alex's and they gave the lever another yank. With Victoria's considerable strength added to his own, the lever easily slammed into the off position. As the lever fell into place, the carousel immediately began to slow, the rapid rotation of the ride gradually decreasing, as did the intensity of the storm. The carousel came to a halt, the wind and rain, although still blowing and falling in copious quantities, began to lessen. Alex looked to Nathan and smiled.

"Zeus's thunderbolts," Daphne said, blinking away raindrops as she looked up at the sky.

"I still don't see what this has to do with finding Leanna," Nathan said, glancing at the clouds and then back at Alex.

"They'll be easier to track without all the rain," Kendra said, watching as the carousel slowed to a stop.

"Even I couldn't track them in this much rain," Eleada said, shaking the collected water off her hat.

"That's what Beowulf is for," Alex said, nodding toward the beagle. "But first, we need something of Esmeralda's. Come on. I'll explain."

Clark and Ben applied the final knots to the ropes binding Melvin the minotaur and then ran to join Alex and the others slopping through the muddy lane. As they sprinted toward the back of the main tent, Alex tried briefly, and succinctly, to explain what they knew about Esmeraldas plans — from her poisoning of Leanna and the other carnies' soul-essences, to the theft of Victoria's father's Wall Walking Belt, and the robbery of something small from the bank vaults. They rounded the back of the giant tent and came to a stop outside the wagon Alex knew belonged to Esmeralda and Mr. Apollo.

"I still can't believe Esmeralda would do the things you've described," Nathan said. "She and Mr. Apollo have always been so nice to me."

"You'd believe it if she'd tried to kill you," Alex said.

"What do we need from their sleeping wagon?" Eleada asked. "A piece of clothing or something?"

"I have something more personal in mind," Alex said as he stepped up to the door. "Clark, can you sniff out any traps?"

"Mmm, sure," Clark said, climbing up the back steps of the wagon and slowly opening the door.

"Careful, Clark," Daphne said. "Who knows what they might have left behind?"

Clark disappeared into the cabin of the wagon. A few seconds later, he popped his head back out into the rain. "All clear."

Alex leapt up the steps to join Clark in the wagon. It was nice to be out of the rain, if only for a moment. It wasn't coming down nearly as hard, but it still sounded like an avalanche of water striking the wagon's tin roof. Alex paused a moment to let his eyes adjust to the darkness within the sleeping wagon. The dim, gray light shining through the windows glittered faintly in the gems of Esmeralda's necklace, hanging around the neck of a dressing mannequin in the corner of the room.

Alex walked over to stand before the necklace. He reached out with his magic-sense, but could feel nothing. He wasn't surprised. The necklace must mask its magic or everyone who met Esmeralda would have sensed it. Then a notion occurred to Alex.

He let his vision change to see the astral aspect of the world and the necklace suddenly blazed like a string of miniature yellow-blue suns. Alex nodded to himself. That was why no one could sense the magic of the necklace. It used astral energy to create the astral barrier. That made sense. Only a Spirit Mage could sense or use the magic of the necklace.

Now that he was looking closely at the necklace with his astral eyes, Alex could see the magical energy it emitted and how it functioned. It pulled astral energy into it like a sponge absorbing water, then used that same energy, altering its nature, to create a barrier that this very same astral energy could not function within. It was like using someone's motion to spin him around and send him in the opposite direction.

Alex looked at the necklace more carefully, trying to figure out how to make it stop its magic. Making a magical device function usually involved speaking a rune-word related to the type of magic involved. To end the magic, one usually spoke the opposite rune-word. For a glow-wand one would say the rune-word for *light* and then *darkness*.

Having no better ideas, Alex said aloud the rune-word for *open*, guessing that the necklace might be activated by the word *close*. To Alex's surprise, the gemstones of the necklace quickly dulled and became dark. Alex let his vision slip back to normal and raised the necklace over the head of the mannequin.

"Ah, open what?" Clark asked, referring to Alex's rune-word intonation.

"Nothing," Alex said, turning to his friend. "This necklace is what Esmeralda was using to create the astral barrier."

"Ah, open for off," Clark said, nodding in understanding.

"Exactly," Alex said. "Now let's see if Beowulf can get a scent from this. Esmeralda's been wearing it for days."

Outside again in the rain, Alex held the necklace up for Beowulf to smell. As the beagle sniffed at the ancient magical artifact, Alex explained to the others what it was and what it did.

"She's worn that for years," Kendra said, squinting at the necklace.

"Ever since she came back to the carnival and married Mr. Apollo," Eleada added, bending down to sniff at the necklace along with Beowulf.

"I guess that's who Madam Fortuna meant," Alex said, scratching Beowulf behind his floppy ears.

"Woof," Beowulf said, wriggling around in the mud and barking again as he pointed his nose to the southeast of town.

"He's got the scent," Nina said, looking in the direction Beowulf's nose pointed.

"So that's what he does when he has the scent," Rafael with a snort. "All that napping he did was for show."

"Great lot of gorping good it will do us," Daphne said, folding her arms across her chest. "Without our bikes, we'll never catch up to Esmeralda and the evil carnies."

"Let's not call them evil carnies," Kendra said with a worried frown.

"They're our friends," Nathan added in anxious agreement.

"Hmm, how about temporarily evil?" Clark said, his voice soft and apologetic.

"Birds," Ben said, looking to the cloud-darkened sky. "Maybe Rafa and Kendra could turn into birds and carry Beowulf to where they are and then come back for us."

"That's even worse than Alex's ideas," Rafael said, staring incredulously at Ben.

"Besides, Beowulf is too heavy, remember?" Victoria said, looking down at the magical beagle as he barked again.

"Heavy," Ben said, smacking his forehead. "I forgot."

"We need to get moving," Alex said, standing up and starting to trudge through the mud. "We don't have any choice. We'll never catch them if we don't."

"We'll catch them, alright," Eleada said, raising her arm and pointing over Alex's shoulder.

Alex turned around and saw a large truck with high wooden railings wrapping around the flatbed at the back. He smiled.

"What?" Nathan said as he and the others followed Alex's gaze.

"We're going to steal a truck," Alex said with a laugh.

"And I'm driving," Eleada said, her laugh even more wild than Alex's.

Chapter Twenty-Two
The Silent Swamp

The rusted Dodge pickup truck bounced along the old dirt lane running along the edge of the fields behind the Millberry family's dairy farm, north of the Silent Swamp. Eleada sat in the driver's seat, hands gripping the big steering wheel. She drove with a reckless abandon that made it clear motor vehicles were normally never entrusted to her care.

Nina sat beside her, holding on to Beowulf, who had his head out the window, long ears flapping in the wind, barking and pointing his nose toward the Silent Swamp. The truck tilted to the passenger side because of Beowulf's enormous weight, and Eleada struggled to compensate and keep the truck from veering off into the ditch.

Alex stood in the back of the truck with everyone else. They all held tight to the wooden railing slats, hoping they wouldn't be thrown from the truck bed with the impact of the next gopher hole under the tires. Victoria stood at his side, clinging to the railing and looking a little seasick. Nathan stood on the other side of Alex, holding on to the truck and looking like he might vomit. Centaurs do not like trucks.

"Slower!" Ben shouted as he tried to stay on his feet. "Slower, you crazy elf!"

"I thought dwarves were sure-footed," Eleada yelled out the open window of the cab.

"Mountains," Ben said. "We're sure-footed on mountains. Things that don't move."

"We're almost there," Alex said, feeling a little nauseous himself.

The rain had stopped when they had passed out of the town, although slate-gray clouds still cloaked the sky. Alex looked over his shoulder and saw it was still raining in Runewood.

Beyond the town, farther toward the north, he could see bright white clouds rising up to join the dark, black ones above. Smoke from the fires of the White Forest. Alex wondered how Batami was handling the fire. He hoped she was all right. He wished there were something he could do to help her, but he knew he would have his hands full trying to stop Esmeralda and the evil carnies in the Silent Swamp.

It was obvious that was their destination. Alex had hoped it might be the Dead Forest, but Beowulf's nose had pointed only in one direction. At least in the Dead Forest, someone could hear you scream.

Alex and the others lurched forward as Eleada brought the truck to sharp stop. Beowulf bounded out of the truck as Nina opened the door and climbed out of the cab. Eleada hopped to the ground and grabbed her bow and quiver of arrows from behind the seat of the truck. She had insisted on taking the time to fetch them before leaving the carnival grounds. Ben had taken the opportunity to grab the small, horned bow he had used in their competitions and a matching quiver. He slung the quiver over his shoulder as he and Eleada strung their bows.

"I thought you said you could drive," Alex said as he climbed over the railing of the truck bed and lowered himself to the ground.

"I knew I should have flown," Kendra said, holding her head between her hands.

"You're here, aren't you?" Eleada said with a snort. "Wherever here is."

"The gorping Silent Swamp," Daphne said, smiling like she had just jumped off a carnival ride.

"Why do they call it the Silent Swamp?" Nathan asked, still steadying himself with the side of the truck.

"Well, because it's silent," Clark said, rubbing his forehead as though trying to stop a headache.

"Really, you don't say," Eleada said with a frown. "What makes it silent?"

"The fact that there are no sounds in the swamp," Rafael said, placing a hand on Kendra's shoulder to steady her. "That's the silent part."

"To be more accurate, sound doesn't travel in the swamp," Victoria said, sliding the strap of her satchel over her shoulders. "I've never been in it myself, but as I've heard it explained, there is simply no sound once you are in the swamp."

"No sounds from animals, you mean," Kendra asked.

"No sound at all," Victoria said.

"Victoria's right," Nina said. "There's no sound from animals or trees or water or your footsteps or your voices or anything."

"Silence," Ben said. "Total silence."

"How do we communicate?" Nathan asked.

"Sign language?" Eleada suggested.

"Thanks to Victoria's father, we have something better than sign language," Alex said.

"Mumbling marbles," Victoria said with a proud smile as she held up her backpack.

It took a few minutes to distribute the mumbling marbles and explain to Eleada, Kendra, and Nathan how they worked. Alex and the rest of the Guild all had their own mumbling marbles, but Victoria had packed spares in her satchel when they left the Guild House. Her father had invented them to allow people to communicate over long distances without sound. He had also given them flavors.

"Sour apple," Nathan said with a frown as he took his marble from his mouth.

"Sorry, that's the last one," Victoria said. Alex could have sworn she smiled when she said it.

"Okay," Alex said as they all assembled at the edge of the swamp. "Beowulf will lead us in. Rafa and Kendra, could you change into birds and scout ahead?"

"Sure," Kendra said, beginning to glow and transform into a raven, her clothes morphing to accommodate her new shape.

"You'll learn to hesitate before volunteering," Rafael said as he glowed red. He popped his marble into his mouth and transformed into another large black raven. Kendra must have explained how to enchant his clothes, because they too changed shape and clung to his large bird body.

"Everyone, stay close," Alex said. "Ben and Clark, bring up the rear and watch where we came from. There's a lot of them and they could be waiting to ambush us. Ready?"

Alex waited a moment for anyone to say something, but when no one did, he bent down to Beowulf and patted the small dog on the head. "Go find 'em, boy."

Beowulf gave a low woof and trotted off toward the swamp. Alex didn't allow himself to hesitate. He had heard too many stories from his father about the dangers of the Silent Swamp. Esmeralda and the evil carnies only added to those dangers. If he had allowed himself to hesitate, he might have thought seriously about turning back. Or at least blowing the whistle around his neck that would call his mother and father to his side. He wanted to blow the whistle, but he wanted to wait until the presence of his parents would really help.

The journey into the swamp was gradual. With Beowulf in the lead, they passed through a narrow margin of slender trees giving way to a marshy field of tall, green reeds. The ground beneath their feet became soggier with each step until they passed out of the reeds and into the weeping willows, drooping maples, and water-logged oak trees of the actual swamp. As they moved through the trees, it became harder and harder to avoid the still and stagnant water surrounding them. Dry patches came farther apart, forcing them to wade through scum-covered water reaching up past their knees.

The disappearance of sound matched their pace through the swamp. It reminded Alex of slowly turning down the volume on a record player. Each step was quieter than the last. The more they trudged through the water, the less they could hear the splashing of their passage.

By the time Alex found himself waist deep in swamp water, he was completely deaf, save for the sound of his own heartbeat in his ears. Ahead of him, Beowulf paddled through the dark and murky water, his wide ears floating out to the side and rippling with the waves caused by each stroke of his small paws.

Alex looked back over his shoulder to find Victoria had accepted Nina and Daphne as riders on the back of her horse half. The water only came to the tops of Victoria's legs and would have been near the necks of Nina and Daphne. Clark had scooped up Ben, who now rode perched atop Clark's broad shoulders. Eleada had opted to stay on her feet in the water, although she walked with her bow held high to keep the string from getting damp. Nathan followed Eleada, looking as wet and uncomfortable as Alex felt.

At least the rainstorm had left them all so water-soaked that the swamp water was not a shock. While filthy, the water was actually fairly warm, likely the result of the unnaturally hot weather of the past few days. However, the stench of rotting vegetation made the slog unpleasant. Alex looked up into the sky and saw Rafael and Kendra circling above as ravens and felt a pang of envy. He couldn't wait to get dry again.

Looking down, he saw his hands. His fingers had become fleshy, brown prunes. Getting dry was nothing that would happen soon. After twenty minutes of silently splashing through the swamp with not even the sound of his own breath in his ears, Alex suddenly heard a voice in his head.

"Mar moo shmur mat mog mows mhere me's mowing?"

The voice sounded like Eleada. He looked back at her and gave her a thumbs-up sign. She rolled her eyes. He took the opportunity to smile at Victoria, because he knew she would smile back and it would brighten his mood. She did and his mood responded instantly. Unfortunately, looking at Victoria meant he was not looking where he was wading through the swamp.

He turned around to see a large snake head staring at him as it floated on the water's surface. His good mood faded fast. Almost as fast as the snake snapped forward, diving down into the water and wrapping around his legs. Alex had only a moment to reach down and grapple with the snake before it pulled him from his feet and down into the black swamp water.

Underwater, Alex kicked at the snake, grabbing it below the neck with both hands and squeezing tight. Even as he did so, half a dozen mangled voices assaulted his head.

"Melp, melp!"

"Makes! Makes!"

"Mare mall mover mu mace!"

215

Alex held his breath as he held on to the snake's neck, its head whipping about as it slowly lost strength. Just as Alex was certain he could hold his breath no longer, the snake abated its attack and relaxed its hold on Alex's legs.

Alex stood up, still holding the reptile by the neck and gasping for air, struck by the silence of his struggle with the snake even as the sounds of his friend's jumbled voices bombarded his head. He gasped again as he saw the entire party was under attack by snakes. Hundreds of snakes. The water churned with the battle between the snakes as they emerged from the swamp and attempted to bite Alex's friends and pull them under.

Alex watched as the heads of two large snakes wrapped around Eleada's waist and dragged her down. Even under attack, she had the presence of mind to hold her bow above the surface of the swamp water. Ben sat on Clark's shoulders and loosed an arrow into a snake's head as a clutch of the reptiles wound around Clark's legs and tried to pull him under.

Beowulf had transformed into his larger, grizzly bear size, and had two snake necks in his massive jaws, thrashing them back and forth. Victoria and Nathan were dancing in the water, attempting to knock the snakes away with their hooves. Victoria raised her hands at a large snake curling up before her and flame suddenly erupted from her palms, engulfing the snake's head. The last thing Alex saw before three snakes twirled around his ankles and pulled him beneath the water was Nathan copying Victoria's attack on the snakes near his own legs.

As Alex struggled beneath the water with the snakes, several thoughts struggled for dominance in his mind. The first was that he needed to get above the surface of the water soon because he had not had time to grab more than a fleeting breath when the snakes had pulled him down. The second was that Victoria and Nathan were the group's only hope of survival. They were the only ones who could perform magic without speaking the words aloud.

Alex had managed to perform magic with only his thoughts when he had saved himself from being drowned in the Azure River by the runaway bicycle, but that had been a simple spell. Creating enough fire to combat the snakes would take far more concentration. Attempting that level of concentration would be a sure way to end up drowned by snakes.

The third thought was how odd it was he had not seen the tail of a single snake in the entire attack. This led to a fourth thought, really more of a memory, that right as they had been attacked, he had seen a tree that did not look at all like the others they had passed, its bark a deep, scaly black.

Alex held one hand around the neck of a snake and used his free hand to pull his pocketknife from his pants, opening it one-handed to slash at the second snake's head that menaced him. The blade made contact, thick, black blood oozing from the snake's hide. Both snakes pulled back momentarily, allowing Alex to surface, spitting fetid water from his mouth even as he used his teeth to hold onto the mumbling marble.

"Ma mlack mree!" Alex mumbled into the marble, trying to gesture with the knife in his hand toward Victoria and Nathan that they should attack the large, leafless black tree at their side. They were still flashing flames from their hands at individual snakes surfacing from the dark water.

Nina and Daphne were clinging to Victoria's horse back as snakes pulled at their waists. In the air above, Alex glimpsed two small dragons, one red and one blue, belching flame at the rippling water. Rafael and Kendra had been able to change form to assist in the defense against the snakes.

"Ma mlack mree miss ma makes. Ma makes mar ma mlack mree."

As the snakes around him redoubled their attack and dragged him once again into the water, Alex hoped Victoria and Nathan had been able to interpret his hasty and garbled pleas. As he thrashed and fought with the snakes holding him in the muddied swamp water, Alex could make out the stone gray clouds above. He could hear his heart pounding in his ears while his mind filled with the frantic and largely unintelligible voices of his friends shouting as they fought off the snakes.

For a moment, he was certain it would be the last and final sound he ever heard as his lungs gave way against the powerful muscles of the snakes squeezing at his chest and air burst from his

217

mouth. Then clouds of tangerine and ruby-tinted fire filled the sky above the water. A moment later, the snakes were gone.

Alex staggered to his feet to see Victoria and Nathan assaulting the black snake-tree with walls of flame even as Rafael and Kenda belched fire into the tree's branches from above. Hundreds of snake-roots writhed in the water, their mouths open in silent shrieks of pain.

The group needed no signal to know what to do. They ran, Victoria and Nathan shooting steams of fire over their shoulders as they fled, Rafael and Kendra continuing the assault the snake-tree and covering the group's escape. When the snake-tree was several hundred yards away, Alex and the others finally stopped and gathered around.

"*Mi mate makes,*" Victoria said through the magic marble voice in Alex's head.

"*Memusa's magots,*" Daphne said. "*Mat mas mlose.*"

"*Mow mid moo mink mov ma mree?*" Eleada asked, wringing swamp water from her hair.

"*Muck,*" Alex said. It had been luck. But it had also cost them more time. Now they would need more luck to find Esmeralda before she and other carnies could find the sword. "*Me mould mo,*" Alex said. "*Me mon't mave much mime.*"

The others nodded and they resumed their trek through the swamp. Nina and Daphne once again took their places on Victoria's horse back while Ben climbed up to Clark's shoulders. Beowulf remained in his bear-sized form as he continued to lead them through the swamp. Alex no longer cared how wet he was. Wet was fine as long as he could breath. They all kept a watchful eye on the water for any more signs of snakes, and avoided the vicinity of any tree that looked like its bark might be even a little scaly.

Alex was beginning to lose hope of ever catching up to Esmeralda, Mr. Apollo, and the evil carnies when Beowulf stopped and held still, gesturing with his nose toward a small clump of trees with knarred roots and wilted branches. The dog only paused a moment, long enough for Alex to see where it was going, then it paddled forward again. As they approached the cluster of trees, Alex could discern movement from within and between them. He motioned to the others to take cover as they approached, moving from tree to tree, as they came closer to the spot where Beowulf led them.

Alex held up his hand for the others to stop as he reached down and placed his hand on Beowulf's collar and halted the dog's hunt. An outer ring of knotted trees circled a single gigantic tree in the center. Around this tree, Alex could see four people — Esmeralda, Mr. Apollo, and the two Siren Sisters, Medea and Elektra.

Esmeralda and Mr. Apollo were hacking at the tree with long daggers, digging into the meat of the tree's trunk, one soundless blow at a time. Alex could not see what they were digging at, but he saw something green and glittery behind the blades of the daggers. Mr. Apollo stopped and pulled at something within the trunk of the tree, straining as he heaved at it. Then the thing was free and Alex could see what it was as Mr. Apollo turned to show it to Esmeralda.

The Sword of Silas.

Nearly four feet long and encased in a rusted metal sheath with rotted leather straps dangling down, the hilt of the blade held a large emerald stone gleaming even in the dull light of the heavily clouded sky. Lord Elvodar's vassal had hid the sword well, apparently strapping it to the bark of a young tree and allowing the trunk to grow around it over time, eventually hiding the sword from any who might seek it out. It made Alex wonder how Esmeralda had managed to find it so easily. It was a conundrum, but one he did not have time to contemplate.

Alex turned to the others, gesturing for them to spread out in a ring. He pointed to Victoria and Nathan, pantomiming with his hands to indicate fire, and then spreading his hands out to show them to circle and attack from opposite sides. He gave similar silent instructions to Eleada and Ben. It was actually easier than trying to communicate with the mumbling marbles.

Alex and the others moved quickly to take up positions around the stand of trees as Esmeralda withdrew the sword from its sheath. Alex was unsure what the Dark Spirit Mage was intending until he saw her swing the sword at one of the nearby trees. The blade was far too big and weighty for Esmeralda to wield with anything like grace or composure, but she could manage to swing it in a wide and wavering arc that bit into the bark of the tree with considerable force.

As the bark of the tree and then the tree itself dissolved into ash around the edge of the blade, Alex knew what Esmeralda was doing. She was testing the sword. Making sure it was the Sword of Destruction she sought. As the large tree rapidly turned to ash and collapsed into the shallow waters of the swamp, Alex saw a wide smile break out across Esmeralda's face. It chilled his heart.

Alex glanced around at his companions and they greeted him with similar looks of distress. He turned back to Esmeralda and waited until she had resheathed the sword before he motioned with his hands to begin the attack. Fire erupted from either side of the clump of trees as two arrows flashed through the air, one striking Mr. Apollo in the leg and the other ripping through Esmeralda's arm.

Alex splashed through the water toward Esmeralda and Mr. Apollo as Beowulf bounded ahead of him. Victoria and Nathan surrounded the trees in flames as Ben and Eleada loosed two more arrows.

Esmeralda and Mr. Apollo hid behind one of the trees as the Siren Sisters, Elektra and Medea, hid behind another. Alex wasn't sure how the next part of this plan was going to work. It was vague in his mind. Somehow, he had to convince Esmeralda and Mr. Apollo to relinquish the sword. How he was going to get them to release a sword that could destroy anything it touched was the vague part.

Esmeralda made a gesture toward Elektra and Medea as Alex reached into his shirt and withdrew the whistle his father and mother had given him. Maybe he and the others didn't need to convince Esmeralda and Mr. Apollo to give up the sword by themselves. Maybe they needed to hold them captive long enough for his parents and reinforcements from the town to arrive. *How long would that take?* Alex thought as he placed the whistle to his lips.

As he started to blow the whistle, a sound miraculously pierced his mind, a sound so hideous and overpowering, he immediately released the whistle to fall back around his neck as he clamped his hands on his ears.

The sound in his head ripped through his mind and tore at his brain, like something wild and vicious digging into his skull — dying animals screaming in pain as metal scraped against stone and a thousand misshapen bells all rang at once. The soundless sound erased all ability to think or react.

Alex could see the sound had an identical effect on the others. They had stopped their assault and were clutching at their heads in a vain attempt to stifle the agonizing noise assaulting them. Even Beowulf shook his head in pain, unable to cover his ears.

Alex could barely stay on his feet with the excruciating wail stabbing into his head. As he watched, the Siren Sisters, Elektra and Medea stepped out from behind the trees to face Alex and the others. Their mouths were open, seemingly in song. Behind them, Esmeralda was helping Mr. Apollo limp away from the trees and back into the swamp. For some reason, they seemed unaffected by the mental shrieks of the Siren Sisters.

They were getting away and Alex could do nothing to stop them. He could barely breathe under the strain of the noiseless screeching in his mind. Somehow, the Siren Sisters' magically melodious voices became warped and transformed by the Silent Swamp into banshee-like howls that, while not carried through the air as sound, could nonetheless shatter the minds of those nearby.

Alex watched through tear-blurred eyes as Esmeralda and Mr. Apollo ran through the swamp behind the Siren Sisters, past a huddled Eleada and an immobilized Nathan. The Siren Sisters could choose whom their voices would normally affect and this skill remained intact in the magical environs of the swamp.

Just as Alex began to think he would pass out from the splitting pain in his head, he looked up to see two dark shapes hurtling from the sky. He blinked tears from his eyes and stared as the two speeding shapes struck the Siren Sisters, one apiece.

Blissful silence.

Alex took a deep breath and shook his head to clear it from the remnants of the Siren Sisters' searing song. As he looked toward the clump of trees that had sheltered the Siren Sisters, he saw them each floating unconscious in the swamp water. Two dragons, one sapphire, one cobalt, flapped above them, reaching down with long talons to drag the women from the water before they could drown.

"Manks," Alex said via the magical marble in his mouth as he stepped over to take Elektra, or was it Medea, from Rafael's claws.

"Monly ming me muould mink muv," Rafael said with a flick of his dragon tail.

"My med murts," Nina said, hands still covering her ears.

"Mow mhat mo me moo?" Victoira asked as she grabbed the other twin siren and held her while Clark removed a length of twine from his knapsack and began binding her arms.

"Mag mem," Daphne said, shoving a handkerchief from her pocket into the mouth of one of the twins and securing it with a length of twine. Eleada swiftly did the same with the other twin. Alex noticed neither handkerchief looked particularly clean, but he didn't mention it. The very least the Siren Sisters deserved were snotty handkerchiefs in their mouths, even if they were under the influence of Esmeralda's Dark Spirit Magic.

"Mhat's miss?" Nina said, pulling a large sheet of scorched paper from the surface of the water.

"Mooks mike ma map," Alex said as he helped Nina hold the creased parchment up to examine it. The size of a newspaper, burn marks blackened the edges of the map. Flames appeared to have punched right through several places in the middle of the paper, likely by the fires Victoria and Nathan had created.

The map looked like it represented part of the Rune Valley. Looking more closely, Alex saw the lines depicting the Dead Forest and the Silent Swamp waver and shift, flickering to a view of the entire Rune Valley, and then back to a closer representation of the swamp. Alex knew what the map was and how Esmeralda had found the Sword of Silas.

He carefully folded up what was left of the map and turned to the others.

"Mhow moo me mrack mem?" Nathan said, frowning. He clearly didn't like sounding like an idiot as the magic marble mangled his speech.

"Me moant mave mo," Alex said. *"Me mow mer may mar mowing. Me must mave mo met mar mirst."*

Alex was thankful everyone seemed to know where he was talking about. There was only one place Esmeralda and Mr. Apollo would be headed now they had the Sword of Silas — the Shadow Wraith's prison cave on the side of the Black Bone Mountains.

Chapter Twenty-Three
Mountain Melee

Alex was thankful for many things — being out of the Silent Swamp and free from its tomb-like silence and stench — the wind at the back of the speeding truck drying him off for the first time in hours — no longer needing to speak with a marble in his mouth mashing his words into unrecognizable mush — standing next to Victoria and feeling the warmth of her hand next to his on the wooden railing of the truck bed, and most importantly, that his friends would be beside him when he reached the cave to deal with Esmeralda and Mr. Apollo.

They had raced to beat Esmeralda and Mr. Apollo from the swamp, but had been too slow. As Alex and the others ran from the edge of the swamp and the sounds of the world returned to their ears, the first thing they heard was the roar of a motorcycle engine.

By the time they reached the dirt farm path near the swamp, they could see a trail of dust from the fleeing motorcycle nearly two miles ahead of them. This would not have been such a problem if they had not needed to run nearly a mile in the opposite direction to reach the place where they had left the old Dodge truck.

Eleada once again at the wheel, the Siren Sisters firmly gagged and tied to the side of the truck bed, they raced after the motorcycle dwindling into the distance. Nina and Daphne sat in the front seat to advise Eleada on the shortest route to the base of the Black Bone Mountains where the Shadow Wraith's prison-cave resided. Beowulf rode with his head out the window, long ears fluttering in the wind.

Rafael and Kendra opted to remain in the form of dragons and clung to the top forward rail of the truck bed, wings clutched to their sides, necks stretched out, enjoying the speed and the wind. Nathan,

Ben, and Clark stood behind Alex, holding on to the truck rails as it bounced over the old farm trail.

It wasn't long before they came upon the dirt road they had ridden along only days before, when they had left the Dead Forest, and not long after that before they crossed the main East Road leading into town and out of the Rune Valley. Eleada took a sharp right turn at the main road and then a quick left turn not half a mile later. This was a more direct road leading to a different path up the mountain than the one Esmeralda and Mr. Apollo were following.

Alex tried to relax even in the mounting tension of anticipation. He didn't know what was coming next, but he knew he had to beat Esmeralda to the cave. If she could enter the cave with that sword…

He felt a warmth on his hand and looked down to see Victoria's hand clasped gently around his own. This eased the tension in his mind about the cave, but replaced it with a different sort of tension. Now, Alex found himself worrying about what would happen to Victoria at the cave. What would happen to all his friends in the Guild and his sister and the new friends from the carnival who had already risked their lives at his side? Alex looked up into Victoria's eyes and she smiled. Alex smiled back and forgot his worries for a moment. How could he worry when Victoria was smiling?

"Was it a map to the sword?" Victoria asked, nodding to the map he had tucked into the belt of his pants.

"Kind of," Alex said. "It's called the Questing Map. It's a magical map that can show you where anything is. The mage who created it used it to hunt for gold in the Copper Blood Mountains. It was stolen from the town museum about thirty years ago. It's a very famous story in town history. It seems somebody has been hiding it in the vaults at the bank the whole time."

"When did you say was the last time the carnival was in town?" Victoria asked.

"Thirty years ago," Alex said, seeing the connection now that Victoria had mentioned it. "Esmeralda would have been in the carnival at that time, as a teenage girl."

"Do you think she could have been under the influence of the Shadow Wraith all that time?" Victoria said, her nose wrinkling in disgust at the thought.

"I don't know," Alex said, thinking about it. "Maybe someone was influencing her when she was young the way she's been influencing the other carnies now."

"Like an apprentice to evil," Victoria said.

"Whoever it was, thanks to them we might have a chance of finding the Rune Tree using this map," Alex said, patting the map with his free hand.

"The map looked badly burnt," Victoria said. "Do you think it will still work?"

"It's got to work at least as well as showing drawings to Beowulf," Alex said.

They were quiet for a moment, Alex reveling in the feeling the wind on his face and Victoria's hand on his. Now would be a good time to lean over and kiss her. If they weren't surrounded by their friends on the back of the truck. If Nathan wasn't lurking five feet away. Why was it so hard to find a good time for kissing?

"Do you have a plan for when we get to the cave?" Victoria asked.

"Keep Esmeralda from getting that sword into the Shadow Wraith's prison chamber," Alex said.

"Ah," Victoria said. "We're improvising. I like improvising. Sometimes it's easier that way. Fewer things to remember. I tried learning to play the violin for nearly a year, but I simply couldn't follow all the notes. I kept wanting add some in. Drove my teacher batty. Daddy says it's because I don't have a linear mind. I think it's because the songs in my head sounded better than the ones I was trying to learn."

Alex stared up into Victoria's blazing blue eyes. Now he really wanted to kiss her. "Maybe you can play for me sometime," he said instead.

"Oh, well, I suppose so," Victoria said, suddenly blushing. "I haven't practiced in ages."

"I'd love to hear the songs in your head," Alex said, finding his face felt as hot as Victoria's looked.

They smiled and gazed silently into each other's eyes. Then the truck hit a large rut in the road and they bounced into the air, jostling against each other. They smiled and looked ahead, down the road the

226

truck raced along. Victoria's hand squeezed Alex's a little tighter where he held the wooden railing.

Up ahead, Alex could see the Black Bone Mountains, and off to the east, the White Forest. There was still smoke rising out of the depths of the woods, but the rain clouds that had been pouring down over the town seemed to have drifted over the forest and quenched the fire. Alex wondered if that had been Batami's doing or the work of Maybelle Merriweather, the town weather witch. Either way, it had probably saved the forest from being entirely consumed by the flames. Alex wondered how Batami was doing.

He could see scorched and blackened trees at the edge of the forest, but it was hard to gauge how much damage had been done. The forest would take years to recover. Alex knew Batami would likely take just as many years to heal from the fire. He thought about slipping into his astral form to check on her, but the truck was very closer to the base of the mountains and getting closer every second. Eleada did not believe in driving at any speed but recklessly fast, regardless of the quality of the road. As long as the forest had survived, Alex knew Batami had, as well.

A minute later, the truck came to a brake-screeching, tire-sliding, halt at the base of the Black Bone Mountains. Alex and the others quickly disembarked from the truck, jumping to the ground as Rafael and Kendra, in dragon form, took to the air.

"Fly ahead and see if you can spot them," Alex said, craning his neck back to shout up at Rafael and Kendra. "But don't let them see you. This path is quicker than the one they took. We might be able to catch up with them."

"Right," Rafael said as he and Kendra flapped their leathery wings wide and flew over the tops of the trees.

"This way, everybody," Alex said, heading for a deer path at the edge of the woods near where the dirt trail had ended. The others formed a line behind him and followed.

Alex ran up the deer path at a fast jog. They needed to move quickly, but it wouldn't do any good to arrive before Esmeralda and Mr. Apollo if they were too exhausted to confront them.

The path they ran along up the side of the mountain was different from the one they had used back in the spring when Alex had first fallen into the cave that held the entrance to the Shadow Wraith's subterranean prison door. From the trail of dust left behind by their motorcycle, Alex knew Esmeralda and Mr. Apollo had taken the path closer to town. The path Alex and his friends followed was closer to the White Forest and would cut considerable time from their assent up the side of the mountain. He hoped it would be enough time.

As he ran, Alex dug into his shirt and withdrew the magic whistle his parents had given him. He had been waiting for the right time to blow the whistle and call his parents to his side. Calling them now would give them his general location and that would be enough to warn them of where he was ultimately going. He blew the whistle. Not loud. He knew the magic that would tug at the sister whistles around his parents' necks did not rely on the volume of sound the whistle made.

"A whistle to warn them we're coming?" Eleada said from right behind him. She ran quietly and easily through the woods, bow in hand, quiver strapped tight to her back.

"To call for backup," Alex said.

"Magic whistles to call our parents," Nina said, pulling her whistle out of her shirt to show Eleada.

"Hyperion's hiccups," Daphne said, running behind Eleada. "Alex is calling for help before there's a fight."

"Yikes," Ben said, his short legs pumping to keep pace. "That's a bad omen."

"Hmm, maybe Alex is finally listening to his parents' advice," Clark said, ducking beneath a low-hanging tree branch.

"Calling for help is very prudent," Victoria said, dashing around a tree. "Let's not discourage it by teasing him."

"I'm actually listening to Batami's advice," Alex said, thinking back to his mentor's words the day before.

"Help is all very good, but where is this cave?" Nathan said, sounding as though he might dash ahead alone. Alex could see from the look on Nathan's face he was concerned for Leanna's safety. They must be good friends, Alex thought to himself.

"We'll be there soon enough," Alex said, glancing up the mountain path and trying to calculate how long it would take them to reach their destination. A few minutes later, when they were about two thirds of the way to the cave, a small, blue dragon swooped out of the air. Rafael.

"We found them," Rafael said, wing flapping to hold him steady, "but Esmeralda and Mr. Apollo took the motorcycle half way up the mountain path. They're almost there. Kendra stayed behind to keep an eye on them."

"Gorping gorp guzzlers," Daphne cursed.

"You can say that twice," Eleada said, leaning forward as she increased her speed.

"Faster, everyone," Alex said, breaking into a full run as the sound of multiple explosions shook the air. More explosions followed and the mountain beneath their feet trembled.

"That can't be good," Victoria said, turning her head toward the sound of the explosions.

"Explosions are never good when we're around," Rafael said, flapping his dragon wings harder to rise above the trees.

"Find out what's happening," Alex shouted to Rafael. The cobalt-colored dragon nodded his head and disappeared behind the tops of the conifers.

"What do you think it is?" Nina asked, nervousness raising the pitch of her voice. "Maybe their blasting into the cave, or maybe they are trying to start an avalanche to crush us, or maybe they're using the sword on the rune seal in the Shadow Wrath's prison already."

"We'll find out in a few seconds," Alex said, trying not to let Nina's imagination infect his already expanding fears. It wasn't that Nina's imagination was wild and impossible. The opposite was true. Any of the things she suggested could be happening and all of them were bad. Alex wouldn't know what was happening until he reached the clearing around the cave. He ran faster as Clark picked up Ben and Victoria swung Daphne and Nina onto her back.

Rafael never returned to them and the explosive vibrations on the mountainside only got louder the closer they came to the clearing. Alex dashed off the thin deer trail and between the trees as he ran up the side of the mountain. When he came to a stop at the edge of the grassy clearing around the old cave, he gasped as much for breath as for what he saw before him — a battle of magical might consumed the little forest glade. It took Alex a moment to gather it all in and understand what he saw.

A tornado of wind whipped around the clearing and the ground rumbled and quaked. Large trees had been felled and stacked around the entrance of the cave, creating a tall, fort-like barrier. Behind this wall stood both of his parents, Victoria's father, and Deputy Dervis. His parents were casting blinding bolts of blue and red magical energy from their long wooden staves while Deputy Dervis sent rocks hurtling through the air like missiles, and Victoria's father lobbed grenade-like balls over the walls.

On the other side of the wall, facing the cave, Esmeralda and Mr. Apollo fought beside half a dozen carnies, fending off the magical onslaught arrayed against them and returning one of their own. George the giant hurled large boulders over the barricade of logs while, beside him, Oanadin the dwarf created a wall of fire, igniting the leaves and bark of the fallen trees in a smoky blaze. A thick layer of black soot covered their torn clothes. Sweat and charcoal smeared their faces. Alex had a very good idea who had started the fire in the White Forest.

There were at least four others Alex recognized from his time spent carousing in the carnival. He watched as they each cast magic of fire and energy at his parents, Victoria's father, and Deputy Dervis.

To one side, Alex caught sight of Leanna, calling down shafts of lightning from above. In the sky over the clearing, Rafael and Kendra dodged lightning bolts even as they spewed jets of flame at the evil carnies.

Esmeralda and Mr. Apollo ducked behind a large outcropping of rock as a blast of blue energy from Alex's father's stave struck the ground nearby. A baseball-sized grenade thrown by Victoria's father hit the ground beside Mr. Apollo and exploded, engulfing the Dark Mage in a tangle of net-like webbing.

"What's the plan?" Eleada said, slipping up beside Alex. He blinked and breathed deep. So much was happening so fast, he had almost let himself get overwhelmed by the moment.

"Attack from behind," Alex said. "Focus on Esmeralda. Ignore the others. We have to stop her from using that sword."

Even as Alex spoke the words, he saw Esmeralda wrap something slender around her waist and race for the barrier of trees, the sheathed Sword of Silas in her hands. As he watched, Esmeralda wavered in the sun like a desert mirage and then vanished through the trunks of the fallen trees. She had used Victoria's father's Wall Walking Belt to run right through the rubble of rocks encasing the cave entrance. In seconds, she would be racing down the spiral tunnel to the chamber holding the rune-seal of the Shadow Wraith's prison.

"Themis's toe jam," Daphne yelped. "That crazy belt really works."

"I keep telling you, Daddy's inventions always work," Victoria said with exasperation. "Even when it was best if they didn't."

"Ideas?" Ben said, peering around a tree at the battle in the clearing. "What we should do?"

"We need to fight them," Nathan said, hooves stamping the ground. "We can't sit here."

"Fighting them doesn't stop Esmeralda," Eleada said, sliding an arrow from her quiver and knocking it in the string of her bow.

"Hmm, and we risk hurting them while they're under her control," Clark added, shielding his eyes from the glare of a lightning bolt striking a rock not far away.

"There's only one way," Alex said, looking at his friends.

"That's totally and completely stupid," Nina said with a frown. "But stupid is all we've got." She stepped up on her toes and gave Alex a kiss on the cheek. "Don't be too stupid."

"What's stupid?" Nathan asked, looking around at the others for an explanation. "What are they talking about?"

"Alex is going inside the cave," Victoria said, stepping beside Alex as he laid down on the pine needles beneath the trees.

"How?" Eleada said, glaring over her shoulder at Alex. "By taking a nap?"

"Something like that," Alex said with a weak smile. "Attack from behind, anyway. Keep the carnies distracted until I get back. Make sure they don't hurt our parents. Victoria?"

"I'll watch over you," Victoria said, taking up a position beside Alex. There was no time to explain to Nathan and Eleada what he planned to do. No time even to think about it. Every second was a second that brought Esmeralda closer to freeing the Shadow Wraith. A second closer to destroying the world.

As Alex closed his eyes, the last thing he saw was Eleada raising her bow and drawing back the string, the knocked arrow bursting into a blaze of blue fire as she let it fly. *No wonder Ben likes her*, Alex thought.

Alex exhaled, pushing out the worries and fears fighting for control of his mind and assumed his astral form. A moment later, he willed himself to the place where he had hoped he would never have to go again — the chamber beneath the mountain containing one of the Shadow Wraith's twelve prison doors.

Chapter Twenty-Four
Astral Assault

Alex appeared in astral form in the center of the circular chamber carved from the granite at the heart of the mountain. The space was empty, but not entirely dark. Thousands of runes etched into the smooth walls of the cavern glowed with a faint golden hue, amplified slightly as they met in the center of the wall to form the final rune of spirit-sealing holding the Shadow Wraith trapped in a prison between the realms of existence.

Alex had no time to contemplate the runes or relive the memories flooding his mind of the last time he had been in the chamber and what he and his friends had faced. He was without his friends, but he was no longer alone. Shimmering, as though made of gauzy light, Esmeralda walked through the solid iron door at the back of the room. She glanced around, a look of worry momentarily flickering across her face. Then she laughed. It was the same laugh Alex had heard when she had tried to trap his soul-essence in Pandora's Box.

"I can sense you, Revenant, but you are too late," Esmeralda said, a vicious smile on her face. "The true Lord comes again, and there is nothing you can do. Except join him."

Alex floated to position himself between Esmeralda and the large rune of spirit-sealing inscribed in the wall as she flipped the clasp at the center of the wide metal and leather belt around her waist. The belt fell to the floor and Esmeralda's body became fully solid once again. She took a step toward Alex and the rune seal, clumsily unsheathing the sword. The blade was nearly three feet long and unwieldy even with both of her hands.

"Prepare to bow down before the All Supreme Shadow, or be destroyed when it is loosed," Esmeralda said as she raised the sword up above her head and lunged forward.

Alex had no plan, could see no rational means of success. So, he followed his instincts. He improvised. Speaking a series of rune words with his mind, he called forth all the astral energy he could command and channeled it through his own soul-essence at his heart center.

Like the light of a noonday sun amplified and focused through a magnifying glass, a beam of blazing luminescent white energy burst forth from Alex's chest and blasted into Esmeralda's own soul-essence at her heart.

Esmeralda staggered back as the iridescent astral energy from Alex's soul-essence bore into the center of her being. She screamed and her face flushed with rage.

"You do not possess the power to stop me, child," Esmeralda shouted. "But I have it in my power to annihilate you."

A thick shaft of onyx-colored energy roared forth from Esmeralda's heart center and slammed into Alex, enshrouding his soul-essence in a swirl of dark, noxious power. Alex reeled and screamed within his mind. The astral energy cast through Esmeralda's dark soul-essence struck at Alex's own being in wave after wave of malignant power. It was like being drowned in an ocean turned putrid and vile from the flesh of a billion of rotting corpses.

Some part of Alex's mind knew this power could not come from Esmeralda alone — there was only one source of such degenerate spirit energy. But how was she able to touch it, much less use it against him? And how long could he hold out against it? Alex still cast a clear white blaze of energy from his heart-center into Esmeralda, but she seemed far less affected by it than before. She righted herself and once again raised the sword above her head.

"Now you perish for all time," Esmeralda shouted. "There will be no more Revenants."

Esmeralda took a step forward, as though leaning into the gale of some tumultuous storm. Alex could feel her dark energy pressing him backward. Back into the large rune engraved in the wall. What would happen to him, to his soul-essence, under the pressure of

Esmeralda's dark energy when she breached the seal of the rune with the Sword of Silas? Would he be thrust into the prison realm between worlds? Is that what Esmeralda had meant by her words?

Alex began to panic. There was nothing he could do to stop her. He wasn't strong enough. The end was inevitable if he could not think of some way to thwart Esmeralda soon. But he had run out of plans, and the space of mind he might need to improvise was consumed with warding off the dark astral energy threatening to devour him.

Esmeralda took another step closer, her long, curly red hair flying around her head like some misshapen and malevolent halo. Her eyes were wide with a rage bordering on righteousness, her teeth bared in a wolfish grin of triumph.

Wolfish. It made Alex think of a wolf he knew. Why hadn't he thought of that before? She had told him he needed to ask for help. He had been trying to heed that lesson.

As Esmeralda took yet another step forward, Alex dedicated a part of his mind to shouting for help from the one person who might be able to save him.

"I can see you, Child," Batami said in his mind, *"but I am too weak to come to your aid."*

"I need your help," Alex pleaded in his mind as he watched Esmeralda take one more step closer to him, and the rune-seal, and his doom.

"You must force her to see your true heart-self," Batami said, her voice fading away.

Esmeralda was right before him now, right before the wall, and she raised the sword back for its inevitable swing toward the rune-seal. Alex saw in that briefest of moments the truth of Batami's words — he had been shielding himself against the warped spirit energy Esmeralda flung at him, when instead he needed to open himself to her, to shine upon her the full nature and depth of his own soul-essence.

Alex reached out to Esmeralda's soul-essence with his own, embracing it with the entirety of his being, the very core of his true-self, the quintessence of his existence — love. He focused on this incandescent blaze of love and radiated into Esmeralda's heart-center.

Esmeralda froze, blinking as she bathed in the glorious light that had once been her own true light. She gasped, her dark spirit energy dissipating with the shock of what she was experiencing. It was an experience mirrored by Alex as he saw how Esmeralda's once pure nature had been slowly corrupted and twisted like a strong and vibrant tree brought down gradually by a malicious blight.

Alex realized two things in that moment. In his true heart, his primal soul-essence, he loved Esmeralda and would always love her for the woman she had once been, the girl who had once held such joy within her heart. A girl on a beach, laughing as the waves broke against tiny legs. Waves and tears and sunsets and smiles and footprints in the sand.

Alex also realized he could not change, in a few moments, the nature of Esmeralda's soul-essence. It had taken decades to become warped and distorted. Seconds would not save her. There were tears in Esmeralda's eyes and her face looked stricken as she spoke.

"Please."

It was only one word, but Alex knew its full import of what she was asking. If he had been in his physical body, there would have been tears in his eyes as well. In astral form, he could only feel a deep ache where his heart would be.

Something wailed dimly in his mind, something he recognized as an echo of the Shadow Wraiths' soul-destroying voice. Esmeralda must have heard it, as well, because she blinked and straightened herself. Alex had no more time. He could not defeat Esmeralda in a battle of Spirit Magic. He had been wrong to try.

She held his gaze a moment more, tears and gratitude in her eyes, and then, as he watched, she let her fingers slip from the hilt of the sword, the long, bright blade falling back to strike her firmly in the shoulder.

Esmeralda cried out in shock and pain as the sword's blade pierced her flesh, but her cries vanished abruptly as her body rapidly transformed to ash and disintegrated.

The ash that had been Esmeralda, only a moment before, swirled around the room as Alex magically gathered the air and used it to cradle the sword before it could fall to the floor of the cavern. Alex spoke more rune-words for gravity and motion and pulled the sheath from the back of the room, carefully sliding the sword into it. He then magically pulled Victoria's father's Wall Walking Belt and wrapped it around the sword. The sword shimmered as though seen though the heat rising off a blacktop road in summer.

Alex turned and used the air of the room to coax the ash that had once been Esmeralda and settle it to the floor of the chamber. He then gently used the air to gather it all into one small pile in the center of the room. It was not a proper burial, but it was the best he could do. Esmeralda had wanted to free the Shadow Wraith and now she would be interred with it forever. Had he not seen how pure her heart had once been, how pure it might one day have been again, Alex might have found it ironic. Instead, he only felt sadness.

"You have succeeded," Batami's voice said in his mind.

"Are you okay?" Alex thought in his mind to Batami's disembodied voice, trying not to think about what he had succeeded in doing.

"Thanks to you, I will have time to recover. Come to me when you can."

Alex felt Batami's presence fade. He looked around the chamber one more time, staring at the pile of ash that had been Esmeralda. It was hard to feel triumphant, knowing he had succeeded only because Esmeralda had chosen to take her own life at the last moment instead of freeing the Shadow Wraith. It did not really help knowing she had made that choice because Alex had helped her see who she might have become, instead of who she was.

Turning away, Alex mentally spoke the rune words for motion and gravity once more and pulled the sword behind him as he floated though the iron door of the chamber and left it behind for what he hoped was the last time.

He did not bother following the spiral tunnel up through the mountain, instead opting to pass straight through the rock itself. It was an odd sensation to pass through something so consistently dense in astral form, but the feeling did not last long and Alex soon emerged into the sun above the grassy glade around the rubble-covered entrance of the cave.

He floated over the clearing, the passage through the air of the Sword of Silas drawing the attention of most of those present. The battle was over. The carnies who had been under the influence of Esmeralda's Dark Spirit Magic were either unconscious or looking around in dazed confusion. Alex saw Mr. Apollo, still covered in the sticky web of Victoria's father's magical grenade, on his knees, sobbing.

"How could she?" Alex heard Mr. Apollo moan. It seemed Mr. Apollo had been one of those under Esmeralda's malignant influence.

He watched as his parents used their magic staves to push the trees of their hastily constructed barricade apart and step out into the clearing, followed by Victoria's father and Deputy Dervis. Alex let the Sword of Silas slowly drift to the ground and land in front of his parents. They both sighed in relief as they looked at the sword and then the air around them.

Alex spun away and took in the rest of the scene on the mountainside.

Leanna wept, crouching next to Nathan, who lay on his side in the high grass, his face tight with pain. Nathan had his hand on her face, stoking her hair.

"I'm so sorry, I'm so sorry," Leanna repeated over and over. Drifting closer, Alex could see blistering burns covering one whole side of Nathan's horse half. As Alex floated past, Nathan leaned in and kissed Leanna.

Alex was shocked, but not as shocked as by what he saw next. Rafael and Kendra had remained in dragon form and sat on a large rock ledge, their dragon wings touching as the leathery lips of their dragon snouts met in a kiss.

"I've never kissed a dragon before," Alex heard Kendra say.

"You've probably never met a dragon worth kissing," Rafael replied.

"I've never kissed a griffin either," Kendra said.

"You poor thing," Rafael said, glowing red and transforming into a creature with the body of a lion and the wings and head of an eagle. Kendra laughed with glee as she glowed and transformed to match Rafael's form. Surprised and amused, Alex grinned inwardly in

238

admiration of Rafael's romantic courage, as he continued to drift over the mountain glade.

Not too far away, Ben and Eleada helped a wobbly Oanadin to his feet. They stared at Raphel and Kendra. Ben cocked his head, looked up at Eleada and then promptly climbed up an outcropping of rock until he was eye level with her.

"You clearly have more courage than brains, Dwarf," Eleada said, staring Ben in the eye.

"Chicken?" Ben said, staring back. "Are you saying you're afraid, Elf?"

"You are the strangest boy, I think I've ever met," Eleada said as she leaned toward Ben.

"Lucky for us, we both like strange," Ben said as their lips met.

Alex floated along, flabbergasted beyond words or thoughts by the daring actions of his friends in facing their infatuations.

Across the clearing, Alex saw Clark and Daphne standing side-by-side in silence. Clark looked down at her. She looked up at him. They both looked at Rafael and Kendra. Then back at each other. Then at Ben and Eleada.

"Cupid's cuspids," Daphne said, looking back up at Clark.

"Ah...well...mmm...that's...hmm..." Clark began to say as he gazed down at Daphne.

"If you're thinking about kissing me, Clark, think again," Daphne said with a frown.

"Ah...well...I was..." Clark started to say when Daphne interrupted him.

"I'm the brave one, remember," Daphne said as she grabbed Clark's shirt and yanked him down until he was bent nearly in half. Then she kissed him.

Alex's mind reeled. It was like watching a line of dominoes falling in some intricate pattern. The series of amorous events he witnessed so stunned him that he nearly slipped uncontrollably from his astral form. It felt like his inner understanding of the world was shifting and tumbling around him.

Nina stood not far away, smiling at the whole scene.

"Only an absolute idiot could not figure out how to kiss a girl after all that," Nina said, seemingly to no one but herself.

Alex looked to the trees at the edge of the clearing and saw where Victoria knelt down beside his body. He could see her gently stroking his face. Something large lay on the ground behind them.

Alex blinked open his eyes and sat up in his physical body, staring at Victoria and enjoying the feel of her hand still against his cheek.

"Oh, you're okay," Victoria said, her face lighting up with a dazzling smile Alex felt instinctually compelled to mimic. "I was so worried. You were gone so long. And you had tears in your eyes. And then the carnies seemed to realize you were a threat and started trying to attack you."

The massive shape behind her momentarily drew his attention. He realized it was the unconscious form of George the Giant.

"Thanks," Alex said, nodding toward George.

Victoria looked over her shoulder briefly. "I felt terrible about that, because he's normally so sweet, but I thought it might be better for both of us if he was unconscious for a while."

"You saved me again," Alex said, looking deeply into Victoria's ocean-blue eyes.

"You saved us all," Victoria said. "Again."

Alex was certain there was something romantic and witty he could say, but looking into Victoria's eyes, he seemed to have lost all power of speech. So, instead, he did what he knew he should have done weeks and months ago, but hadn't for reasons that now seemed impossible to comprehend. Alex leaned over and kissed Victoria. He felt his power of thought vanish as quickly as speech has evaded him moments before. A single notion remained and seemed to be all his mind could hold — kissing Victoria was the best thing in the world.

Alex wasn't sure how long the kiss lasted, but his powers of thought were returned to him as the sound of someone's throat insistently clearing continuously erupted from nearby. Finally, Alex could ignore the sound no longer and broke away from Victoria, looking up to see the source of the disturbance that had drawn him back from the little world he and Victoria had silently created between themselves.

"Mom!" Alex said, his power of speech returning more quickly than his thoughts. "Dad!"

"Daddy!" Victoria echoed beside Alex.

Alex's mother and father stood beside Victoria's father, all three of them standing awkwardly above Alex and Victoria. His father held the Sword of Silas in one hand.

"It seems a little victory has gone to everyone's heads," Alex's father said, gesturing toward the clearing where Clark was still bent over kissing Daphne, Ben still stood on a rock kissing Eleada, and Rafael and Kendra still traded kisses between transformations from one animal to the next. They glowed and turned into baby elephants as Alex looked back toward his parents.

"Or their lips, as the case may be," Victoria's father said, his blue eyes twinkling.

"Probably all well-deserved," Alex's mother said, pulling Alex up to his feet and into an embrace.

"I'm so glad you're safe," Victoria's father said as he helped her up and into his arms. "I was ever so worried you'd do something dangerous."

"Daddy, you're the one who was in the middle of the fighting," Victoria said.

"Yes, but everyone knows I'm prone to doing dangerous things," her father said. "I rely upon you to be the level-headed one in the family."

"Sounds like someone we know," Alex's father said, embracing Alex.

"An interesting match," his mother said.

"I was talking about you," his father said to his mother.

"So was I," his mother said with a grin.

"How did you all get here so fast?" Alex said. "I only blew the whistle when we reached the bottom of the mountain."

"That's how we knew to expect company," his father said.

"We headed here right after we checked the bank," his mother said. "We figured this was where they would eventually come and we hoped to stop them."

"Unfortunately, my Wall Walking Belt proved a bit too efficient," Victoria's father said. "I was certain it wouldn't work for anything as thick as the boulders blocking that cave."

"You're too smart for your own good sometimes, Daddy," Victoria said.

"Another comment that could be applied to someone else," Alex's father said.

"Not that we aren't glad you did whatever it was you did," Alex's mother said, "but we're supposed to be the ones who save you, not the other way around."

"He's too stupid for something that simple," Nina said, walking up and giving her brother hug. "But not too stupid for other things," she whispered as she nodded toward Victoria. Alex frowned.

"How did you stop Esmeralda?" Victoria said. "Is she still in that cave?"

"Forever," Alex said and slowly explained what had transpired after he entered the cave chamber and faced Esmeralda in her attempt to use the Sword of Silas to shatter the rune-seal holding the Shadow Wraith in its prison. When he was finished, the others were silent. Victoria reached out and took his hand.

"Seeing hard things does not need to make us hard people," his father said, placing a hand on Alex's shoulder and looking him in the eyes.

"Especially considering the alternative," his mother added, kissing his forehead.

"There was some small good in her after all," Victoria said, squeezing his hand.

"Very small," Nina said firmly.

"That may be so, but things are rarely ever so simple as that," Victoria's father said. "Her husband is devastated his wife betrayed him, but I'm sure he will be even more devastated when he learns of her death." They all turned to look at Mr. Apollo, still sobbing as several of the carnies tried to free him from the sticky web holding him fast.

"What are we going to do with this?" his mother said, staring at the sword in her husband's hands with a mixture of horror and fascination.

"Make sure it never touches anything again, I imagine," Victoria's father said.

"You're quite right, Daddy," Victoria said.

"Yes," Alex added. "And we have a way to do exactly that."

"What are you talking about?" Alex's father asked.

"Are you sure you want to know?" his mother said.

"We'll have to tell you about some pretty stupid things Alex did before it makes sense," Nina said. "But you should be used to that."

Chapter Twenty-Five
Carnival Conclusion

A cool night breeze, the first in days, blew gently through the open door and windows of the Guild House. This was good, as the Guild House was crowded, packed with more people than it could comfortably fit, especially as two of them were centaurs.

Alex stood next to Victoria as Nina and the rest of the Guild gathered around the rusted cauldron sitting atop the old woodstove, a fire blazing within, adding to the warmth of the room. Alex's parents and Victoria's father were also present. Victoria's father was very excited by the prospect of examining the magical cauldron close up and observing as it performed a transformation.

Alex's parents had been visibly displeased with his and Nina's recitation of their adventures in the Dead Forest and the manner by which the Guild came to possess the cauldron. However, as the cauldron had seemed abandoned, and as it would be helpful, and as Alex had risked his life to save the town, his parents had postponed any decision about possible groundings.

Eleada, Kendra, and Nathan had guided the other carnies back to the carnival where Alex's father and Deputy Dervis had conducted interviews with all those who had been under the influence of Esmeralda's Dark Spirit Magic. They had all told a similar story of being able to remember exactly what they had done, but unable to explain why they had thought so strongly they should try to help Esmeralda free the Shadow Wraith. They all reported still feeling dark and violent thoughts, but not knowing where they came from. Alex suspected it would be a long time before their soul-essences were free from the effects of Esmeralda's magic.

Clark, Ben, and Daphne had been briefly reunited with their parents and Rafael with his aunt, but they had all insisted to their guardians it was important for them to be present at the final act that would end the hopes of freeing the Shadow Wraith. This was how, even though it was nearly midnight, they were all assembled in the Guild House.

"Ready," Ben said. "I think the fire is hot enough." Ben, as usual, was responsible for the fire in the woodstove.

"What happens now?" Victoria's father asked, peering curiously into the cauldron's deep interior.

"Hmm, we put the sword in," Clark said, gently holding the sheathed Sword of Silas in his hand as though holding some living animal.

"And then we concentrate," Daphne said, looking brightly at the others. "On what we want to turn it into."

"Any ideas?" Nina asked, scratching her head in thought.

"Something harmless," Rafael suggested, frowning as he stared at the sword.

"How about a soup ladle?" Victoria suggested, looking around the room.

"Brilliant," Alex said with a smile.

"A fitting choice," Alex's father said, his arm slipping around Alex's mother's waist.

"The Soup Ladle of Silas," Alex's mother said with a laugh. "It has a nice ring. And I could use another soup ladle."

"Let's hope its magical properties are transformed, as well," Victoria's father said, watching intently as Clark lowered the sheathed sword into the bowl of the cauldron. The sword was too long to fit completely, resting against the lip of the iron pot at an angle.

"Everyone concentrate on a nice, shiny soup ladle," Daphne said, staring at the cauldron.

"Concentrate," Ben said with a shuffle of his feet. "Don't get distracted. Getting distracted is bad."

"Shush," Nina said as they all gazed intently at the sword in the cauldron.

Alex focused his mind on imagining a soup ladle and was surprised when the sword began to slide down into the cauldron as though it were melting. A moment later, the Sword of Silas disappeared into the depths of the cauldron, never to be seen again. There was no smell or light or any other indication of the transformation that took place within the black bowl of the cauldron, but Clark, by virtue of his height and proximity, could see when the conversion was complete.

"Mmm, done," Clark said as he reached into the cauldron with a gloved hand and withdrew a gleaming silver soup ladle.

"You should test it," Victoria said. "To be safe." Clark tapped the soup ladle on the side of the woodstove with a metallic ring.

"Amazing," Victoria's father said, stepping closer to examine the soup ladle.

"Harmless," Daphne said, a prideful tone in her voice.

"Hmm, makes me hungry," Clark said, still holding the ladle.

"Food," Ben said, quickly snuffing out the fire with a wave of his hand and muttered rune-word. "Always food."

"We're lucky it didn't transform with soup in the ladle, knowing Clark," Rafael said, patting Clark on the shoulder.

"It's still a little warm outside for soup," Alex's mother said, a sugar-craving glint in her eyes, "but there's enough root beer and ice cream for floats."

"Excellent idea, Mom," Nina said, bouncing on her toes. "We may have to let you in the Guild House more often."

"We may take you up on that offer if you keep bringing home magical artifacts," Alex's father said, raising an eyebrow at Nina and Alex.

"What makes you think that would ever happen again?" Alex said with an innocent smile. His father frowned for a moment and then burst out in a hearty laugh.

Looking again at the soup ladle, Alex thought about the magical necklace and whether his decision to keep it rather than destroy it in the cauldron was wise. His parents and the Guild had agreed with him that it might be useful in a future confrontation with followers of the Shadow Wraith, but as they pointed out, it was still a dangerous magical artifact. However, he had convinced them he knew exactly how to keep it safe.

Later that night, after they had all devoured their root beer floats while sitting around the table in Alex's kitchen, Victoria, her father, and the rest of the Guild headed to their respective homes. Alex and his family retired to their rooms shortly thereafter.

At the door to her bedroom, Nina paused.

"You haven't forgotten about tomorrow, have you?" Nina asked. It sounded more like a threat than a question.

"No, I haven't," Alex said and rustled his sister's hair.

"Good," she said with a smile and headed to her bed.

There was an almost chilly breeze wafting through the window of Alex's room and it was a profound relief from the oven-like heat of the last few days. Sinking his head deep into the feather pillow, Alex closed his eyes, but resisted the temptation to fall directly asleep. Instead, he willed himself into his astral body and then to Batami's hut.

Alex floated outside Batami's hut and thought her name clearly in his mind. She opened the door of the hut a minute later, and leaned against the wall. She looked exhausted beyond anything Alex had imagined, but she seemed physically well.

"It is good to see you, Alex," Batami said. "I'm afraid our lessons will need to be in person for a time. I am too weak for astral travel."

"Are you okay?" Alex asked, feeling his concern for Batami tug at his heart.

"I will recover," Batami said, "but it will take some time. Nearly half the forest was destroyed in the fire. It will be years before it, or I, return to our full strength."

"I'm sorry I woke you," Alex thought.

"No apologies, Alex," Batami said.

"I'll visit tomorrow," Alex said. *"I have something I need you to keep safe for me."*

"Ah. The necklace." Batami sighed and nodded. "You outshined even yourself today. Thank you. You should get some sleep, as well." Batami gave a small wave and then stepped inside and closed the door.

Alex returned to his body a moment later, feeling the tension in his stomach finally relax. Batami was not well, but she would get better. And her words had filled him with a warm sense of pride. It felt good to accomplish things that needed doing. Especially things few others could undertake.

Alex was about to drift off into sleep when the sound of a rock striking his window roused him. He went to the window, expecting to see Victoria or one of the other Guild members in the yard. Instead, he found the mysterious figure in black, hooded cloak still concealing its identity, staring up at him. The figure raised one arm to point and then walked toward the back of the house.

Alex slid on his sneakers and quietly snuck downstairs and slipped out the back door, crossing the backyard in a run, stopping only when he stood beside the figure in black, outside the Guild House door. Alex was surprised when the figure raised its hands and slowly lowered the cowl of the cloak to reveal the bald head of a very old man. The man's wrinkles hung from large cheekbones and his deep-set, gray eyes looked past Alex even as he spoke.

"I have come for what is mine," the old man said.

"Who are you?" Alex asked. "And what do you think is yours? And why have you been helping me?" Alex did not fear this man, although the way he refused to look directly at Alex was disconcerting.

"So many questions," the man said with a gentle smile. "I have come for my cauldron."

Alex blinked in surprise. "We thought it was abandoned. It was rusted. It looked like no one had been in the hut for years."

"It was abandoned. And I had not seen it in years. But it is still mine. Get it for me. Please."

Alex didn't know what to say. He had been certain the cauldron's owner was long dead. Was it possible the man was some kind of ghost? He didn't look like any ghost Alex had ever seen. Alex whispered the secret password to the Guild House door.

"Voluptuous vermin vomit." Maybe once Nina was officially a member, she would start coming up with more respectable passwords. Alex struggled under the weight of the cauldron, but managed to carry it outside to the strange man in black.

The old man grasped the handle and lifted the cauldron with apparent ease. He was obviously stronger than he looked. He turned to go and Alex stepped in front of him.

"Who are you?"

The man looked past Alex again and licked his lips before speaking.

"I helped you because I could. Because I might have been you rather than who I am."

"Who are you?"

"My name is Andrew."

"But why do you live in the Dead Forest? You're a Spirit Mage. Does Batami know you?"

"She does. She is part of the reason I live in the Dead Forest. I did not heed her lessons and now it is only place I can bear to be because it is the only place where I know I will not see other people."

"Are you afraid of people?"

"Afraid of what I see. I see too much. Even now, I can hardly abide being near you. Especially you. You shine so brightly. So bright it burns. Dew-tipped leaves at sunrise. A still mountain lake reflecting the cloudless sky above. Tree blossoms blooming in the light of a clear spring sunrise. So...beautiful."

The old man turned away, wiping tears from his eyes. Alex knew what the man spoke of. And while he did not know who Andrew was, he knew his affliction. The old man had looked into the souls of others too many times and now could only see the souls, touch and share the soul-essence, of everyone he encountered. Alex wondered how Andrew had avoided going mad. Maybe he hadn't. The old man began to walk away.

"Thank you," Alex said. "Without your help, I don't know..."

"You are welcome," Andrew said as he paused and turned back. "And tell my mother I said hello."

Andrew disappeared into the shadows before Alex had time to think through the old man's last words. His mother? Then it struck him. He hadn't thought of the possibility, because of Andrew's age. But it did make sense. Who better to learn Spirit Magic from than Batami? Who better to learn from than one's mother?

Alex stood in the dark a moment longer, letting the thoughts tumbling through his mind settle. Then he snuck back inside the house, snuggled into bed, and fell into a deep sleep.

The next day was Monday, a day of three important events. The first of these was the departure of the carnival. As the noon day sun reached its apex, Alex and the Guild gathered at the edge of the field behind the Town Hall, watching the carnies pack the last of their trucks and wagons while saying their farewells to four, in particular, whom they had come to think of as friends — or more than friends, in some cases.

Eleada, Kendra, Nathan, and Leanna joined Alex and the Guild beneath the shade of the sycamore tree. While the weather had returned to normal, the sun no longer quite so hot, the shade of the tree made a natural spot to gather for goodbyes.

"We should write," Kendra said, smiling Rafael, "but I'm in a traveling carnival."

"I'll address my letters to the most exciting girl in the world," Rafael said, grinning back. "I'm sure they'll find you."

"Or, I'll hand them to her when they come to me," Eleada said with a wink.

"Exciting," Ben said with a laugh. "Rafa said exciting, not exacerbating."

"Big word for a little man," Eleada said, squinting down at Ben. "And don't even think about writing me."

"Write?" Ben said, leaning back to look up at Eleada. "Why would I write when I can come see you?"

"Is that a threat?" Eleada said, raising her chin.

"Nope," Ben said, holding Eleada's gaze. "It's better than a threat. It's an aspiration."

"I'm sorry," Leanna said, stepping over to Alex. "It was me who dropped the ride on you."

"You weren't yourself," Alex said, his voice forceful, yet forgiving.

"That's the thing," Leanna said, staring at the ground, tears in her eyes. "I was myself. My worst self. If the noise of the ride crashing down hadn't drawn the other carnies so quickly, I don't know what I might have done. If it weren't for you and your friends, I don't know what might have become of me."

"Yes, we are all very thankful," Nathan said, stepping up and taking Leanna's hand.

"Very thankful," Leanna said, looking up as she squeezed Nathan's fingers in her own.

"Thank you, in particular," Nathan said as used his free hand to shake Alex's.

"We're very thankful to all of you, as well," Victoria said as she cantered over to stand beside Alex. While it was clear to Alex why they might be thankful to Eleada and Kendra and Nathan, he knew Victoria was thankful in a different manner toward Leanna. He knew because he was thankful to her for the same reason.

"That thing you asked me to see about is all seen to," Eleada said with a mysterious tone as she shook Alex's hand.

"Thank you," Alex said.

"What thing is that?" Victoria asked, looking quizzically at Alex.

"It's a surprise," Alex said, trying to keep his face from betraying what that surprise might be.

"A well-deserved surprise, from what I understand," Eleada said with a husky laugh.

There were goodbye hugs and more than a few goodbye kisses, which Alex took as a good excuse to kiss Victoria again. Now that he had finally realized nearly any excuse for kissing was a good one, he intended to come up with as many as possible.

As the carnies piled into their colorful trucks, Mr. Apollo stepped around a dust-crusted Ford flatbed and walked toward Alex and the Guild. He moved slowly, using his cane to compensate for a limp in his left leg, acquired from Eleada's arrow during the fight in the Silent Swamp. As he stepped up to Alex, Mr. Apollo removed his black-felt, stove-pipe hat and held it in his hands. His eyes were bloodshot, his face drawn tight. He paused for a moment, seeming to collect his thoughts.

"Alex," Mr. Apollo finally said. "I want to thank you. You, and Victoria, and your brave friends,"

"I'm sorry," Alex said, knowing Mr. Apollo would know the source of his sorrow.

"You bear no fault," Mr. Apollo said with a sigh. "I am indebted to you for finally freeing me. Me and all the others. Without your actions, and those of your friends, my friends and I would still be under her sway." He paused again, swallowing slowly. "I don't know if I ever really loved her, or if it was all her dark magic. An odd feeling not to know what is real in your own heart. If ever you and your friends are in need, you have only to ask."

"We could use a carnival next summer," Alex said with a grin.

"Yes," Mr. Apollo said, the tightness in his face loosening into the hint of a smile. "I believe that can be arranged."

"Take care of yourself," Victoria said as she stepped forward to hug Mr. Apollo.

"And you, the same," Mr. Apollo said, stepping back from Victoria's embrace, donning his hat with a flourish and showman's smile. He turned smartly on his heel and strode toward the lead truck of the carnival caravan, his limp a little less pronounced.

Alex and the Guild waved to the carnies and watched them climb into their trucks and begin the long drive out of the Rune Valley, out into the world beyond, and on toward the next secluded well of magical energy that would become their temporary home. As they watched the dust trails of the trucks billow in the air, Clark ushered in the second momentous event of the day.

"Well, so then, are we all ready for the big transformation?" Clark said, standing beside Daphne, holding her hand. After their miraculous kiss the day before, Daphne seemed oddly insistent on holding Clark's hand at every opportunity. Clark seemed to think he was in a waking dream and simply smiled like he hoped he would never wake up every time she grasped his massive palm with her petite fingers.

"Blazing banshee bogeys," Daphne cursed. "I almost forgot."

"Seriously?" Ben asked. "With all the constant reminding, how could you forget?"

"She seems to have something else on her mind," Rafael said, nodding toward Daphne and Clark's entwined fingers. Daphne looked at Rafael and stuck out her tongue.

"You've all had something else on your minds," Nina said with a slight frown, "and now it's time to have something more important on your minds so I can get something off my mind and we can all start thinking about more vital things."

"Right," Alex said, chuckling at his sister's words. "Would you like to do the honors, Victoria?"

"I would be honored to do the honors," Victoria said, turning and looking solemnly at Nina.

"Do you, Nina Ravenstar, swear by the Runes of the Runestones to always abide by all the rules of the Young Sorcerers Guild?"

"I do and I will," Nina said, straightening her back and standing to her full height, augmented by leaning forward on her toes.

"All those in favor of Nina being accepted as a full member of the Guild, say, 'Aye,'" Victoria said.

"Aye!" everyone shouted together.

"Unanimously approved," Alex said to Nina. "Welcome to the Young Sorcerers Guild, Sis. How does it feel?"

Nina cocked her head in thought. Scrunched up her face. Then sighed. "Not very different, actually."

"What were you expecting, a parade?" Rafael said in a teasing tone.

"Parade?" Ben repeated, excitement in his eyes. "A parade is an excellent idea."

"You're right," Alex said, grabbing his sister and hoisting her into the air by her waist. It took only a moment before everyone else in the Guild grabbed a limb and held Nina aloft as they made their way back along the edge of the field toward town.

"I want a parade for every birthday," Nina said, laughing as the others carried her aloft.

At the front of the field, near where the main entrance to the carnival had been, and a short distance behind the Town Hall, Alex spotted a group of people. His father was among them. Mayor McClint stood in front of Alex's father, shouting and pointing in the direction of the Guild and their parade. Behind the mayor stood Anna, Dillon, and the rest of the Mad Mages. They looked very smug and Alex could guess why. Technically, Alex and the entire Guild were all still grounded and supposed to be confined to their homes until the conclusion of the investigation into their supposed burglary of the town museum.

It seemed Alex's father had not informed Mayor McClint of the decision to allow the Guild to forgo their confinement in celebration of their victory at the cave the day before. From what Alex's father had told them the previous night, Mayor McClint was disinclined to give much credence to his description of the events at the cave.

Alex and the Guild saving the town from the Shadow Wraith again wasn't as appealing a story as Alex and the Guild getting caught in the middle of robbing the town museum. Of course, Alex and the Guild had not stolen anything, and with Eleada's help, Alex had returned the stolen property that had fallen into his possession.

"Are you ready for your birthday present?" Alex asked his sister as he began the third exceptional event of the day.

"Does it taste like chocolate?" Nina asked, still giggling as the Guild neared the rear of the Town Hall where his father, Mayor McClint, and the Mad Mages were clustered.

"Nope, but you're going to like the smell of it," Alex said as he reached in his pocket and clasped his fingers around a coin. Then he spoke the rune-word for fire as he focused on the coin in his pocket — the coin that he had linked to his great-great grandfather's tracking coins — coins that now burst into flame.

Anna and Dillon screamed and shouted as the pockets of their shorts smoked and flames flared up around them. Alex and the Guild could not help but laugh.

Alex causally pulled his hand from his pocket as they passed by. Anna and Dillon slapped at their shorts, each yanking a coin from their pockets and tossing them on the ground, staring at the currency like it might combust again at any moment.

"Let me see those coins," Alex's father said, bending down to pick the coins up from the grass. As Alex's father stood up straight and examined the coins, a frown crossed his face. "These are the magical tracking coins that were stolen from the town museum. How did you two come to have these in your pockets?"

"What?" Mayor McClint said, lumbering over to stand next to his son. "What stolen coins? Let me look at those. Stolen coins in my son's pocket. Nonsense."

Alex and the others continued to carry Nina past as Alex's father held Anna and Dillon in his steely gaze. Alex glanced back and caught Anna's eye for a moment. He didn't smile. He didn't laugh. He simply held her eyes for a moment.

She wouldn't be able to explain how she had the stolen coin in her pocket and she couldn't possibly blame Alex. Neither he, nor anyone from the Guild, had been near her in two days. Eleada had, however, and she was as deft at slipping things into pockets as, she had assured Alex, she was at slipping them out of pockets.

"That was the best birthday present ever," Nina said with a laugh once they were out of earshot. She was still laughing as they finally lowered her to the ground. Alex took Victoria's hand as they walked side by side down the sidewalk.

"So what do you want to do with the rest of your birthday, Sis?" Alex asked. "Keeping in mind, of course, that we have to go home and pretend to be grounded and confined to the Guild House."

"I was thinking about another root beer float," Nina said, "but I suppose I could be convinced to spend the afternoon pouring over some old burnt up magical map trying to figure out how to get it to reveal the location of the Rune Tree, so we could get into more trouble trying to find it than we've managed to get into so far."

"Funny, that's exactly what I was going to suggest," Alex said as he and the others laughed.

"Hereditary," Ben said. "Crazy runs in their family."

"Apparently, Alex wasn't the only one dropped on his head," Rafael said.

"Hmm, maybe he's a bad influence," Clark said.

"Maybe she's the gorping bad influence," Daphne added.

"It's entirely possible Alex and Nina are a good influence on all of us," Victoria said, giving Alex's hand a small squeeze. The others, Alex and Nina included, turned and looked at her in astonishment. "I said it was possible. I didn't say it was very likely."

Alex laughed again and the others joined in as they headed back to the Guild House and the beginning of what he hoped would be a great adventure.

www.ingramcontent.com/pod-product-compliance
Lightning Source LLC
Chambersburg PA
CBHW061610170626
46811CB00001B/377